SWIFT'S TEMPTATION

J.R. LOVELESS

Copyright 2011 by J.R. Loveless

Cover Design by Sara York Copyright 2013

All rights reserved.

No part of this book may be reproduced in any form or by any electronic or mechanical means, including information storage and retrieval systems, without written permission from the author, except for the use of brief quotations in a book review.

ACKNOWLEDGMENTS

Trademarks Acknowledgement

The author acknowledges the trademarked status and trademark owners of the following wordmarks mentioned in this work of fiction:

Corvette: General Motors Company (GM)
    Rolex: Rolex SA
    Camaro: General Motors Company (GM)
    BMW: BMW AG, Munich Germany
    Mercedes: Daimler AG
    Toyota: Toyota Motor Corporation
    Lincoln Town Car: Ford Motor Company
    Jack Daniels: Brown-Forman Corporation
    Coca Cola: The Coca-Cola Company
    Red Ryder BB Gun: Daisy Outdoor Products
    VHS format: JVC Kenwood Holdings
    Spencer's Gifts: Spencer Gifts LLC
    Disney World: The Walt Disney Company
    Greyhound: Greyhound Lines, Inc.

1

Let me start by introducing myself. I am Fagan Swift, born and raised on a small farm in rural Iowa. Every morning I would have to get up to milk a cow or feed the chickens. Nothing ever happened in that boring little town, so I moved to this exciting place called New York City about nine months ago with my best friend Trinity. We've been friends since kindergarten and both hold the same opinion of our home town. She developed a crush on me in the ninth grade, but alas, to her consternation and dismay, I'm gay. Yes, my name is unusual and I know you're thinking 'a fag named Fagan, how ludicrous', but my mother wanted to name me after her grandfather, who raised her after her parents passed. And there was no possible way for her to know I would turn out to be gay. After I came out to my classmates, my given name certainly took on a whole new meaning for them.

Trinity eventually got over me and moved on. We are now roommates together in a small two-bedroom apartment overlooking a huge park.

They're right about how this city never sleeps! You can

hear sounds from every direction at any time of the night. The first night here, neither of us could sleep for all the noise, but now nine months later we don't even hear it. I'm 24 years old with blonde shaggy hair that pisses me off all of the time because it's always falling into my eyes. I constantly threaten to cut my hair off and Trinity constantly threatens to kick my ass. She says it looks sexier longer rather than shorter. I am six-foot-two and I have what Trinity dubs 'foamy sea green' eyes. My body is pretty much in shape from all the heavy hauling I used to do on the farm, and of course, tan from all the labor in the sun.

Like I said, I couldn't take living in that small town anymore. Not only am I gay, but I also want to be an artist. My dad was pretty pissed off the day I told him I was going to the city and he has never really forgiven me for not wanting to be a farmer like him. Let me not even go there with the whole gay factor.

I am currently standing in the middle of the sidewalk in front of where I work. I can't believe what I have been doing for the last six months. You would never guess in a million years what a farm boy like me does for a living. I work for an escort service! Don't go freaking out just yet. My job isn't one of those escort services you hear about, since I'm not required to have sex with the women that come through the agency. Some of the other escorts do by choice, but I had explained to the owner early on I was gay and he'd been fine with it. Victor Harrison is the greatest boss I have ever had. He is breathtakingly gorgeous, but alas, straight.

The job had fallen into my lap. Literally! Six months ago, give or take a few days, I was sitting outside a small cafe enjoying my coffee and scanning the classifieds yet again. I had already had six different jobs but none of them suited me. I would either get fired or quit after a few weeks of being treated like shit. Anyway, my cup was sitting on the table while I was circling an advert with potential when there was loud barking. A man shouted and suddenly a dog was in my lap, coffee flying everywhere. I sat there stunned, looking at this two-ton gorilla sitting on me.

"What the hell!" I exclaimed just as the gorilla decided to clean the coffee off my face. I spluttered and gagged when its tongue accidentally slipped inside my mouth because my lips were open. Disgusting!

"Hercules! Get off of him! Now!" The dog whined and leapt off my lap to sit beside me, wagging his tail. It was a huge Saint Bernard. In New York City! How inappropriate is that?

I looked up and suddenly found the most gorgeous man standing there with an apologetic expression on his face. "I'm so sorry. He gets excited sometimes, and tends to run away from me. I'm Victor Harrison."

He was about an inch or so taller than me, with shoulder-length dark brown hair, wire-framed glasses, and gleaming bright blue eyes. I felt myself begin to drool and wiped my lips. "Fagan Swift. That's all right. I'm kind of used to large animals." I laughed and gestured for him to sit.

"At least let me buy you a cup of coffee to replace the one Hercules spilled," Victor offered, motioning to the pretty waitress standing a few feet away.

"It's fine. I was almost finished anyway." I stood up with a sigh as I looked at my coffee splattered clothing and the newspaper on the table.

"Hercules, I oughta make a carpet out of you!" When Victor saw the classifieds sitting open on the table he asked, "Are you looking for a job?"

His eyes ran over my body in an intense perusal I could feel straight to my bones. Those blue eyes were sliding down my legs and back up again to my face. I almost fainted from the lust that shot through me. Down, boy, I barked at myself mentally. He's probably straight.

"Well, yeah. Kind of. Why?" I raised a hand to brush my hair away from my eyes and then rub sheepishly at the back of my neck.

"I run a service that you look like you could be perfect for. Would you be interested?"

"That depends. What kind of service?" I was suspicious at first. You never know exactly what someone's offering, especially after the way the guy checked me out.

"Why don't you walk with me back to my office? I'll explain it to you once we get there." Victor handed the waitress a twenty and grabbed Hercules' leash to lead him away. He stopped to smile back over his shoulder. "Come on."

I trailed behind slightly, my eyes straying to the hard ass rippling beneath his slacks. I couldn't help myself. He was made like a god! We walked for a few blocks while he asked me questions about why I had come to live in the city. I explained about the small town and how I just couldn't take living there anymore with how isolated it felt. He understood, to my surprise, because he was also from a small town in South Dakota.

A few blocks later, we stood in front of a huge building with a sign at the top in big red letters stating, 'Temptation'. My eyes widened as I took in the impressive structure before me. I looked at him questioningly and he motioned for me to follow him inside.

I stared around me in awe the instant we passed through the plate-glass doors. Just inside was a huge reception area with a fountain and everything. I could hear the water trickling over the rocks and there were even fish swimming around in it! The security guard tipped his hat towards Victor and a receptionist looked up from her switchboard to smile at him. "Good morning, Mr. Harrison," she called cheerily before picking up another call.

"Temptation is a business where we attempt to satisfy our customers' fantasies." Victor pressed the button for an elevator and turned to smile at me.

"This is an escort service?" I asked in shock.

"I don't like to call Temptation an escort service, but in plain terms, it could be deemed as such. There are several floors of fantasy rooms where men and women can enjoy anything they desire. However, no sex is allowed inside these walls nor is any money to exchange hands for those kinds of services. If I find out anyone has broken these rules, then the one who accepted the money will be fired and the customer will be banned from our premises. It's up to the customer and the escort as to whether or not they will go to a more intimate level." The elevator dinged to a stop and we both stepped on.

"See, Mr. Harrison—"

"Victor."

"Victor, I... um... I'm gay. I don't like women," I said, hoping he would understand.

"That's fine. You don't have to like them sexually. None of our members are required to sleep with our customers, only to do what it takes to satisfy their fantasies of the perfect evening or weekend. Whatever that may be, outside of sex." Victor stepped out and led the way into another office that was obviously his. He took a seat behind the huge desk in front of the windows. "You're the right build, the right facial structure, handsome, and have a great body. You'll definitely add to the atmosphere around here."

I practically glowed at his words and felt my pants tighten a little with desire. "I see. What does the job pay?"

"You'll be well taken care of. Your pay depends on the customer's request. Each date can range from five hundred to ten thousand for your services, depending on what the customer desires. You receive a percentage of the fee based on what the arrangement is. You'll be supplied with clothing, shoes, and anything else we deem necessary to satisfy our clientele. There are several large dressing rooms where we have all types and sizes of clothing for men and women to use. They are dry cleaned after each use and we ensure it is a sterile environment in order to make certain our members remain healthy." Victor looked up at me as I stood there, dazed. "Are you interested?"

"I… I… it sounds great. I suppose I can give the job a try and if I don't like it then I can just find something else," I mused, totally lost in everything he had told me.

A knock came at the door before he could speak again and the man who would become my most detested adversary waltzed in without waiting for a reply. "Victor, Tyrone's been at it again. He's in the hospital."

Xavier James. The man was the kind you could spend your life worshipping with every inch of your body. He had long black hair that fell to his waist, tied back with a white string. His body was well-toned and he had a very arrogant tilt to his dark head. He was an inch or so shorter than me, but with such broad shoulders, he would never appear small. I felt my mouth water as I stared at him. Sensing my gaze on him, he turned his head to glare at me with piercing gray eyes. They ran over me in disdain and then flicked back to Victor. Anger and hostility radiated from him. The instant dislike baffled me and I was starting to get pissed off at his attitude.

"I see." Victor sighed, rubbing the bridge of his nose between his thumb and forefinger. He stood and smiled apologetically at me. "Why don't you take a day or two to think about it? Here's my card. Just give me a call when you decide. I have to go take care of this." He handed the small white rectangle to me and stepped around the desk, motioning for me and the other man to precede him out the door.

I tapped the small card against my palm as the elevator descended; the other two men were absorbed by their own private conversation. I couldn't believe what had happened to me today. Looking back over at the two most gorgeous men I had ever seen, I bit my lip and made my decision. "Mr. Harrison?" I queried softly.

Victor looked up, his eyes smiling kindly. "Mr. Swift?"

"I think I'd like to try."

"Excellent. See the receptionist on the way out. Explain who you are and she'll give you instructions on what to do. I look forward to seeing you tomorrow morning." He shook my hand again before the doors opened on the first floor.

The two men quickly exited the building without a backward glance. I approached the receptionist to receive a booklet and a small bag before she went back to her phones. Outside on the sidewalk, I looked back up at the name. Temptation. Such an appropriate name, for there were, undoubtedly, many tempting things hidden inside those glass walls. I headed towards the apartment, eager to tell Trinity my news.

2

"You what!?" Trinity shouted, her amber eyes flashing and her long black hair tossing in the breeze as we stood looking out over the bay. "But you don't even like girls!"

She could be a real spitfire when she wanted to be, and right now was she angry at me! She only came to my shoulder in height, but she sure could pack a wallop when she threw a punch. I guess that's from all the martial arts training she had gone through in the four years of college she spent away from our home town.

"It's not like I have to have sex with them. I just have to wine and dine them. Come on, Trinity! It sounds like a great paying job and he said there is no sex involved unless the customer and the escort agree to it without exchanging money. I would never agree, so there will never be sex involved." I pleaded with her for understanding and sighed, wondering if maybe she was right, but it sounded like a great job. You get to go out, eat for free, ride in a limo, and go to parties while getting paid for it all. Where would you get a better job?

"You know, if your father found out about this, you'd be slaughtered and fed to the cows, yes? He's still not entirely over the fact you moved out here and you don't intend to provide him with an heir," she pointed out sarcastically, causing me to grimace with guilt.

"I can't help the fact I'm gay, Trinity. It's not like I suddenly decided to piss my father off one day by declaring I'm gay. Besides, he has my sister to provide him with an heir to the farm. She loves the place, so let her have it. I don't want it, Trin. Besides, I'm only trying the job out, not making it my permanent occupation. If I don't like it, I'll quit." I hugged her and grinned broadly as I saw her stubborn expression melting.

"Fine. But don't say I didn't warn you. Where do you want to go for dinner?"

I shrugged as we started walking towards the diner we frequented. It's not like I had the money to afford fine cuisine, so we almost always had the cheap, early-bird dinner for four dollars and ninety-nine cents there. The food was pretty good, though. I read through the packet of paperwork that night and by the time I got to the end of it, my head was whirling with all the details you had to remember. Things like the customer is to never be denied what they desire within reason (no sex), you must always make sure to be well-groomed, and a whole lot more. There were instructions on where to go two hours before your assignment in order to be dressed and polished in the correct type of clothing for the outing. The packet gave no information on what to expect from the assignments, but I suppose it was pretty cut and dry. Take them out, make them laugh, dance with them, feed them, etc. I was pretty sure I could handle that.

The next day, I reported to the front desk in the lobby. The receptionist was busy and I had to stand by her desk for about ten minutes before she was able to speak with me. While waiting, I looked around and saw people coming and going. What a busy place! There were all types of men and women. Some had a refined air around them, while others had a furtive and secretive attitude. It was almost as though they were embarrassed to be there. I have never understood why someone who is uncomfortable with doing something would do it. I mean, you either want to or you don't. Why else would you bother? One woman in particular caught my eye, because when she stepped out of the elevator her gaze immediately zeroed in on me. She was a beautiful woman, tall, slender and elegant, with large violet eyes and blonde hair she had pulled back in a tight chignon. I felt my skin crawl with the way her eyes ran over my body. It was like I was on display and she was choosing a piece of meat. I hoped I wouldn't have to get used to that feeling.

Her thin lips twisted into a small smile and she walked gracefully towards me, stopping in front of me. She held out her hand and I looked at her with surprise. I took her hand and shook it. Her smile tightened a little around the edges causing me to wonder if I had done something wrong. "You must be new." Her voice was husky, like wood-smoke, and the words rolled off her tongue in an English accent.

"I just started today," I told her nervously, unsure what to do with her.

"I see. I am Brianna Newberry. Duchess Brianna Newberry." She stated her name like I should know who she is.

I just looked at her. "It's nice to meet you. I'm Fagan Swift. Just plain Fagan Swift," I tried to joke, but her violet eyes flashed with temper and I swallowed hard. Apparently the joke hadn't been funny.

"I'm sure I'll be seeing you around, Mr. Swift," she replied and left with a flourish, her long white coat swirling around her ankles.

Seriously, who wears a long white coat in the middle of the summer in New York City? I shook my head and turned back to find the receptionist staring at me as though I had grown two heads. "What?"

"You just managed to ruffle the Duchess. I didn't think anyone would be able to. She's commonly referred to as the Ice Queen around here." The receptionist grinned. "Welcome to Temptation, Mr. Swift."

"I wish everyone would stop calling me Mr. Swift. It's Fagan." I smiled back and held out my hand.

"I'm Georgina." She wasn't a plain woman, but nowhere near as striking as the Duchess who'd just left. In my eyes, though, she was more beautiful than the Ice Queen, because her inner beauty was much more apparent than the other's obviously cold interior. Georgina had sparkling blue eyes and mousy brown hair pulled back into a ponytail, and she was wearing very light makeup. She was your typical girl-next-door kind of woman. "Here are the basics you need to know. You'll have to be trained for two weeks before having your first assignment. And—" I cut her off.

"Trained?" I asked curiously.

"In table manners, dancing lessons, all the things you'll need to know to make a woman's fantasy come true." She winked at me and I pursed my lips.

"I see."

"Anyway, you'll be trained for two weeks before you're assigned your first client. Your first time out will be a double with one of our other more distinguished members. Probably Tyrone. Although we won't know for sure until it's time. I'm afraid he's a little... shall we say, mentally unstable? He's always in and out of the hospital, having hurt himself countless times. But he's able to seduce a woman faster than any other man I've ever met." She blushed at this and looked away from me.

It was obvious something had happened between this woman and the man named Tyrone. Tyrone was the same name mentioned yesterday when that hateful man had come into Mr. Harrison's office. "I see. Georgina, can I ask you something?" She nodded expectantly and perched her chin in her hand. "Yesterday, while I was in Mr. Harr...I mean Victor's office, a man came in. An inch or two shorter than me, with long black hair, and to die... uh... I mean cold gray eyes. Do you know who he is?"

Her eyes narrowed a bit when she heard me trip over my words, and I flushed, knowing I had just given away my orientation to her. "Well, he sounds like Xavier James. He's Victor's cousin and pretty much runs everything behind the scenes. He's the accountant for the company, but he also ensures the clothes are sent out for dry cleaning, there are enough outfits, and scheduling the assignments for all of our escorts." She looked at me speculatively. "And he's single."

"Oh, really?" I asked eagerly, but then stuttered. "Uh, I mean, it doesn't surprise me."

"Calm down, Mr. Swift. I was merely teasing." Georgina smiled slightly, her blue eyes dancing with laughter.

I laughed and shrugged. "You caught me. I have no interest in women whatsoever."

"Don't say that too loudly," she warned. "And never admit that to a client. Does Victor know?"

"Yes. I told him yesterday."

"Well then, take the elevator to the fifth floor and when you get off the elevator, make a left, go to the fifth room on your right, and you'll find Winston. He's to be your trainer for the next two weeks. I think you'll fit in quite nicely around here, Fagan, and I have high hopes for you to become Duchess Newberry's personal favorite. Not many people have managed to accomplish upsetting her." She winked again and went back to her phone.

I considered myself dismissed and headed towards the elevators. Pressing the button, I leaned my back against the wall, lost in thought. The ding signifying the elevator had arrived at the bottom floor came and I turned without looking up to enter the elevator. Someone was exiting the elevator at the same time. I ended up bashing into a strong chest and a pair of arms automatically locked around me to keep us both from falling.

"I'm so sorry!" I cried, pulling back to look at the person I had just run into and swallowed. My throat was suddenly dry when I found myself looking into those same hard gray eyes.

"You should watch where you're going," he snapped at me harshly. "You could have run into a client."

"I said I was sorry. It was an accident." I glared at him and then I realized his arms were still around my waist. "Would you mind letting go of me?" I asked sarcastically, looking down pointedly at his arms.

A flush worked its way over those beautifully tan, high cheekbones and he immediately released me, stepping back hastily. I gloated that I had managed to embarrass him. He didn't say another word, just stalked by me and walked towards the exit. I stared after him for a brief moment, my eyes drawn to his long legs and the way his slacks hugged his ass. Sighing, I entered the elevator and hit the button for the fifth floor. When he'd dropped his arms, I had been engulfed by a sense of loss that shocked and horrified me. What the hell? How could I possibly be attracted to someone who was so rude and arrogant? Shoving the man from my thoughts, I counted my way down the doors to my left until I came to the door Georgina had directed me to. Taking a deep breath, I knocked and waited.

The door was flung open and an owlish-looking man stood there with huge wire-rimmed glasses. A pair of dazed brown eyes looked up at me. Several strands of blond hair fell into his face. "Yes?"

The voice squeaked out of the thin man and I grinned down at him. "I'm Fagan Swift. Georgina told me to come see you."

The eyes registered recognition and he stepped back. "Yes, yes. Come in. I need to take some measurements and send them over to wardrobe. Then I need to find out what you know."

"What I know?" I asked, looking around the very large room. Winston ignored me, still muttering under his breath.

There was a dining table set for a party of four and a large dance floor to the left with a piano nearby. But what caught my attention and lifted my brow was the huge four-poster bed in one corner. "What's with the bed?" I demanded, my gaze turning to the thin, shorter man.

"Oh, the bed? That's just for whenever a member has not had enough rest. We force them to lie down and get some sleep before an assignment. It's nothing to be concerned with. I'm sure Victor explained there is a no-sex-for-money policy." He waved his hand as though dismissing the bed from my thoughts, but my eyes kept straying to the dark blue sheets. Images of a certain gray-eyed man and me wrapped up together kept popping into my head.

"Now, Mr. Swift—"

"Fagan."

"Huh?" He blinked behind his glasses.

"My name is Fagan. I hate being called Mr. Swift. That's my father, not me." I walked over to where he stood.

"Uh… okay. Fagan, let's start with the measurements. Stand straight with your arms at your sides," he instructed.

I did as he directed and started laughing when he started measuring the inside of my thigh, as it was the only place I was ticklish. He gave me an impatient look and went back to measuring again, only causing me to laugh harder. "I'm sorry," I managed to gasp out in between. "I'm very ticklish right there."

"Please try to hold still. I need to get these measurements done as quickly as possible."

I bit my lip and managed to hold still long enough for Winston to finish measuring. The next two hours went by so quickly that by the time we were done, my head was spinning. He had asked me countless questions about my background, and table manners. He also told me how he was going to be putting me through a rigorous training each day, as well as set me up on an exercise and diet regime to keep me in shape. I raised an eyebrow at the diet part, but didn't say anything, because there was no way this little man could possibly watch me all day, every day. "We'll start tomorrow. For now, I'll take you on a guided tour of the office and the Suites of Fantasy."

"Suites of Fantasy?" I parroted.

"Yes. Those are where our members and clients can enter into their fantasy worlds. You'll see what I mean while we're going through the tour." Winston led the way to the sixth floor, up a flight of stairs.

He was puffing by the time we got to the next floor but I was barely out of breath. "I see you're in good shape," Winston replied enviously.

"Yep. Working on a farm for twenty-three years will do that to you. Milking cows, feeding chickens, putting up new fencing will definitely keep you in shape," I said, my eyes drawn to a door labeled 'Chains of Love'.

"I see you noticed this room immediately. Into S&M, are we?" he asked, opening the door to reveal a chamber of torture devices.

My jaw dropped and I couldn't do anything but stare at the assorted whips, chains, manacles in the walls, sawhorses, and tables with shackles as well. "Th… this is… a torture chamber?" I swung around to stare at him.

He started laughing and threw his head back, holding his belly as he laughed harder. "No, Fagan, this is an S&M room. It stands for Sadism and Masochism. Basically, when a member or a guest wishes to inflict painful pleasure on their partner, they come to this room. It's booked months in advance. Right now, the room will be sterilized in a few moments and that's why it's empty. I see you have no idea what all this is. You truly are a farm boy." He wiped tears from his eyes that had formed from laughing so hard.

I glared at him and just kept my mouth shut. Painful pleasure? Whips? Chains? I don't know. I was doubtful I would ever enjoy pain. I hoped I never had to find out! I followed him to room after room: rooms for dining, rooms for dressing in historical costumes and enacting those time periods, others for music, so many ways to indulge. I couldn't believe all the rooms they had, and what each room contained. By the time we were done with the tour, it was almost four in the afternoon. He dismissed me for the day and I went back downstairs, bewildered by all I had seen. For the second time, I found myself running into someone.

"Do you ever look where you're going?" Xavier snarled and stepped back, his hair disheveled from the collision.

"Look, I think we got off on the wrong foot." I smiled, holding out my hand. "I'm Fagan Swift."

But he didn't reach for my hand, just gave me a snobbish look and went to move around me. "What the hell is your problem?" I asked angrily.

Xavier looked at me with distaste. "I don't like you. It's more men like you that this company doesn't need. Concerned with nothing but money and sex."

"You know nothing about me." I was truly starting to dislike this man.

"I don't wish to know anything about you, Mr. Swift." He turned on his heel and stalked away.

I shook my head and started walking home. I couldn't believe the man! I could feel the rage flowing through my veins. So he assumes just because I'm going to work as an escort I'm going to resort to having sex? Damn it! I clenched my fists and dug my nails into my palm. Why do I even care? I resolved to ignore him and started whistling on the long walk home.

3

The training began the next day and Winston started with table manners. Every time I did something wrong he would slap the back of my hands with a ruler; elbows on the table, wrong fork or knife, etc. The first time I was stunned and almost slapped him back, but I controlled myself. I'm not a violent person by nature. I'm actually pretty laid back unless I'm provoked. Winston sniffed at my question and replied, "It's the only way you'll learn to do it properly."

The backs of my hands hurt so badly by the time we took a break, I wanted to wring Winston's neck, but couldn't because I could barely clench my fists. "Anyone ever tell you that you could be a great Catholic-school teacher?" I asked, rubbing the backs of my hands. They were extremely red.

"We'll continue with the training by moving on to dancing for now. You better practice your table manners at home, because for the next two weeks we'll be doing the same lesson on table manners until you get it right. Grab yourself a cup of coffee, take a five-minute breather, and then we'll continue. Coffee's in the next room over."

Winston dismissed me and I rolled my eyes at his back. I exited Winston's room of torture and found the room he'd indicated. I poured myself a large cup of coffee before stepping out into the hall again. Looking to my right, I saw another door at the end of the hall, an exit sign above it. Upon opening the door, I found a fire escape that led up to the roof. Anticipation set in at the idea of being able to have a smoke. I took the stairs two at a time in eagerness for the rush of nicotine through my system. I hadn't realized how high up the building actually was until I looked down from the roof. Dizziness assaulted me for a moment before I pulled back slightly and looked out across the city instead of down to the ground beneath.

I grabbed a cigarette from the pack in my pocket and lit up, dragging deeply. I knew smoking was a foul habit, yet I couldn't kick it. I'd tried. I would quit for several months, but the moment I'd feel pressure or stress I would reach for a pack. Trinity was always bitching and nagging me, but I still did it anyway.

I set my coffee cup on the edge and leaned against it. I tend to daydream or get lost in thought a lot, one of the many things that had always earned me my father's ire. He'd tell me to get my head out of the clouds and keep my feet on the ground. Granted, I almost wound up chopping my leg off one time because of my daydreaming, but it's not like I did it on purpose. It just kind of happens. My daydreams take over my mind, and before I know it, I'm staring off into space with my mind anywhere but the present.

I wonder what my father is doing. Is he thinking about me or wondering what I'm doing? Ever since Mom died things hadn't been the same at home. She had been diagnosed with leukemia and I, my father, nor my sister, were a match when they tested us to be bone marrow donors. Man, did that shit hurt when they took the sample! But the pain would have been worth it if she'd lived. I miss her something fierce. She was the complete opposite of my dad; loving, kind, and never disappointed in me for being who I am. She would have supported the fact I was gay, and probably even gone so far as to start finding me boyfriends. She died when I was twelve and my sister was ten. I remember her favorite perfume. It always reminded me of summer. The smell was like fresh linens drying in the sunshine and made me think of the flowers, with the bees buzzing around them that grew in the field behind our house. She had been truly beautiful, inside and out. It's actually because of her I could see a person's heart instead of just the outside beauty.

Looking over, I caught sight of a figure standing near the door leading onto the roof. "Well, well. If it isn't the grumpiest person I've ever met," I said dryly, turning my head back to look out over the city.

"What are you doing up here?" The deep, husky voice spoke of hot nights of pleasure on pure silk sheets and, even though I despised him, caused a shiver to travel down my spine.

"I was taking a five-minute break. Winston has practically filleted the skin off my knuckles," I replied ruefully, rubbing the back of my right hand again. Taking the last drag off my cigarette, I tossed the butt into my cup.

I didn't look at him but I could feel his eyes on me. "You shouldn't be up here."

"Yeah, well, I could say the same thing to you," I tossed casually over my shoulder, smirking with humor. I didn't let anything get to me for very long, even though he'd been nothing but rude to me. I saw his mouth tighten in disapproval and I sighed.

"You really need to learn to loosen up a little there, Xav. You might actually smile for a change and make everyone else forget you can be such an asshole." Snatching up my empty coffee cup, I didn't give him time to reply before I sauntered back over to the fire escape and took the stairs nimbly back down to the fifth floor door I'd come out of.

Winston was waiting impatiently for me. "I told you five minutes, not fifteen!" He had his arms crossed and reminded me so much of my father I couldn't help but laugh. He frowned in confusion. "I don't know what's so funny."

"You look so much like my father when you do that," I explained when I had stopped laughing.

He blinked and dropped his arms. "I do?"

"Arms crossed with a disapproving look on your face like I disappointed you. Well, don't expect much else from me. I tend to disappoint everyone." I felt the smile on my face fading as I finished speaking and I think something clicked inside Winston because he suddenly smiled. It was the first one I'd seen from him and caused me to blink.

"Well then, let's get back to it. I have Samantha here to help you with your dance training." He pointed to a young woman standing by the window.

I smiled at her and as she approached me, I stuck out my hand. THWACK! I howled in pain and glared at the evil sadist standing near me. My knuckles were throbbing. "What the hell did I do now?" I demanded grouchily.

"You never greet a lady in such a manner! And don't swear in front of them, either!"

A small, gentle laugh came from the woman standing in front of me, and I looked at her, feeling sheepish, and rubbing the back of my neck. "I'm sorry. As you can tell, I'm not exactly refined."

"That's quite all right. That's what Winston is here for." She presented her hand and when I reached to take it, Winston stopped me.

"You are to accept her hand in yours, bend low over it, and kiss the back of her hand. Like this." He shoved me out of the way and accepted her hand with a smile. Bending at the waist, he pressed his lips gently to the back of her hand. "It's a pleasure to meet you." He lifted his head, still bent over her hand, and smiled at the girl.

She gave a small nod and he stood up, letting her hand go. I lifted an eyebrow at Winston before stepping in front of her. She held out her hand expectantly. I accepted it, gave an overly dramatic bow as I pressed my lips to the back of her hand, and said, "It's a pleasure to meet you, Samantha. I'm Fagan Swift." I looked back up at her, winking teasingly.

She laughed and gave a small nod. I stood straight and released her hand. Winston immediately piped in, "Very nice. Although a little overplayed. You'll have to calm the playfulness down when you meet a client for the first time."

Samantha was a petite girl. Her head just came to my shoulder. She had long auburn hair pulled back in a French braid, green eyes, and a beautiful smile. "So you're my dance partner, hmm?"

"Have you danced before?" Samantha asked merrily.

I gave her a mischievous grin and grabbed her hand. With a twist of my wrist, I twirled her around expertly, causing her skirt to flare out and bare half of her upper thighs. Winston's eyes were glued to the exposed flesh immediately and I couldn't help but laugh as I dipped her low to the ground. From what I could see in her eyes, she was pleasantly surprised. "My mother taught me the basics. She loved to dance. And my father was always too busy with chores around the farm."

"She must be a lovely woman," Samantha commented.

"She was." My voice went low as I remembered her again.

"Was?" she queried gently.

"Yeah, she died when I was twelve. After that it was just

me, my sister, and my dad." She gave me a sympathetic look but I grinned widely. "It's okay. I still miss her but that was a long time ago, and I still have my dad, even though I didn't turn out to be the way he wanted."

"Well, let's see how well you can keep up with me, then," she teased and signaled to Winston to put on some music.

I had been to a lot of the barn dances they had almost every other weekend, so I'd learned a lot of different styles of dancing. Plus, I loved to dance so I was pretty sure I wouldn't need a whole lot of training. I heard the piano start to play and turned my head to glimpse Winston sitting at the keys. My eyebrows lifted for a second, but I took Samantha by her hand and bowed. "May I have this dance, milady?" I purred as she smiled, curtseying before me.

I pulled her against me and slid an arm around her waist, my hand splayed across her lower back. I started with a basic waltz and transitioned into more intricate dance steps. Each time Winston would switch the style of music, I would switch my style of dance. Samantha was a great dancer and kept up flawlessly with each change.

"You're really good," she commented breathlessly as we whirled to a stop.

"Thanks." I could feel sweat dampening my skin and stepped back from her to keep from getting any of the salty fluid on her. "This was a lot of fun. I haven't danced like that in months."

"Well, it appears you have superior dancing skills." Winston stood from the piano and approached both of us, repositioning his glasses on his face. "So, we'll skip dance lessons then."

"Aww. But I had a lot of fun, and of course, I had a lovely partner. But I suppose I could just dance with you, Winnie." I grabbed his hand and whirled him around playfully. When he tried to pull away, I refused to let him go.

"You really need to lighten up, Winnie. You're too uptight." I twisted him back around until he was against me and bent him back over my arm, laughing at the consternation on his face.

"I think it's you who needs to learn how to stop playing games so much." The harsh voice sounded from the doorway. I looked up to find Xavier standing there, his arms crossed on his chest with an angry look on his face.

I glared at him, slowly pulling Winston back up before stepping back to allow him his personal space. I ignored Xavier and turned to Samantha. "I had a great time dancing with you, Sam. Winston, I'm kind of hungry and wouldn't mind getting something to eat. Would it be all right for me to take a lunch break?"

Winston nodded and opened his mouth to speak, but Xavier cut him off. "Victor wishes to see you, Winston."

"You know what, Xav? Like I told you earlier, you need to relax. Maybe you need to get laid," I taunted, pulling Sam close to my side. "Seems like it's been awhile." I thought he was going to explode. His face turned bright red and his eyes flashed with fire. I just grinned serenely and walked towards him, pulling Sam behind me. When we reached him, his fists were clenched at his side, and he wouldn't look at me. "See ya, Xav."

I sauntered breezily through the door, Sam in tow. Sam looked at me with shock. "I can't believe you did that!" she cried.

I just started laughing and let her go. "I'm going to get something to eat. Want to come?"

"Sure. But do you know who that was?" she asked me as we waited for the elevator.

"I have not a care in the world for who he is because without so much as a greeting, he copped an attitude with me. For nothing. Only because I'm going to be working here.

He thinks I'm going to be sleeping with each of my assignments. Only the joke's on him, because I'm gay," I replied cheerfully as we stepped onto the elevator.

I probably should have thought about how I said it, because she squeaked at my admission, and I looked over at her to see her eyes bulging out of her head. I closed my eyes and shook my head, sighing. "Are you disgusted? It's all right if you are. We don't have to be friends."

"No! That's not what I meant. I was just surprised is all and saddened the world of women has lost such a great guy to the world of men." Sam sighed dramatically causing me to crack up with laughter.

"I like you, Sam. You remind me a lot of my best friend Trinity."

At lunch, I told her about Trinity and moving to the city. I also told her about my life on the farm, how I figured out I was gay, my father's disapproval because I didn't want to continue tradition on the farm, and how I'd been suffocating there. She told me about her current relationship, her career goals, and why she was working for Temptation. She never slept with her clients no matter how much money they offered her. In her spare time, she was going to college to become a lawyer. "I was thinking maybe this job will give me the chance to go to school to become an artist," I admitted, not looking her in the eye as I twirled my straw in my glass. "I've always loved to draw and paint. I see things in a way others don't, or can't. And I'm continually struck by a person's beauty. I don't mean just the outside. There are some women who look like the Venus de Milo, but inside they're uglier than sin."

"That's a great goal. Why not give it a shot? Once you start doing assignments, you can enroll in one of the local colleges and give painting a try. If you don't like it, you can always pursue something else," she encouraged, her eyes twinkling.

"You truly are a beautiful person, Sam. I can tell that even in the short amount of time we've spent together." She beamed at me, and blushed at my compliment.

"Thank you."

4

Back at the agency, I made my way upstairs to see Winston, my mind on what I had revealed to Sam. Since the move to the city and trying to get a job I could keep, I'd neglected to pursue what I really wanted to do. Hopefully with this job I could actually have the money and time to take a few courses. I decided to drop by one of the campuses in the area and grab a couple of pamphlets on what they offered. The rest of the day passed by very quickly, and soon Winston told me to call it a day. "I'm proud of your progress already, Fagan. You're certainly more accomplished at some things than I expected."

"Thanks. I think that was partly my mother and partly my best friend Trinity. Hey, do you know where the closest college campus is from here?" I asked.

"Yeah, about five blocks west of here. Why?" Winston was putting away the dishes and silverware we'd been using for the table manners training. He really was an attractive, if slightly dorky, man.

"I wanted to see what kind of art classes they offer. Take a few if possible."

"That's great!" He lifted an eyebrow at me in surprise. "Is that why you came to the city?"

"Sort of. It's one of the reasons. I've always felt I have an eye for beauty. There are certain things in this world that amaze me with their simple grace. One of the best things about living on the farm was all the beautiful sides of nature you get to see. But then again, there are ugly sides of nature too. Forest fires, droughts, blizzards."

"You sound like you miss it," Winston observed and I backtracked quickly.

"No. Not at all. I love the city life. The sounds, the sights, and so many people. There's never a dull moment." I grinned at him, and tapped a finger against my chin. "Say, Winston, are you into men or women?"

Winston choked and I laughed. "That's kind of an impertinent question, don't you think?" He looked at me regally.

I shook my head. "Nope. I was just wondering. I have no problem admitting I'm gay. I prefer men over women."

Winston's expression was priceless. He looked like he had swallowed a toad. "You're gay?" he squeaked as he spoke sending me into a fit of laughter.

"Yep. One hundred percent. Of course, only you, Victor, Sam, and Georgina know. So let's keep that fact to ourselves, hmm? I figure since you're supposed to be my mentor then I should tell you. Plus, it'll help you understand me a little bit better."

"You really angered Xavier earlier," he mused.

"Xav really needs to relax. I told him the same thing when I was on my break. He judged me before he even knew my name. And that irritates me. I can't stand people who judge others without knowing anything about them, based on what they assume is the correct way to think. I know that I don't like him because of his attitude and rudeness. He's very haughty for someone who helps run this place," I pointed out, practically sulking.

Winston laughed. "I think you're attracted to him."

"What? Never! He's a bastard on the inside which makes him ugly on the outside," I spluttered, standing up from the chair with an indignant sound. "I'm going home."

"I'll see you tomorrow, Fagan."

I left the building and headed west towards the campus Winston had mentioned. The sun was hanging low in the sky, splashing purple and orange hues across the tops of the skyscrapers. There was something so pure about the sight, and the colors made me sigh with pleasure. I found the campus easily and located the administration offices to find out if they had any brochures on the art classes offered. There were classes for beginners that steadily increased in skill. I was getting excited and I held onto the papers tightly as I went to meet Trinity at the diner. Things were looking up. I could hardly wait for the next day to begin.

The two weeks of training went by fairly quickly and they left me with a sense of refinement. Of course, I felt like an idiot through most of the lessons, but I suppose when in Rome… you know what they say. Anyway, Trinity convinced me to sign up for the classes, so when I got my first paycheck, I went straight to the college and enrolled in the beginner's class. I had a tour of the campus, spoke with the art teacher Professor Klein, and was given a list of all the materials I would need. That took up more than half of my paycheck, but the expense would be worth it in the end.

I had to get Professor Klein's signature in order to add his course. His artwork was simply amazing. Several of his pieces were on display in his classroom. I think at one point he was hitting on me, but I ignored his advances, even though I found him relatively attractive with his shaggy brown hair, which could use a trim. He was about my height, give or take an inch, and had these ocean-blue eyes you could almost drown in. Okay, that sounded a little melodramatic, but he was definitely hot. Not overly muscular yet nicely shaped.

After I left the college armed with my list, I went straight to an art supply store and bought everything on the list. By the time I was finished, I had two huge bags of supplies and could barely carry them as I walked out of the store. A horn blew to my left and I turned my head to find Victor leaning over the center console of a fire-red Corvette to shout out the passenger window. "Hey, Fagan! You want a lift?"

My arms were already aching, so I nodded and walked to the car. He popped the trunk and helped me stow the two bags before we both climbed into the front seat. "Wow! This is a great car!" I slid my hand along the leather seat and gazed around in awe.

"Yeah, but I'm thinking of getting rid of it. Hercules can't fit in here so I also have a truck. Which way to your home?" Victor requested as we pulled back out into traffic.

"Uh…" I didn't really want him to see where I lived but I gave him directions anyway and about ten minutes later we were pulling up in front of my apartment building.

Victor didn't say anything, just put the car in park, turned the engine off, and climbed out of the car to get my bags. As he helped me, he asked, "What are all the art supplies for?"

"Oh! Yeah! I just signed up for an art class at the college a few blocks from Temptation!" I felt so excited about going to school.

"That's great. I didn't know you were interested in art. My

cousin—" Before he could go any further, I interrupted him rudely.

"Thanks for giving me the opportunity to work for you, Mr. Harri... Uh, I mean Victor. The job couldn't have come at a better time. I've had a lot of fun with the training, although I'm a little nervous about tomorrow night's assignment."

"Oh, don't be. Tyrone will walk you through what you have to do and point out any problem areas we need to work on. So don't be nervous!"

I took the bags from him, bid him goodbye and trudged up the stairs, sighing when I finally got the apartment door open. The place really wasn't much. Our small, two-bedroom apartment was sparsely furnished with an old beat-up leather couch and loveseat, a scarred wooden coffee table, and a small television. We hardly watched TV so we didn't really need cable. We only watched movies on the DVD player we had indulged in once we arrived in the city. Trinity wasn't home and I was disappointed I wouldn't be able to tell her my news just yet. I walked into the kitchen to make myself something small to eat for dinner, since I wasn't overly hungry, and settled down after popping a movie into the player.

Tomorrow was my first assignment and I was anxious. Once the movie was over, I went out onto the fire escape and lit up a cigarette to try and relax. I stared out over the park and listened to the sounds of loud music booming from cars rolling by, shouts of laughter, and bursts of conversation. There was a certain allure to this city I just couldn't seem to get out of my head. Ever since we had moved here, I'd felt more at home than the entire time I'd lived on the farm. I mean, I love my family and all, but I had felt so stifled back home. Like I couldn't breathe. Ironic isn't it? I felt freer in a city of millions of people than I did back home. I admit I do miss the stars. You couldn't see very many of them here with the city lights reflecting off the sky. I used to sit out on the porch swing at home and just listen to the crickets, watch the fireflies as they darted around the yard, and count the endless amount of bright specks in the sky while wondering if one of them contained another form of life.

I truly believe life on other planets exist. Otherwise, it just wouldn't make sense for there to be all those other planets or space out there. I just hope it's not like those movies such as Independence Day. That would suck. Besides, I'm in one of the cities they attacked first! I took a drag of the cigarette and inhaled the nicotine deep into my lungs, relishing the buzz that ran through my veins. Tossing the butt to the ground below, I turned and climbed back inside the window.

Trinity was just coming in the door and wrinkled her nose at the smell of smoke coming from me. "You've been smoking again, haven't you?"

"Don't I always? How was work today, Trin?" I yawned and flopped down on the couch.

Trinity had gotten a degree at college for accounting and finance, and now worked for a very prestigious accounting firm in the city. She made good money, but she had huge student loans to pay off so we were both pretty strapped for cash most of the time. "It was all right. Nothing exciting happened. How about you? Isn't tomorrow night your big night?" she asked, dumping her purse and briefcase onto the nearby easy chair.

"Yeah. I'm a little nervous but I'm sure I'll be fine. I signed up for my classes today though. Those start next week." I yawned again and closed my eyes, my breathing deepened as I succumbed to sleep. I felt Trinity brush my hair back from my face just before I lost consciousness. I really did love her. Sometimes I wished I could love her the way she wanted me to, but I guess my life isn't meant to be easy. Trinity shook me awake a little while later, and helped me stand up to go in my room. My eyes were blurry and I didn't even bother to remove my clothes, I just crashed onto the bed and fell back into oblivion.

Fingers trailed over my skin, caressing the hot flesh. Lips followed those fingers mere seconds later. My head was thrown back in pleasure and little pants of breath were escaping me. My body felt like I was in an inferno, my blood pounding through my veins, my hands buried in the long hair of the owner of those fingers. I arched my back when I felt those lips feasting on my inner thigh, followed by little flicks of the tip of his tongue. I groaned when that hot, wet mouth engulfed my achingly hard shaft and pushed my hips up, desperate to bury myself in the moist heat. I opened my eyes to gaze down at my lover and met those deep, enchanting gray eyes.

Wait a minute! Gray eyes?

I shot up in bed, gasping for breath with a serious hard-on, and covered my face with my hands. I couldn't believe I just had an erotic dream about Xavier James. What the hell! I looked at the clock and saw it was only five in the morning. I flopped back down among the sweaty bedclothes. My hands clenched in the sheets because I refused to jerk off to thoughts of that arrogant man. I breathed deeply and could feel every nerve ending in my body alive with lust. Damn it! How the hell could I have had such a sensual dream with him as the featured man? It didn't make sense. I detest him.

I had seen him at work yesterday and been on the receiving end of the same disdainful, haughty look. The bastard still thinks just because I'm getting paid to take a woman out I'm going to have sex with her. But he doesn't know you're gay, my mind whispered to me and I shoved the little voice away. Shut up! I refused to ever tell him. Let him think what he wanted. I finally managed to fall back asleep and woke up at eight when the alarm went off. Winston wanted me there early, so he could walk me through exactly how the date should go and to introduce me to Tyrone. I still felt nervous, but I decided to try and do my best. Hopefully that would be good enough.

5

I stood in front of the mirror Winston placed me in front of and he slowly handed me clothing to put on. He briefed me on my assignment as I dressed. "Her name is Abigail Grayson. She is the daughter of Walter Grayson, the CEO of a huge oil company. She has blonde hair, blue eyes, about five foot, four inches, and she loves to dance. She's been to our agency several times in the past, usually when she has some function to attend with her father. Tonight, her father is giving a reception to some foreign business tycoon and she is requesting our services. Her cousin will also be attending, which is why Tyrone was commissioned to go with you. He has been assigned to Abigail many times in the past, but she requested someone new."

When I was fully dressed, I could hardly recognize myself. He had put me in a pair of black slacks, dress shirt, suit jacket, and shoes. Then he slicked my hair back, gave me a Rolex watch to use for the night and a diamond stud earring to put in my ear in place of the simple silver ball I wore every day.

"Now, Tyrone is going to be with you as well. So he can help smooth over any moments of awkwardness. Once the date is over and you've escorted the women to their respective homes or hotels, you'll come back here to change into your own clothing and return any other accoutrements we gave you," Winston instructed, stepping back to admire his handiwork.

The person in the mirror just wasn't me and I knew it. I was a plain ol' blue jeans and t-shirt kind of guy. And to see myself in a monkey suit with a Rolex watch and a diamond chip in one ear made me grimace at the picture I made. Stepping down off the small block in front of the mirror, I turned around to see a very tall, very sexy, black stud entering the room. He was beautiful: my height, muscular, tight pants, a drool-worthy body, shaved head and dark brown eyes, with a walk like a proud lion stalking its mate.

Winston saw me looking and turned around, smiling at the man. "Ah, Tyrone. I see you're doing better."

The man oozed sex appeal and I couldn't help but stare. He was definitely what they called eye-candy. The voice issuing from those lips was pure silk and slid over my skin like the touch of sheets on a hot summer night.

"I am. So this is the newbie huh? Are you sure he's ready?" Tyrone looked at me dubiously.

His eyes raking my body caused my knees to weaken and I steadied myself on a chair nearby. "I'm ready," I piped up, stepping forward once I had my wits about me. I held out my hand. "I'm Fagan Swift."

"Tyrone Drestler." He took hold of my hand, engulfing it in his hard grip. His skin felt wonderful against my own, and I wondered if he would feel just as good all over. "Let's get a move on, Swift. We don't want to keep the ladies waiting." He dropped my hand and strode back the way he'd come, leaving me to follow behind.

I glanced nervously at Winston and followed Tyrone out the door, into the elevator, and out the front entrance of the agency. The sun had set about an hour ago and the city was just starting to liven up for its nighttime partying. A limo waited at the front for us and I grinned with glee. "I've never ridden in a limo before!" I said excitedly.

Tyrone just shook his head and climbed into the door the driver held open for us. He didn't seem to like me. I was starting to develop a complex with all of these people who disliked me before we'd even held a proper conversation. I followed him inside and settled into the plush seat, unable to believe this was happening to me. "So, Winston tells me you're the best they have. How long have you worked at Temptation?"

"Two years." Tyrone didn't elaborate, just looked out the window with a bored expression on his face.

I studied him and wondered what I had done to irritate him. Shaking my head, I turned to gaze in silence at the scenery passing by. Ten minutes later, we pulled up in front of a huge mansion and I couldn't help but gape at the impressive home. I had never seen such lavish splendor before. It actually kind of made me gag, the way the rich lived their lives. The driver opened the door for us to step out. Tyrone led the way up the walk to the front door. The door opened as we approached and a maid stepped back to allow us entrance.

"Milady will be right down." The maid curtsied and left.

The house was gorgeous inside as well. Marble floors, stairs with a rich oak banister that would have been perfect for sliding down, but I doubted the banister had ever been used for such purposes. Large paintings and sculptures decorated the room. There was a painting of a beautiful sunset over the ocean that drew me in like flies to candy.

"Such a beautiful piece." I saw the loving strokes of the

brush and the way they had captured the almost surreal beauty of the sunset. The picture was signed in the corner by the artist, but I didn't recognize the initials. LJ.

"You have good taste."

I heard a soft, feminine voice behind me. I turned to see the woman who was to be my first assignment standing at the bottom of the stairs, an amused expression on her face.

"Miss Grayson, I presume?" I moved over to her side, and smiled down at her. "Abigail? A beautiful name for such a beautiful woman."

A slight flush broke out across the high planes of her cheeks as she offered her hand. I proceeded to bend over, kiss, and introduce myself. "I am Fagan Swift. And I look forward to spending the evening with you."

"Abigail Grayson. And I can see you are an impertinent young man, but adorably so." She giggled behind her hand and I wanted to gag. I hated fake innocence.

I offered her my arm and saw Tyrone conversing with another young woman, similar in features to Abigail. Abigail kept pressing her breasts into my arm as we headed out the front door and down the steps towards the waiting limo. I just wanted to laugh. She truly thought that would turn me on. Of course, she couldn't know that I was gay, but it was amusing to see her try. As the limo brought us to the reception hall, she kept sliding her hand along my thigh, pressing closer to me. "So Abigail, what do you like to do?" I asked.

"You know the usual. Shopping, dining, going to plays. I hope you don't want to stay too late at Daddy's party tonight. It's so boring being around those stuffy old people. I mean, all they do is talk business and none of them want to really party. I hate these things. Have you been to a lot of them?" she asked me curiously.

"A few," I replied vaguely.

The conversation continued in pretty much the same

way. She would ask me questions and I would answer as vaguely as possible. I didn't want to get her interested in me any more than she already was because she was too vapid for me, even if I was straight! She reminded me of the cheerleaders in my high school, the ones who used to tease the unpopular girls and screw their football boyfriends up on Tyson Point. Tyson was the name of our town mascot, a goat. A goat for cryin' out loud! I mean, how small town can you get? I don't know how many times the sheriff would catch them at it and take them home to their parents.

I used to make it a hobby to call the sheriff and tell them about the cars parked up there. Aw, don't look at me like that! I know it's pathetic, but come on! There was nothing else to do! And if my life was a living hell, and they helped make it worse, why wouldn't I want to share a little of it? These same girls would tease me about being gay. One even went so far as to try and seduce me one night, pretending she had broken up with her boyfriend and needed a shoulder to cry on. It turned out to be a bet between them to see how far she could get me to go with her. Needless to say, that left some scarring.

Now, here I sit, returning to the mental state of those times. My skin crawled at the thought of being with this woman, but I held it back and just grinned at her stupidly. When we arrived at the reception hall, I breathed a sigh of relief and exited the limo, helping her out gracefully. Flashes popped off as we stepped away and I blinked dazedly. I saw several men standing with cameras outside the hall. I wondered who they were and just shrugged as I guided Abigail towards the building. I could hear string music coming from the room we approached and I almost groaned. I hated classical music. Damn, I had better be getting paid well for this! Classical music was like water torture to me!

There were dozens of men in tuxedos or business suits

and women in cocktail dresses milling around the room. Trays of champagne were carried around by white-jacketed waiters. I grabbed two off the nearest one and handed one to my assignment, taking a sip of the foul liquid and smiling as though I were enjoying it. Abigail dragged me over to meet her father, which was right around when I started sweating. Tyrone disappeared and I sighed, knowing I was on my own. Her father was intimidating, but I didn't show that I was affected, I just introduced myself and then dragged her off to dance, setting the glasses on a nearby table.

The orchestra began playing a waltz and I led her right into it, moving easily around the room. She gazed up at me, her hand on my arm, and the other hand in mine. "You don't seem like the others," she mused.

"What do you mean?" I asked her, spinning us both towards the opposite side of the dance floor.

"The others have this arrogant confidence around them. You seem like you're confident, but not arrogantly so. I like that. And I can tell you aren't comfortable here, but you're hiding it well."

I couldn't help but stare at her amazement. "How did you know?"

"I'm not just a socialite, you know." She laughed, her blue eyes sparkling. Her pale blonde hair had been pulled back into a bun at the top of her head and several long strands were left to dangle over her shoulders. She had on a sparkling red dress that clung to her curves, leaving nothing to the imagination. The dress flowed to her ankles, but the slits up the side to the tops of her thighs made it obvious a miniskirt would have been more decent.

She leaned forward, enclosing me in her perfume, and whispered, "I hope you're the same way in the bedroom as well." Her laughter tinkled like shattering glass along my nerves.

I gave her a tight smile and just kept my mouth shut. No sense in ruining my first assignment by refusing her immediately. At the end of the song, we made our way over to the table we were to sit at. The food was horrible and the speeches being given about one thing or another were boring. Is this what these people did on a nightly basis? I stifled a yawn at one point, and I felt her foot sliding up my leg along my inner thigh. I bit my lip and reached under the table to gently push her foot back down to the floor. She pouted, but I ignored it and took a sip of the soda I had ordered with my meal.

Finally, the evening was over! We met up with Tyrone and Abigail's cousin at the front of the hall. The limo was waiting outside and I gratefully climbed in after Abigail, sighing with pleasure as I sank into the plush seat. Abigail immediately attached herself to my side the moment I took my seat beside her. The smell of her perfume was suffocating and I began to wonder if this was how all the assignments would be. Because if so, I knew it wouldn't be something I could enjoy doing for long. It was something I would have to force myself to do just long enough to finish off those art courses.

Abigail leaned closer and whispered into my ear, trailing her fingertips along my thigh. "I know you aren't supposed to be paid for anything other than your services as an escort but I wouldn't mind throwing in a little extra for a bit of 'dessert'. If you know what I mean."

I clenched my jaw and grinned tightly. "I'm afraid I'm a little tired. I don't much care for dessert."

I saw her eyes blaze and sighed inwardly, wondering if Victor would find out I had refused her and fire me. Even if he did say there was a no sex policy, it was obvious I had displeased her by refusing her offer. I mentally shrugged and figured if I was to be fired, then so be it. There is no way I could have sex with her even if I wanted to. Women totally turned me off.

"I see," she said, her voice almost a growl. "Well, then I guess we'll call it a night."

Tyrone stopped me part way up the walk and said quietly, "It's fine if you don't want to stay with her tonight, but I'm staying here so you can take the limo back to the agency. I'll make sure that Abigail has her dessert."

He winked at me and then turned serious. "You did a good job tonight, kid. You kept her satisfied through most of the night. I'll make sure Victor knows."

He headed back towards the ladies. I followed slowly behind to bid Abigail a goodnight before getting back into the car. On the way back to Temptation, I couldn't stop from thinking back over the evening. I prayed all of my assignments weren't like this one. It had been extremely boring and Abigail had been too clingy for my taste.

6

The agency was mostly deserted by the time the limo arrived. A different security guard than the one who was usually there stood just inside the door he opened for me. I smiled wearily at him and walked over to the elevators. Normally I would have introduced myself, but I was too tired to be my usual cheerful self. I pressed the button and leaned my head against the wall with my eyes closed.

"Back already?"

Shivers raced down my spine and I frowned because it wasn't like the voice was friendly; it was more sarcastic than anything else. I turned my head to glare at the man who was still haunting me in my dreams at night. "I'm sure you can see I'm back already. Dumb question."

There was a slight tightening of his mouth at my words but the elevator dinged. "Night, Xav." I smiled mockingly as I stepped into the elevator and hit the button for the fifth floor.

A hand snaked in between the doors and Xavier pushed them open. "You really are irritating."

"Did you stop me just to tell me that?" I asked, tiredly rubbing my eyes. "Look, can you for once just leave me alone? I'm tired and want nothing more than to change and go home."

"Job ain't working out for ya?" he mocked.

I opened my eyes, lowered my hand and gritted my teeth, refusing to give him the satisfaction of knowing he'd angered me. "Oh, it's nothing like that," I replied silkily, smirking. "A nightmare woke me up extremely early this morning."

I stepped forward and placed a hand on his chest, satisfied to see his eyes widen slightly. "You want to guess who the monster in the nightmare was, Xav? No? You."

I shoved him backward slightly. He stumbled a moment before he regained his footing. His eyes were flashing something undefined and were locked on me as the doors closed. I sighed shakily and rested my forehead against the cool metal. I rubbed my hand against my leg, trying to get the feel of his broad chest off of it. My emotions were on a rollercoaster and I needed a cigarette badly. Instead of heading to Winston's room, I went to the end of the hallway where the fire escape was and took the stairs two at a time to the roof. I pulled the pack from my pocket and lit one up, dragging deeply.

This job might be harder to handle than I expected. If things didn't start to get more comfortable I knew I'd have to leave. I didn't want to give up so easily because that's just not the person I am. The smoke I blew out curled up towards the night sky. The few stars visible twinkled at me almost mockingly. Whenever I was angry or depressed back home, I would take a cigarette and a cup of coffee out to the porch swing and just stare up at the sky, searching for answers. But here, things were different. I wondered if Trinity was home yet. I pulled out my cell phone and dialed our number, sighing as I waited for her to pick up.

"'Lo," a sleepy voice answered.

"Aw, shit, I'm sorry, Trin. I didn't mean to wake you. I thought you'd still be up. I'll let you go." I went to disconnect the call but she stopped me.

"What's the matter?" I could hear the rustle of bed sheets and the click of a lamp as she fully woke up.

"Nothing. I just don't know if I can do this job, Trin." I dragged deeper on the cig, watching the tip flare up in embers.

"What happened tonight? Did you have a good time?"

"She was all over me, pressing her breasts against me and hinting at other things all night. You remember those cheerleaders in our senior class?"

"How could I forget," she said wryly. They'd teased her too, especially in gym glass.

"She reminded me of them. All giggles and twirling the hair. I almost wished I could call the sheriff to break it up!" She laughed on the other end and I started to feel better. She always had a way of cheering me up. I sank down to sit against the wall. "I'm going to tough it out for a little while, see if it gets better, but I don't know if I can keep this up for long. I thought it would be so easy and all. I was so uncomfortable tonight."

"It was your first night, hun. Just take it easy and go with for flow. I'm sure it will get easier. You were just nervous."

"Yeah, I guess. I can't wait to attend my first art class." I stubbed the cigarette out beside me and stared up at the stars. "Trin?"

"Hmm?" She yawned.

"Do you think it was a mistake to come to this city?"

Trinity was quiet for a moment and then spoke up with a low tone of voice. "I think this was the best thing we ever did, babe. I know everything is so unsettled right now and you haven't had a job that lasted longer than a couple of weeks, but things are going to work for us here. We have each other and together we will succeed."

"I guess you're right. All right, let me go. I got to report back to Winston and change back to my street clothes. I'll see you in the morning." I clicked off the phone and dragged myself up, slowly making my way back downstairs.

The hallway was still empty and I entered Winston's room, where I found him lying on the bed in the corner, fast asleep. I grinned and tiptoed over to look down on him. He really could be an attractive guy, but I didn't go for the nerdy types. I saw my clothes hanging on a rack and quietly pulled them off the hangers, slung off the suit and dressed in my jeans and t-shirt. I slid my sneakers on and just stuffed the shoelaces inside. I left the Rolex, earring, and suit on the bed next to Winston with a note, letting him know the night had gone okay. Tomorrow I didn't have to report to work, since I'd had my first assignment tonight and training was over. I was so glad tomorrow was my first art class.

I quickly headed back downstairs and exited the elevator, sighing when I saw the rain pouring down outside. It must have come out of nowhere, because a few minutes before, the weather had been fine. I stood at the front entrance looking out morosely. Shit. I didn't want to get sick. I only had fifty bucks left of my check until I got paid again, but I guess I was going to have to call a cab. I turned to look at the guard and started when I found Xavier a few feet away from where I was. I didn't acknowledge him as I pulled out my cell and called information. "Yeah, can you connect me to a cab company, please?"

"One moment, please," the operator stated.

There was a click and the ringing on the other end began. Before anyone could pick up, my cell phone was plucked from my hand and closed with a snap. I stared, flabbergasted at what Xavier had just done. "What the hell did you do that for?" I demanded, snatching at my cell but he pulled it away, an amused look on his face.

"Aren't you a little old to be playing keep-away?" I asked sarcastically. His amusement trailed off and the arrogance flared back up.

"Follow me." He turned on his heel, my cell phone still in his hand. I had no choice but to follow him.

"Would you give me back my cell and stop playing games?" I was exhausted and wanted nothing more than to go home.

He led me to a door at the back of the building that opened into a parking garage. He walked towards one of the few cars left, a dark blue 1969 Camaro. Totally unexpected! I would have thought he'd be driving a BMW or a Mercedes. To find out he drove such a classic car left me astounded.

"Nice car." I slid my fingers over the hood, admiring the sleek look of the front. "A little surprised, Xav. This car seems a little too cool for a stuffed shirt like you."

Xavier ignored my comment and slid into the driver's seat, leaning over to unlock the passenger side. "Get in."

I balked at the idea of accepting, but it was either that or use the last of my money to take a taxi. Sighing again, I opened the door and climbed in. The leather seat was amazingly comfortable and I breathed in the smell of the interior. "This reminds me of the car my dad used to own. Great car. But he had to sell it one year, because we needed the money to keep the farm from going into bankruptcy."

"Farm?" Xavier started the car, its engine roaring to life with a growl as he stepped on the gas.

"Yeah. My dad owns a farm back home. He wanted me to inherit it, but I just wasn't one for that kind of life. That was his, ya know? My sister loves it. I told dad to let her have it." My words were getting a little slurred with how tired I was feeling. I tried to sit up straight to keep from falling asleep.

"So you left a farm boy life to become an escort?" Xavier's voice was dry with sarcasm and I turned my head to glare at him.

"You try living on a farm for twenty-four years and see how boring it can be," I snapped before I directed him where to go.

The headlights cut a swath through the pouring rain and the wiper blades were rushing back and forth, clearing the window of water. It pounded against the roof, and combined with the smooth ride of the car, started to lull me to sleep.

"Hey, wake up." Xavier shook me roughly as I started to doze.

"Damn. I'm sorry. I'm really tired." I yawned and shook my head, trying to keep myself awake yet again.

"So I was in your dreams?" he asked me and I knew he was being an asshole again.

"Yep. It didn't become a nightmare until you showed up in it," I replied, smirking.

Xavier didn't say anything more until we pulled up in front of my apartment. His hands were clenched on the wheel and I wondered what the hell his problem was, but anything I did or said irritated him.

"We're here," he grated.

"Thanks," I said before I reached for the handle and thrust the door open, slamming it shut behind me. I rushed out and into the apartment building. I heard the roar of the engine as he sped off.

The first art class was great. Professor Klein was patient and enthusiastic. He talked through most of the first hour about his course and what he expected. The second hour he gave us the opportunity to paint or draw whatever we wanted. He wanted to get a feel for where we stood. I hadn't had any training, so I stuck with drawing for the time being. I just started sketching and before I knew it, I was staring down at the man who was beginning to haunt me. I couldn't believe it. I picked it up and was going to rip it up when the professor stopped me.

"You're not going to destroy that, are you?" He took it away from me and held it out to observe it. "The natural talent you have is amazing. These lines here show your deep feelings for this man. The expression you gave him here, in his eyes, is one of arrogance, yet there is something more. Almost a hint of desire for the one who caught his eye. This is a beautiful sketch. I refuse to let you destroy it. This is going to be saved for display at our art festival in May."

I stared at him in horror. "You can't!"

"But of course I can. This is a beautiful piece." Without another word, Professor Klein walked away from me, leaving me staring after him in panic.

Oh shit! This wasn't good. Where the hell did I get that image from? I would have to talk with the professor after class. There was no way I could let him display my drawing. May was almost a year away. I had to be able to convince him by then! I let it go for now, but the fact I had drawn that irritating man was enough to set my teeth on edge. I picked up my charcoal and started sketching again. This time I pictured Trinity and started drawing her. I was proud of it once it was done. I had given her the faraway look she sometimes gets when she becomes lost in her daydreams. She only does it when she's upset about something. I guess it's her way of processing whatever happened to make her upset.

Professor Klein asked me to stay after class once it was time to leave, so I loitered around his desk at the front until all of the students were gone. He perched on the edge of his desk and looked at me, his blue eyes studying me intently. "You seem upset that I'm going to display your drawing."

"Well… yeah." I shifted uncomfortably. "I don't even know why I drew him. Argh! He aggravates me to no end."

"Passion is best displayed in the form of art. Even if you deny it, there are feelings buried inside you for the man you've drawn. If, by the time the art festival comes around you truly do not want the drawing displayed, then I will hold it back and submit something else. But the greatest piece an artist can do is one filled with passion and desire. I hope that is one thing I will be able to teach you through the next several months. I'll see you tomorrow, Fagan." He smiled at me, pushing away from his desk.

I nodded and left, my backpack with my supplies slung over my shoulder. I was lost in thought as I walked towards home. Maybe that was why I didn't notice the man approaching me from behind.

7

I was halfway home when suddenly someone slammed into me, knocking my backpack from my shoulder to catch on my wrist. He grabbed my bag and I instinctively clenched my hand, glaring at the offender who was trying to steal my stuff. Before I knew it, the bastard had whipped out a blade and sliced at the strap of the bag. When I refused to let go, he stabbed me in my upper arm, causing my grip to loosen as I screamed in pain. Blood started spilling everywhere as the son-of-a-bitch took off. The knife had gone deep and I could feel unconsciousness creeping in on me as I stood there shaking with adrenaline.

I reached automatically for my cell phone, but it wasn't there! Son of a bitch, that bastard still had it. Xavier had never returned it to me the night before and I had been too tired to notice. I pressed my hand tight against the gushing wound on my arm, trying to stem the flow, as I stumbled towards the convenience store on my right. The man behind the counter stared at me in horror as I slowly bled to death in his store. I collapsed against his counter, knocking several of the small racks down. "Call… an ambulance," I gasped out as I lost consciousness and hit the floor.

The next thing I knew, I woke up in a hospital room with my arm stitched up and bandaged. Trinity and Victor stood off to the side, quietly talking, when I opened my eyes. I squinted against the painful light and rasped out, "Damn, I feel like I got stabbed."

"Fagan!" Trinity's eyes were red-rimmed and she rushed over, hugging me tightly, wrenching a groan of pain from me.

"Easy now. I'm still in pain here." I brought my good arm up to wrap around her. "Hey, babe. It's okay. I'm fine." She was sobbing into my neck.

"You idiot! You almost died. You lost so much blood they had to do a transfusion. If you'd have left me alone in this city, I'd have come after you just to kill you again."

I laughed and then groaned in pain as the stitches in my arm pulled slightly. "Victor, man, I'm so sorry. I just start and already I'm messing up."

"It's all right, Fagan. We just want you to concentrate on getting better. Tyrone told me what a great job you did the other night, and I'm glad to know you'll be okay working at Temptation."

"The other night? Wasn't it last night?" I asked, confused. The two of them looked at each other and I moaned. "How long was I out?"

"Twenty-four hours."

I let out a profanity that would have burned Mother Teresa's ears. Then I remembered what he got away with. "Shit. He got all of my art supplies and I don't have the money to get them again." I brought my hand up to my eyes. "Why do these things happen to me?"

Trinity gave me a watery smile and patted my good shoulder. "Because you're a magnet for trouble."

Victor stepped forward and handed me five hundred dollars in cash. "Here, this is your pay from your first assignment. So you'll have enough money to get your art supplies again."

I stared at him in shock. "Just from one assignment?" I asked in surprise. Five hundred dollars for one night?

"Yes. See, this kind of job has its benefits." He winked at me before looking at his watch. "All right, I have to get back to Temptation. Xavier's probably tearing his hair out. I am glad to see you're awake. Take your time getting better and we'll have an assignment waiting for you when you get back."

Victor left and I looked up at Trinity. "Wow." It was all I could manage.

"Why didn't you just let him have the bag, Fagan?" she demanded, her eyes flashing at me in her fury at my stupidity. "Nothing in that bag was worth dying for. And why didn't you have your cell phone on you?"

"Because Xavier took it from me the night of my assignment when I refused to accept a ride from him. He held onto it, but he never gave it back. I was so tired by the time we got to the apartment, I forgot," I mumbled sheepishly.

I saw her anger flare up higher and she smiled tightly. "I see. I think now that you're awake they probably will let you go home either tonight or tomorrow. But visiting hours are over in about ten minutes so I need to get going. I'm so glad you're okay, Fagan."

Trinity hugged me again and then left. I couldn't believe this had happened. Gee, what a way to almost screw up another job. I really was a disappointment. A nurse came in a moment later to check me over and told me they would send me home in the morning. Great, then at least I can attend my art classes. I fell back asleep after the shot she gave me.

I woke up around two in the morning gasping for breath and in the midst of a panic attack. I had been having a nightmare about the mugging, the remembered pain, and even though I would never admit it out loud, the fear. I sat up with my heart pounding. I dropped my head into my hands and tried to catch my breath. When I had calmed down a bit, I reached up to turn on the little lamp by the bed and saw my cell phone on the nightstand with a note. Strong, bold cursive writing splashed across the page.

Your friend came to see me and told me what happened. I apologize for not returning your cell phone the other night. I cannot help but feel a small amount of responsibility for not making sure you had it before you got out of my car. I am truly sorry for my lapse in judgment. Get well soon. Xavier James.

Shaking my head, I ran the tip of one finger over the writing and then realized in horror at what I had just been doing. I crumpled the note up and tossed it into the garbage can by the bed. That was bullshit. He didn't know how to feel guilty, because he had no emotions other than his own arrogance and feeling of superiority. It unsettled me the bastard had been in there while I was asleep and looking at me in such a vulnerable state. I tried to fall back asleep but couldn't. I lay there awake until the sun started to slowly filter into the room.

A nurse came in with breakfast shortly after seven. I grimaced at the nasty powdered eggs and watery oatmeal. Do they really feed this shit to people? I mean, couldn't they at least make someone who's sick something appetizing, so they aren't feeling even more depressed about being sick? I hate hospitals. I remembered all the time I spent in them when my mother was sick. The smell of antiseptic and the sight of so many ill people was nauseating.

Once the breakfast was taken away, I stood up and walked over to the small closet in the room, pulling out my clothes. There was blood on them, but I didn't care. I slowly and carefully pulled on my jeans, buttoning and zipping them up, before taking off the hospital gown and sliding the t-shirt on. I tried to bend over to tie my shoes once I had shoved my feet in them, but I couldn't because it pulled the stitches in my arm. So I just stuffed the laces into my shoes with my good arm and grabbed the rest of my stuff. I headed down to the nurse's station and stopped in front of it.

"Sir! You can't be up and around yet! You're supposed to be taken out in a wheel chair. Hospital policy," the nurse said heatedly, rushing around to try and get me to sit down.

"Don't touch me," I bit out through clenched teeth. "If you don't let me out of here NOW I'm going to start throwing a fit. I hate hospitals more than you could ever understand, lady. And I want out."

She looked at me in shock and with a tiny bit of fear. "Um... sir, please just have a seat in the chair and as soon as I get your discharge papers ready, we'll take you out. I promise. Just twenty minutes."

I looked at her, but nodded stiffly and sat in the wheel chair she had provided. She quickly settled everything, gave me several things to sign and motioned for an orderly to take me to the front entrance. Once outside the sliding doors, I stood up, waved off the orderly and opened my cell. "Trinity, it's me. I'm out. I couldn't take it there a moment longer."

"I was surprised you didn't do it last night," she commented, her voice wry. "How are you getting home?"

"I was going to take a cab since I have the money now." I grinned, even though she couldn't see it. "Can you get me the phone number to the school? I need to call and speak with my teacher about what happened."

"I already did," she replied.

"What?" I was surprised.

"He called here when you didn't show up for class yesterday. I explained the situation and he understood. He said to tell you he hopes you feel better and it wasn't worth risking your life for art supplies. He could have provided you with them until you could afford them," she pointed out, anger once again seeping into her voice.

"Yeah, yeah. It was just reflex, Trin. I couldn't help it."

We finished the call and I hailed a cab, climbing into the back seat and giving the driver my address. Things certainly had a way of working out like that for me. Trouble followed me everywhere. I used to get into all kinds of it back home. People knew about me before I even met them because of all the stories they had heard about me and my escapades. It was funny actually. It wasn't like I ever intended for any of it to happen. It just kind of did.

I spent the rest of the day lying around in bed resting. The following day, I went out to buy the items I needed to replace. I was able to buy a little better quality since Victor had given me such a large amount of money.

The store was great. It had everything an artist could possibly want or need: canvases, easels, paints, books, charcoal, and so much more. I splurged on a small watercolor kit and whistled happily as I left the store. I grabbed a quick bite to eat, then decided to stop by to see Winston, since Temptation was around the corner from where I was. My bags were in my good hand as I entered Temptation and the security guard rushed forward to take them from me. "Mr. Swift, they told me what happened. Leave those here with me so you can give your arm a rest."

I grinned and clapped him on the back. "Thanks, Tom. My arm was getting a little tired. And how many times have I asked you to call me Fagan? I hope everything is good with your wife and kids."

"Yes sir! Everything is good. The wife just gave me the good news, our third child is going to be on its way soon." He grinned broadly, proudly.

"That's great! Congratulations! Hey, why not name it

after me?" I winked at him, jokingly. "I'm just kidding. I wouldn't wish my name on anyone. It was a horror in school."

Tom laughed and I waved to Georgina as I walked towards the elevator. I pressed the button and looked down at my arm wrapped in bandages as I waited for it to arrive.

When it dinged, I looked up straight into those piercing gray eyes. Those eyes widened slightly at seeing me. I shrugged and stepped inside since it didn't seem like he was going to be exiting.

"What are you doing here?" he demanded as the doors closed and started to ascend to the fifth floor.

The tone grated on my already stretched nerves and I snapped, "Not that it's any of your business, but I came to see Winston."

"You should be at home resting. Not running around."

"Thanks for the advice, Xav. But I don't need it. I'm a big boy, and I can handle it."

"Yeah. I'm sure. Since you handled it so well and managed to get yourself cut up," he pointed out, crossing his arms over his chest.

I tightened my mouth and turned my head away, refusing to look at him or acknowledge his words. "You know, you're a lot like my father." I saw Xavier's body jerk slightly at my words. The elevator stopped and before I stepped out, I finished what I'd started saying. "Nothing I do is ever good enough for you."

Winston was in the midst of walking a new recruit through his table manners when I walked in. He looked up and his face brightened. "Fagan! What are you doing here? You're off duty until you heal."

"I know. I just dropped by to say hello and make sure you got everything back the other night. I didn't want to wake you since you were sleeping so peacefully."

He blushed and nodded. "Yeah. I got everything. Thanks. So how's the arm?"

"All right. Still painful. Are you torturing a new victim?" I raised an eyebrow when I saw the young man rubbing his knuckles.

"I don't torture them," he protested.

"Come on, Winston, you know it's true. My knuckles were practically bleeding by the time I got it down right."

The guy's eyes widened as he looked at Winston with fright. New respect glittered in his eyes and I grinned. "I just wanted to check in with you. I'll talk to you later okay? I should be back by next week."

"Get some rest. It'll take time for your arm to heal." He went back to his newest kitten and I left him to it. This time I took the stairs instead of the elevator, since every time I used the elevator I seemed to run into Xavier. I grabbed my packages from Tom and headed back home. The week away from work was boring and I spent a lot of time drawing. I even tried painting with the new watercolor kit. When I went back to get the stitches removed and the doctor told me I was going to be able to return to work, I was happy about it. I never sat around doing nothing. I was always on the go.

8

The first day back, I was given a new assignment. This time it was Duchess Brianna Newberry. I rolled my eyes, knowing she was going to be worse than the previous assignment. She'd had a predatory look in her eye the day I'd met her in the lobby. I found out she'd specifically requested me. I reported to Winston a couple of hours before the arranged time. This would be my first assignment on my own. I didn't know if I would be able to do as well as the first time, despite the fact Tyrone really hadn't been around much that night. He did help at the end, though, when I refused Abigail's request. I dressed in a tuxedo, gold cuff links, and another diamond stud in my ear. "Where am I off to now?"

"The duchess attends all of the up-and-coming events. There is an art gallery opening tonight and she has been invited by the artist personally."

"Art gallery?" I asked excitedly. Now that I could get used to!

"Yes. A new artist has put together an event tonight. And she wants you to escort her."

All right! I was getting excited about tonight's event, even if I did have to deal with the duchess. I almost skipped down the hall to the elevator once I was ready to go. A wide grin was on my face and I waved to Tom as I left the building to climb into the waiting Lincoln Town Car. We pulled up in front of the Excelsior Hotel and I took a deep breath before exiting the vehicle.

The duchess held out her hand in greeting and this time I bent low over it, pressing my lips against the back of her hand.

"Ah. I see they trained you well," she purred and I nearly gagged with the amount of perfume she'd splashed on herself.

I merely smiled with no comment and escorted her from the building, helping her to enter the sleek dark-colored car. The driver watched over us solicitously as she slid over and I scooted in next to her. The scent of her perfume immediately engulfed me. The only thing saving this night was the art exhibit, I thought as we sped towards the gallery.

"So do you like art?" she asked me, a predatory look in her eyes.

"Yes. I signed up for some classes at one of the colleges," I replied excitedly.

"Hmm. Well, you'll have to show me some of your paintings one day. Perhaps I can open some doors for you," she hinted suggestively. I almost shuddered, but caught myself in time. I knew what she wanted and why she offered the opportunity to me. But she was going to be sadly disappointed when I refused her.

When we arrived and stepped from the limo, there were flashing cameras and paparazzi waiting for us again. I hoped my dad or sister didn't see these photos. With a new girl every night, they might think I turned straight. I almost laughed out loud at that one! I saw the name of the artist on the placard by the front door as we entered and started in shock. Trace Klein. The artist was none other than my art teacher, Professor Klein. Trace. What a name. It fit him well, though. I grinned in eagerness and the duchess clasped my arm tighter. She pulled me to group after group of people to introduce me and chat about the latest fashions or the latest scandals. They had to be the most boring, trivial conversations I had ever had to listen to. She clung to my arm the entire time, showing me off to her friends. I looked around me, dying to go look at the artwork, but knew I was working and this wasn't a pleasure jaunt.

"Fagan?" I heard behind me, and turned, smiling when I saw my teacher.

"Professor Klein! I saw this was your show. You're a wonderful artist. You didn't tell me you were showing your paintings tonight," I accused gently.

"You know Trace Klein?" Brianna asked me in surprise, as though I were nothing but a hick and couldn't possibly know someone who was the slightest bit famous.

"He's my art teacher at the college I attend." I looked at Professor Klein in awe. "I didn't know he would be the artist tonight."

"And what do you think of the work?" The duchess was obviously putting me to the test.

"So far, the one over there, the abstract with all the vivid colors and interesting lines, is my favorite. But of course, we haven't walked through the gallery as of yet."

Professor Klein smiled softly and I could see a hint of interest in his eyes but, no matter how much I wanted to, I didn't feel any attraction in return.

"I think one day you'll be where I am, Fagan. Good evening, Brianna. I didn't mean to ignore you. How's your father?"

I stood there and listened to the two of them chat like

they were old friends. Then, finally, we got to view the paintings. There were some that literally took my breath away. Professor Klein followed along, explaining each one as we walked, and it made it all the more exciting. I changed my mind about my favorite one when I stopped short in front of a painting of a low-hanging moon with stars over a lake and trees surrounding it. There was a solitary cabin in the distance. The tiny windows were lit up with warmth, beckoning those viewing to join the occupant inside.

"Wow. This is beautiful," I whispered, entranced by the expert brush strokes and the haunting loneliness expressed by the painting. I looked at my teacher and wondered if he felt that way.

"This is my favorite as well." Professor Klein stepped up beside me, and said, "Did you notice anything about the woods?"

I stared harder and saw shadows as well as yellow eyes peering from between the painted trees. "Wolves!" I exclaimed and then looked closer.

Creatures were hidden cleverly throughout the painting. It gave it less of a lonely feeling. It was as though those animals were comforting the owner of the cabin.

"I painted this in one of my odd moods," he explained running the tip of a finger down the frame it was set in.

"I can see why you aren't selling it," I murmured, having noticed the red sticker affixed to the info card. I couldn't help but become totally consumed by the painting.

"Well, it's one of the few out here not for sale, but I'll make you a deal, Fagan. You excel in the class, paint me something of show quality, and I'll give it to you."

I stared at him in shock. "You can't just give me something this wonderful."

"Of course I can. I'm the artist." He smirked arrogantly.

"You should accept his offer, Fagan. It's not often an artist of Trace Klein's caliber extends an opportunity to own a piece of his work for such a small price," Brianna advised, her eyes shrewdly examining the canvas.

She gave him a brilliant smile and we moved on to the next painting, but my gaze kept straying back to that one.

Later, Professor Klein gave a short speech, followed by a longer one by the gallery owner, and it was obvious his show was a huge success. I can't believe the way this night turned out. It was amazing. Even though I had to make sure Brianna was entertained, it hadn't been too bad. She actually was pretty intelligent, not an airhead like the previous assignment. She knew a lot about the older styles of artwork and had even done a few herself, but it turned out painting wasn't actually her calling. She told me about the charity work she did and I found it admirable. The rest of the night went quite well and we arrived back at her hotel. As I knew she would, she invited me up, but I declined, politely mentioning the rule of the agency and my desire to keep my job. I made sure she got inside the hotel and as I was about to leave, she leaned up and kissed my cheek, pressing her breasts against my chest. I was cloaked in her perfume and couldn't wait to take a shower to get the smell off of me when I got home.

Back at the agency, Tom opened the door for me and I greeted him with a huge smile.

"A great night?" he asked me.

"Yeah. The gallery was great. And it turns out the artist is my professor at the college I attend." I headed towards the elevators and saw Xavier standing at the end of the hallway.

He was walking with a pretty woman about a head shorter than him and talking animatedly. A shaft of jealousy spiraled through me and I quickly turned my head back to the elevator, watching the numbers counting down. When I could not stop myself from glancing back, he was standing a few feet away, staring at me with a disgusted look in his eyes.

"I can see and smell you had a great night," he said sarcastically. "Thought you were claiming to be different from the others?"

I frowned and looked into the metal doors reflecting my image. I had lipstick on my cheek from where Brianna had kissed me. He probably could smell me clear across the lobby as well. I looked back at him and shrugged. "Believe what you want. You already have it set in your mind anyway."

I stepped into the elevator before the doors had even finished opening, slamming my palm on to the fifth-floor button. I begged the doors to shut and slumped back against the wall of the elevator when they finally did. I rushed through changing my clothes, giving everything back to Winston and racing from the building like the hounds of hell were at my heels.

Basically, that's the way the next six months went. We kept bickering like little kids. Every time we saw each other it was like two tomcats fighting over a tabby. I couldn't stop myself from saying things just to goad him into a response and to see the way his firm lips would tighten as his gray eyes would grow stormy with anger. The job got easier, though, and I became the duchess's favorite even though I never consented to sex. I guess talking with me was more stimulating than the other brain-dead escorts in the business.

My art classes were going great and I was improving every day. Professor Klein kept coming onto me, but I kept rebuffing him. Just yesterday, he'd asked me to stay after class and once everyone else had vacated the room, he asked me something that blew me away.

"Are you seeing someone?"

I couldn't stop my start of surprise at his question. "I'm sorry?"

"Are you seeing anyone?"

"No. Not in the sense you mean," I said wryly, thinking of the way I was 'seeing' someone. Lots of someones.

"I'd like to take you out to dinner," he said, stepping closer to me and I backed up until my shoulder blades were against the wall. He placed his palms on the wall beside my head and leaned in. "I like you. You're smart, talented, and attractive. I've been trying to hint at what I've wanted, but you didn't seem to notice, or else didn't want to. So I've decided to stop playing around."

"I'm sorry," I said honestly. "I just don't feel the same way."

"Then there is someone else," he said sadly, stepping back from me.

"No. Not at all. I just don't find myself attracted to you in that way," I protested, pushing thoughts of a certain gray-eyed someone from my mind. As I looked at Professor Klein, I could see my words had gotten through. I figured it would be a little uncomfortable in class, going forward, but I was trying not to let it get to me. I liked and admired him. I just wasn't interested in him physically.

So now here I stood in front of Temptation, bundled up against the cold, as Christmas approached. It was almost the end of December and tonight was the company holiday party. They had it at this time, because some of the escorts went home for the holidays. I knew I had to go home as well, otherwise, I would never live it down or hear the end of it.

It was just beginning to snow and I felt several flakes catch on my eyelashes. I grinned as I lifted my gaze to the sky, staring at the white blanket that was falling to the ground. I could hear Christmas music and the bells the Salvation Army Santa rang all day long. There were colored lights everywhere. It was a beautiful sight. One I have to say I will never tire of seeing. I was leaving next Friday to go home for a week for Christmas and would truly miss all of this. It was almost dark and I saw Tom standing at the entrance, waiting to open the door for me. I grinned excitedly at him. I was meeting Winston to ride with him. We were going to stop by Trinity's job and pick her up to go to the party. "Evening, Tom. Are you going to the party tonight?"

"No, someone has to be here to watch the building." He grinned. "And it's overtime for me so I can afford a new bike for my daughter."

I took a Christmas card out of my pocket and handed it to him, along with a small gift-wrapped bottle from my other pocket. "Merry Christmas, Tom."

"You shouldn't have!" he exclaimed, trying to refuse to take it, but I insisted, pushing it into his hands.

"I know I didn't have to. I wanted to. You've been great since I started here and I wanted to say thank you." I tilted my head to the side and smiled. "I like making people happy, and knowing I can provide someone with a little bit more cheer for their Christmas makes me happy. I can hardly wait to go home. My sister is going to absolutely love the diamond earrings I bought her. And my dad, well he's a little harder to shop for, but he likes to smoke pipe tobacco, so I bought him this really great hand-carved pipe that's shaped like the head of King Neptune. Christmas is going to be great this year!"

"It sounds like a great gift for your dad. I hope you have a wonderful Christmas." Tom tipped the bottle towards me in thanks when the elevator dinged.

Winston stepped out as I turned and my mouth dropped open. He wasn't wearing his glasses and his hair was combed back. He was dressed in a tuxedo with a long black trench coat over it. I whistled and he blushed. "Damn, if you weren't straight, I might have to take advantage of you tonight."

Then I thought of Trinity and started scheming. "You know, you'd be perfect for my roommate."

He stuttered and I clapped him on his back, laughing. We entered the parking garage where his little Toyota was parked. When he turned the car on, the radio was playing soft carols. Trinity was standing out in front of her office building with a co-worker when we arrived. She said goodbye to her friend and climbed into the back seat. She smiled when she saw Winston and I could see immediate sparks between the two of them.

9

The best thing about Christmas is mistletoe. It gives you the excuse to shed your shyness or your fear of rejection and just have the courage to go for it. When we got to the reception hall Victor had rented for the party, Trinity and Winston entered first. I spotted the mistletoe above the entrance. "Hey! You two are beneath the mistletoe! You have to kiss! It's tradition."

Everyone noticed and turned around starting to chant. "Kiss, kiss, kiss."

I was laughing, because even Trinity was blushing. Winston leaned down and gave her a chaste kiss on the lips, but Trinity wasn't the type to settle for half-assed and decided to take things into her own hands. She reached up, gripped the back of his head and pulled him in deeper, kissing him passionately. That was Trinity. She always did everything with all her heart and soul, no matter what it was. The crowd let loose with a chorus of wolf whistles, applause, and laughter as she pulled back to smirk up at his cherry-red face. "And you haven't even been drinking yet!" I crowed, delighted to see both of my friends happy.

The band played a mixture of Christmas carols and regular soft music. The food was excellent, but of course, Victor's taste was impeccable and he wouldn't have it any other way. I danced with Trinity and then coerced Winston to dance with her, pretending I was too tired to continue. I sat at a table watching the two of them dance and talk. I could tell they were attracted to one another. There are always little hints when two people were into each other. You just have to know what to look for: little looks, touches, body movements, the way someone speaks out of their normal pattern. I picked up my champagne glass and downed it in one gulp, suddenly engulfed by the Christmas blues. It had been a long time since I'd had a boyfriend and seeing the couples on the dance floor, pressing close to one another, was depressing. Sighing, I signaled a waiter and grabbed two more glasses of champagne when he approached. I downed the first one and then sipped the second one.

"Are you drowning your sorrows in champagne, my friend?" Victor slid into the seat beside me, his full lips pulled into a smile.

"Eh. Not really. I don't have anything to be sorrowful over," I said, swirling the champagne in the glass and watching the liquid swish around. "I have a great job, wonderful friends, a great beginning to a career as an artist, money, and my health. What more could I ask for?"

Victor studied me closely for several long moments, and then said, "Love."

I snorted. My depression made me pessimistic. "I don't believe in love, Victor. The one time I thought I was in love it turned out to be he was just using me."

"This isn't like you to be so down." He frowned and I shrugged. "You are one of the most happy-go-lucky people I have ever met. That's what I like about you so much. Cheer up, my friend. Life is too short to live it waiting for things to happen. You have to make them happen yourself. I told Xavier the same thing the other day."

"Ah, now there is a man who is never in a good mood, at least not around me. It's like I bring out the worst in him, and I don't even know why." I swallowed the rest of the champagne and grabbed another one from a waiter walking by. "I can hardly wait to go home. Just to hear my father tell me what a disappointment I am to him."

Victor stood, placed a hand on my shoulder, and said, "I'm sure that's not what he'll do. You've been gone a long time. He'll be happy to see his son, especially for Christmas. Relax, Fagan. Things may not always seem like they're going to work for you, but they wind up doing so in the end. Merry Christmas."

He walked away and I just kept drinking, the room kind of swirling a little as the alcohol started to take effect. The lights twinkled a little brighter and the laughter seemed muted. I stood up, wobbling a little on my feet, to walk out onto the back veranda of the reception hall to have a cigarette. I grabbed another glass on the way; I'd lost count of how many I'd downed, and once outside, leaned against the railing looking out over the gardens behind the hall. The chill bit through my clothes causing me to shiver, but I pulled the pack out of my pocket and lit one anyway. The snow was still falling slightly, little flakes here and there. I couldn't see the stars and it pissed me off. My lungs were burning from the cold but I didn't care. I wanted someone to care about me, for me. Without needing to change who I was.

I could hear the soft music playing behind me and it made me feel very melancholy. I started thinking about my mother. She had passed away the week after Christmas. I could still remember how we spent Christmas morning in her hospital room. She'd been pale and very thin. The sickness was eating away at her, taking away the little strength she had. I'd made a card for her, and she'd exclaimed over it, her smile tired. I didn't understand it at the time, but her eyes had filled with tears and a few days later she was gone. I could still remember dad telling me and my sister, how my sister had started crying, but I could only stare at him, numb inside. I didn't break down until the day we laid her in the ground. I remember watching the casket being lowered and I suddenly realized she was gone. I tried to throw myself onto it, to stop them from putting her in there. I'd screamed how she'd be cold and lonely. We couldn't leave her alone. My dad had pulled me back, hugging me and sobbing as I punched at his back to let me go, so I could be with her. Christmas was never the same after that.

Turning around, I headed back inside and grabbed more champagne. Trinity and Winston were nowhere to be found. Everything became a blur.

The next thing I knew, I woke up to a blinding headache and the sound of a shower. My body felt achy and I had no clue as to where the hell I was. Shit! I hung my head in my hands, groaning as I realized I'd gone home with some mysterious person and from the way my body ached, I knew I'd had sex with him. Dragging myself out of bed, I located my clothes—they were strewn around the room—and quickly pulled them on, wincing as my head pounded. I needed to get out of there. But curiosity stung me and I tiptoed over to the door to peek inside and see who exactly was in the shower.

I almost fainted. I couldn't believe it. The man stepping out of the shower was none other than the man who'd done nothing but torture me since the day I came to Temptation.

Xavier James! I covered my mouth with my hand and stepped back, racing from the room and out the front door, slamming it behind me. I practically flew down the stairs, too anxious to get away to wait for the elevator.

Oh my God! Oh my God!

My mind kept turning the phrase over and over inside my head. I couldn't believe I had gotten so drunk that I had gone home with that man and wound up having sex with him. And what the hell was he thinking!? Let alone me! I was drunk, but was he? I couldn't believe he'd be able to let himself go enough to get drunk. Unless the bastard wanted something to hold over my head!

I was halfway home when my cell phone rang, and I picked it up. "'Lo?"

"Where the hell are you?" Trinity screamed into the phone and I put a hand to my head.

"Please don't yell, Trin. My head is splitting wide open right now. What's wrong?"

"Fagan, you need to get here now. Your sister called late last night. Your father was in a car accident."

I stopped in the middle of the sidewalk. People bumped into me as they hurried past and I suddenly couldn't think. "What?" I whispered.

"He's in the hospital. They don't know if he's going to make it. I already booked you on the first available flight home. It's at one o'clock. You've got three hours. Get your ass here, pack your bags, and get home!" She hung up.

I hailed a taxi and gave the driver the address, unable to really process what she was saying. It was happening again. I was going to lose my father like I did my mother. I was numb and felt nothing as I paid the driver. Trinity threw the door open and was standing there, her hair a mess and her eyes red.

"Where have you been?" she demanded, taking in the

same clothes I wore the night before and the obvious signs of a hangover.

"I don't want to talk about it," I growled and entered my room to hastily throw some clothes into a bag.

"Winston will take you to the airport," Trinity said from the doorway, her eyes sad.

I placed my gifts for my family in my bag. "I need to make a call." I picked up the phone in the apartment and dialed Victor's number. "Victor?"

"Fagan? Are you okay? You sound upset."

"I won't be back for a while. My father's in the hospital. He had an accident last night," I said quietly, no emotion.

"Is there anything I can do for you? Do you want me to call Xavier?" Victor asked with concern in his voice.

"Why would I want you to do that?" I demanded.

"Well… because I saw you two last night, kissing each other underneath the mistletoe. I thought—"

"No. Don't tell him anything, and you know what? Nothing happened. I'll call you when I know what's going on." I hung up the phone, suddenly feeling very exhausted.

Winston stood by the door, wearing the same clothes from last night, and I merely raised an eyebrow but didn't question it. He helped me down the stairs and out to his car. We were just pulling around the corner when a car pulled up in the spot we vacated. I was too far gone to notice.

"Everything's going to be all right." Winston tried to reassure me but I ignored him.

It was twelve-thirty by the time we got to the airport and I had to rush to make the flight. Once on the plane, I just closed my eyes and tried to rest. It was going to be a long flight from the city to Iowa. I was beginning to hate Christmas even more than before. Things always seemed to get bad around this time of year. I managed to sleep for a while and woke up just as we were about to land. My sister,

Rayne, met me at the airport. She looked tired. I sighed, stepping forward to hug her tightly. "Hey, sis. How is he?"

"He's still unconscious. They don't know if he'll wake up." She started to cry and I wrapped her in another hug.

"Come on. Let's get my bag and we can head to the hospital, all right?"

She nodded as we turned towards the luggage carousel. I hated hospitals. The thought of entering one willingly made my body shudder with distaste but I had to, for my dad.

On the way there, Rayne gave me the only information she knew about Dad's accident. He'd been coming home from visiting a friend when a drunk driver ran him off the road. The truck hit a telephone pole and knocked Dad unconscious. His right arm was broken and a couple of his ribs were fractured. The worst part was that he hadn't awakened yet.

As we walked down the hospital corridors, I couldn't help but notice the lonely people in the rooms we passed. It made me sad to see so many sick people during the Christmas season, especially the ones without families. When we reached our father's room, I took a deep breath and stepped inside, praying he would be okay. He looked so pale lying against the white hospital sheets, and the bandage that slashed across his forehead appeared even whiter. I had never seen him look so frail. I bit my lip and blinked back tears.

"Hey, Dad. Can you hear me? You stubborn old goat. Wake up." I took his hand in mine and sat down in the chair next to the bed.

"He hasn't responded since he was brought in." She placed

her hand on my shoulder. We just stayed there for a long time, no words spoken.

We headed back to the house when visiting hours ended. Both of us needed some rest. I held my sister close as we left. At that moment, she seemed so small next to me.

"Let me drive home," I said, taking the keys from her and opening the passenger door for her.

It was dark when we got back to the house so I didn't notice the car in the driveway at first. Snow had already covered a good portion of it. When I walked up the porch steps, I saw a figure step forward from the darkness, and jumped, almost knocking my sister off the porch. A few seconds later, I realized it was Xavier! What the hell was he doing here?

"What the hell are you doing here?" I demanded, pulling my sister behind me.

"Would you mind if we went inside first? I've been freezing my ass off out here for the last two hours."

His eyes glittered in the darkness and I knew I couldn't make him leave, so I opened the front door. I let Rayne enter first, followed by me and then Xavier.

"Rayne, why don't you go get some sleep? I'll see you in the morning and we'll head back over to the hospital," I said wearily, rubbing my eyes with my thumb and forefinger.

"Fagan, who—"

I cut her off. "Just go, Rayne. I'll explain later."

I heard her hesitate before she turned and headed upstairs. As soon as her door shut, I wheeled on him. "What the hell are you doing here?"

"I want to talk to you," he stated simply, as though that were good enough.

"You flew all the way out to Iowa to talk to me? This should be good. About what?" I crossed my arms over my chest, glaring at him.

"Last night."

"There was no last night!" I exclaimed. "Nothing happened."

"Oh, something did happen. You just don't want to admit it," he replied, his silky voice causing a shiver to race through my body. His next words surprised me. "How's your father?"

My head spun at the abrupt change in subject, causing me to snap back at him. "Like you care."

Xavier's mouth firmed into a flat line, his eyes narrowing at the corners. "Do you really think I'm that cold?"

I gave an exhausted laugh. "Aren't you? I haven't seen anything else since I met you. What makes now any different?"

Anger stirred in Xavier's gaze. "Maybe after last night, things changed."

A snort of disdain left me. "Why? Because we had sex? That doesn't instantly make us best friends or lovers."

"What if that's what I want?" Xavier growled shifting closer to me, intent evident on his face.

My eyes widened and I moved backward instinctively. He stalked me and I kept stepping back farther and farther until I hit the wall. He stopped in front of me, pushing his face close to mine. "I remember every detail, every moan, every sigh, and every orgasm. I remember the tight, hot feel of your body wrapped around mine. Your screams, as I made you come."

I stared at him, wide-eyed. I felt my face heating up and knew I was blushing. "What do you want from me?"

"I want more of the same."

"Why?" I demanded. "You don't even like me."

"Because, like you said a few months ago, I need to get laid. And I think you'll do nicely." He smirked.

Pain shafted through me and I couldn't believe he'd be so callous as to say those words. "Get away from me," I said through clenched teeth. "Don't come near me. I wouldn't let you touch me again if I was on fire and needed you to put out the flames."

"I think that's what you begged me to do last night."

"I was drunk." I shoved him away, stepping away from the wall and towards the stairs. "You can stay here tonight, but then tomorrow you will leave."

I stalked up the stairs, waiting at the top for him to follow. When he started to climb, I continued forward, throwing open the guest room door. "You can sleep here."

Then I turned on my heel, stalked to my room and shut the door, locking it. I collapsed against the door, suddenly overwhelmed with all that had happened these past few days. I didn't want this. I slid down to the floor and wrapped my arms around my knees. Tears welled up and I blinked, willing them away. Unable to force them away, they trickled down my cheeks. They felt hot against my chilled skin and then splashed onto my jeans. I leaned my forehead on top of my knees, willing myself to stop crying. Crying was weakness and I hated to show weakness. When they finally subsided, I dragged myself towards my bed, kicked off my boots, and pitched forward to bury myself in the pillows. I fell into a deep sleep and didn't wake again until the sun was shining in the windows.

10

I sat up and stretched with a loud groan. That was when I remembered the bastard was still in my house. And my sister! Shit. I bolted out of the bed and down the stairs, skidding to a stop when I saw them sitting at the table. They were eating together and laughing. I glared at him. "Finish eating and get out of my house."

"Fagan!" My sister reprimanded me. "You don't talk to a guest like that."

"He is not a guest. A guest is someone who is invited. He was not invited. I want him out." I walked back upstairs, took a hot shower, and dressed again.

The snow was heavier when I stepped out the back door to get firewood and I frowned. The clouds were rolling in and looked very ominous. "Rayne," I called as I stepped through the back door again, my arms full of blocks of wood. "We better get moving. There's a snowstorm heading in. It looks like it might get worse before we get back."

I dropped the wood into the bin next to the fireplace and turned to find Xavier standing in the doorway. "What the hell are you still doing here?"

"I told you. I'm not leaving unless you do." He crossed his arms and leaned against the doorjamb.

I stared at him, flabbergasted at his stubborn refusal to listen to me, in my own house no less! "I don't have time for this. I want you gone by the time we get back from the hospital."

He just smirked and when I approached him, did not move out of my way. "Move," I demanded my gaze hard.

"Make me."

I closed my eyes, trying to will my patience to last. "Are you trying to make my Christmas suck more than it already does?" I growled, opening my eyes and shoving past him.

"Name your price," he said.

I stopped, dead still. My shoulders tense. "What did you say?" I whispered.

"Name your price. You sell yourself to those women, why not me?" he demanded, his hand coming down on my shoulder. "If that's what it takes to get you into my bed, then tell me how much you want."

I had never felt so insulted in my life. I didn't think before I reacted. I turned around, brought my arm back and then punched him. Hard. I watched him stumble backwards, and turned away again. I grabbed my car keys and called for my sister. She came back down the stairs. I ignored Xavier completely. I didn't say a word to him as he followed us to the car. I hoped it had hurt like hell. Those words had torn something inside me and I tried to numb myself from how much it had hurt. It was the only way to survive it. I didn't speak the entire ride to the hospital. I concentrated on the road, trying to keep the car from sliding into a ditch.

As soon as we walked in, they told us Dad was awake. I felt so relieved, yet hollow inside. Xavier was still following us. I continued to ignore him. If he wanted to waste his time like this, then so be it. "Hey, Dad," I whispered as I stood next to the bed, smiling down at him. "How are you feeling?"

"How do you think I'm feeling?" he said grouchily.

"Much better, I see," I replied dryly.

Rayne straightened out the bed sheets and fussed over him. Xavier stood leaning against the wall by the door, just watching us. I couldn't believe he was callous enough to follow us all the way to the room.

"We can't stay long, Dad, because there's a huge snowstorm heading in, but we'll come back to see you soon," Rayne soothed him.

"Who's he?" Dad demanded and I grimaced.

"He's no one, Dad. Just someone I work with." I used the word work lightly since Xavier couldn't seem to stand me.

"Is he your gay lover?" he accused, glaring angrily at me.

I was mortified and started to cough. Before I could get out more than a choking sound, Xavier stepped forward, grinning at my dad.

"Hello, Mr. Swift. Even though he's too shy to admit it, yes. I am his lover."

I spluttered in protest. "You are not!"

"Come on, Fagan. You know you don't have to hide it from your family." He pulled me against him. I struggled to get away, but he tightened his grip on me painfully. "I think we should leave and let your father get some rest, don't you?"

My father glared at both of us. "As if it's not bad enough you refused to inherit the farm and you moved to that godforsaken city, but you bring your male lover home at Christmastime. What the hell are you thinking?"

I looked away from the disappointment and anger in his face. I was angry myself, but I didn't want to cause him to have some kind of relapse. What the hell was wrong with Xavier? I couldn't believe he would tell my father something like that and it was totally not true. "Apparently, when it comes to making you happy, I never think."

I shoved away from Xavier and stalked from the room, straight towards the front of the hospital and out into the already heavy snowfall. I was staring off into space, lost in thought, when my sister and that man walked out of the hospital. As they got closer, I lost it. "What the fuck were you thinking?" I yelled at him, my fists clenched at my side. "Why would you tell him something that isn't true? Are you trying to kill him? Or are you trying to make my Christmases suck more than they already do?"

"We'll talk back at the house." He ignored what I was saying in his arrogant manner and I stepped forward, ready to hit him, but Rayne stopped me with a hand on my arm.

"Calm down, Fagan. You don't have to hide the truth from your family. You know how Dad is. He'll be fine the next time you see him. He just needs time to process everything."

"But I'm not his lover!" I exclaimed, looking at her like she had grown two heads.

She just patted my hand and said, "Let's just get home before the snow gets worse."

I couldn't believe this. I didn't speak the entire way home, my hands clenched on the wheel. I was hunched over it, trying to peer out the windshield. When we got home, I didn't say a word as I slammed up the porch steps and into the house, straight up the stairs to my room. I shut the door and locked it.

That prick! I wanted to wring his neck with my bare hands. I picked up my cell and dialed Trinity. "Hey, Trin." I flopped down on the bed.

"Hey, babe! How's your dad?" she asked with concern.

"He's doing all right. Grouchy as ever. He's still in the hospital."

She whistled on the other end of the phone. "When are you coming back?"

"Probably after Christmas. I miss you, babe."

"I miss you, too. Tell your dad I hope he feels better and I expect him to be all better when I get there," she said.

After I hung up the phone, I pulled myself up off the floor where I had slumped down, intent on going down to the kitchen to help Rayne fix dinner. I jumped in surprise when I opened my door to see Xavier standing there, a dark, angry look on his face. "What now?" I asked angrily, sick and tired of dealing with his constant crap.

"Who were you talking to?" he snarled.

"Were you listening to my call?" I exclaimed, shocked he would stoop to invading my privacy.

"I couldn't help but hear your conversation. I was coming to talk to you."

"I don't want to talk to y—hey!" I cried out as he shoved me backwards, stepping into the room and kicking the door shut behind him.

He threw me roughly down on the bed, immediately covering my body with his. I jerked with the suddenness of his actions and stared up at him in horror. "What the hell are you doing?"

"I told you what I want." He lowered his head, but I pushed frantically at his chest, panic flaring through me at the thought of letting this man dominate me.

"Well, I don't want it," I protested, turning my head away from him.

"That's too bad." He lifted up slightly to look down on me. "I mean, after all, you wouldn't want your father finding out what kind of job you've been doing for the last six months. It might send him right back to the hospital."

I froze, perfectly still as I lay there. I couldn't believe what he threatened to do. I turned my head to look up at him. I was almost certain my pain was reflected in my eyes, but I didn't care. "You son-of-a-bitch," I breathed, staring into those cold-as-steel eyes. "You'd threaten me with my own father's health? You truly have no heart." I blinked, trying to will my tears away.

"I always get what I want, no matter how I have to get it." Xavier smirked down at me before lowering his head to capture my lips with his.

I refused to respond at first, but the tip of his tongue probed lightly at the entrance to my mouth and I couldn't stop myself from opening to the soft flesh, moaning low in my throat. I started kissing him back. I could do nothing but scream at myself mentally to stop. Only my body seemed to develop a mind of its own. I felt his hand slide under the hem of my t-shirt and press its heat against my stomach. His fingers caressed me lightly, hot against my chilled skin. I was getting hard from the stimulation and his lips traced a path of liquid fire to my throat, pressing tightly against the skin there, sucking gently. I felt the tugs on that sensitive skin all the way to my groin. Tiny shudders raced through my body. I arched my back, gasping and pressing harder against him.

"See, even though your mind rebels, your body responds to my touch," he whispered against my ear, his tongue tracing the outer shell.

I tensed at his words and pushed against him frantically. "Get off of me," I ground out.

"No," he stated simply and shifted just enough to bring his pelvic area in contact with my own, causing me to cry out as our erections rubbed together.

He rocked his hips against me and I groaned, my head tossing back and forth at the sensations roaring through me. I couldn't believe how expertly he was playing my body, forcing me to feel things I had never felt with anyone before. I had only had sex with one other person, my best friend

Jared, and it had been a long time ago. Xavier's mouth latched onto mine again. His tongue pushed its way inside, brushing erotically over my own before he pulled away. He shoved my shirt up and his hot, wet mouth closed over my nipple, ripping a cry of pleasure from my throat. I couldn't believe how traitorous my body was. "I don't want this," I panted. I pushed weakly at his shoulders, almost grabbing him to pull him tighter against me.

His tongue flicked over the hard nub and then swirled around it, pulling hotly on it. "You don't want me to stop," he murmured, sucking it deep into his mouth.

"Yes! I do," I hissed out, my fingers tangling in his hair and yanking out the white cord to let it fall in sheets around us. The inky darkness contrasted starkly with my tan skin. I would have ravished him if he had intended this as something other than to hurt or use me. My heart lurched and I shoved him, hard, forcing him off me.

I scrambled off the bed and stood there, drawing in deep breaths and glaring at him. "I am not a whore nor am I a slut. I do not sleep around and I don't intend to start!" I shouted, my hands fisting at my sides.

"You won't be sleeping around because I'll be the only one," he stated calmly, raising himself on one elbow to smile darkly at me.

I realized he was serious. "What if I don't give in to you?"

"I'm sure it wouldn't be helpful to your father's health if he were to find out about your recent employment." He was serious. I could see it in his eyes.

I held myself stiffly afraid to give in to the panic I was feeling. "So basically I'm nothing but a fuck toy?" I asked in a whisper.

"Basically," he replied tracing a pattern in the quilt on my bed.

Numbness settled over me and I replied listlessly. "Fine." I turned and left the room.

I felt like the small amount of happiness I had finally managed to secure for myself had been sucked away. And at Christmastime. I truly hate this holiday. I couldn't stay in the house. I grabbed my jacket off the peg behind the back door and crammed my feet into my boots, hurriedly lacing them up. I opened the door with a jerk, shivering at the cold chill that rushed into the warm kitchen. I stepped off the back porch into the snow and immediately sank ankle-deep into it. Damn, it was already quite a few inches deep. Trudging through the cold snow that sucked at my boots, I made my way to the barn. Once inside the relative warmth, I shook off the snow that had gathered on my clothes. The cows nervously shifted in the hay and a couple of the horses let out a brief neigh at the burst of cold air that blew through the barn. I approached Oscar, the big farm horse. "Hey, Oscar. How's it going, bud?" He nudged at my chest and I wrapped my arms around his neck.

"I can't believe what just happened," I whispered against his coat. "To be treated as nothing but a common whore. I don't want to hurt my father again. Not when I've already done that enough. And now, someone is taking advantage of that fact, boy. What do I do?"

I stayed in the barn for as long as I could. I made sure all the animals had food and water before I even thought about returning to the house. Thankfully, a few of Dad's friends had volunteered to help out with the animals. Rayne couldn't take care of them all by herself and once Dad was home, I would have to return to the city and my job. I glanced at the clipboard Dad kept on a peg for any of the animals requiring special attention, but it seemed all of the animals were healthy. Standing there, I looked around for anything else that needed tending to and found nothing to keep me there any longer.

If you can't tell, I was stalling because I didn't want to go back inside. What I didn't know was at that moment my sister was telling him everything about me; about how hard I'd found it being in this small town and how I'd wanted to escape it. I would have cheerfully wrung her neck if I had known at the time. I finally decided to leave the barn and found the snow had increased into thick flurries I was barely able to see through. The inches on the ground had increased in the hour I was out there, and I sank knee-deep as I carefully picked my way back up to the house. I saw my sister standing in the doorway. My body shivered with the cold and the damp wetness that seeped through my clothes as I stepped inside the back door.

"What the hell were you doing out there?" I heard Xavier's harsh demand and I flinched, turningan emotionless gaze on him. He was leaning against the kitchen sink, his arms crossed over his chest and a disapproving look on his face.

"Nothing. Just checking on the animals." I kicked off my boots, slung my jacket on the hook and padded up the stairs to my room. Entering my adjoining bathroom, I switched the water on steaming hot and shed my wet jeans and t-shirt. I stayed in the shower for a very long time, trying to warm the very depths of my core. I felt as cold as the freezing wind whistling outside. When the water started to turn cold, I turned it off, wearily dragged myself out, dried off and yanked on a pair of sweatpants and a t-shirt.

11

I wasn't hungry, so instead of going back downstairs to face the demon haunting me, I walked down the hall to my mother's sitting room. We had left it the way it had been the day she was admitted to the hospital the final time. I sat down in the window seat and just looked out at the swirling snow. I pulled the quilt I'd grabbed from the chair tighter around me. Sometimes I would come to this room when I needed to feel her presence, and today was definitely one of those days. "I miss you, Mom," I whispered, tipping my head forward to rest my forehead against the cold window pane.

So much had happened in these past nine months, and it seemed like it started as a dream but had done a complete downward spiral to become a nightmare. What had I done to deserve this? I'd never cheated anyone or done immoral things. My heart felt heavy with the knowledge of the choice I would have to make. I couldn't risk letting my father find out about my job, because it might cause a relapse he might not recover from. It came down to me becoming Xavier's lover until he tired of me. Those thoughts did not bring me happiness. Instead, they caused a shiver of fear to run down my spine. I knew if I became his lover that when it came time to end it, I'd wind up broken inside. Because I knew, deep down, I could fall in love with him. I must be a glutton for punishment, because how could anyone love someone like him?

I was so wrapped up in my thoughts I didn't even hear the door behind me open or close. The carpet muffled the footsteps and the next thing I knew, a hand landed on my shoulder and I jumped in fright. "Shit! You scared the living hell out of me!" I glared up at the man who'd been haunting my thoughts.

His gray eyes glinted in the simple light given off by the lamp on the nightstand. "You didn't come down to dinner." His voice sounded accusing and I stiffened.

"I wasn't hungry."

"Have you made up your mind?" he asked me, his hand tightening on my shoulder slightly.

"There is no choice, Xav. I can't risk my father's health by revealing what my job is, so I am forced to become your lover until you get sick of me," I said, my voice resigned and my posture radiating sadness as I turned back around to gaze out at the snow.

I felt his lips settle over the side of my neck and I protested, "Not in here." I stood up, forcing him to step back.

I couldn't look at him. Shame and embarrassment flooded me. I felt something shut down inside as I led the way back to my bedroom. He shut the door behind us and came up behind me, slipping his arms around my waist and kissing my neck again. I closed my eyes as I felt my body responding, and within seconds he had me panting for breath. His hands roamed over me, sliding underneath my shirt to rub over my stomach and up to my chest. I gasped when I felt his palms scrape roughly over my nipples.

"I love those noises you make," he whispered in my ear, and I swallowed hard.

He grabbed the hem of my shirt and yanked it over my head, tossing it aside as he took his own off. He spun me around and pulled me flush against him. A groan ripped from my throat at the feel of his hard chest against my own. His lips pushed hard down on mine, his tongue thrust deep inside my mouth, tasting me. I kissed him back, our tongues dueling. My hands trailed over his broad back, the palms caressing the rippling muscles. I dug my nails in as he trailed his hot mouth back down to my throat, pulling a part of my flesh into his mouth. I reached up with one hand to rip the band from his hair, letting it fall to the ground as his beautiful hair swirled around us. Running my fingers through it, I reveled at the feel of it over my skin.

Xavier pushed at my sweatpants. They fell around my ankles, baring my entire body to his piercing eyes. His tongue flicked over his lips, wetting them, as he took in every inch of me. Suddenly, I found myself on the bed as he pushed me down, the backs of my knees pressed against the edge of the bed. He climbed next to me, and started touching and kissing my body again. His lips locked onto the nipple closest to him and my back arched off the bed when his fingers closed around my stiff flesh. I flung an arm over my eyes, not wanting to watch his face as he touched me.

Little fingers of fire raced over my nerve-endings. I felt each touch, each caress, to my core. I almost fainted from the pleasure when his wet mouth closed over my hard length, sliding down the shaft to take me deep into his throat. Little cries escaped my mouth, with nervous pants in between, and my body shuddered with each sweep of his tongue. I tensed as I felt his finger probing at the entrance to my body, but I forced myself to relax as it pushed inside me. Pleasure soared through me at the simultaneous feeling of penetration and moist heat wrapped around my shaft. One finger became two as he continued to finger my tight canal while pleasuring me with his mouth. Finally, he pushed a third inside and I felt my orgasm rising. I pushed at his shoulders to get him to pull off in time, but he stubbornly refused to release my cock and I stuffed my fist in my mouth to muffle my scream as I came. Another cry wrenched from my throat as he swallowed convulsively around my pulsing length, taking every drop into him. My cries tapered to small sighs while slight shivers wracked my body. I groaned when he finished cleaning me off and his lips left my cock.

He moved over me, quickly donned a condom he'd taken from God knew where, and pulled my legs over his shoulders. I felt his hard length pressing at the entrance to my body and winced as the large head pushed inside. A small groan tore from my throat as he penetrated me slowly, deeper and deeper, until he was fully seated inside me.

"You feel so tight!" he gasped, and gripped both my hands as he started fucking me harder.

His hips thrust faster with each downward plunge until he was slamming into me, the bed creaking slightly with the force of his flesh pounding inside me. My own cock had hardened again and I tightened my fingers on his as I felt my orgasm rising once more. My moans of passion filled the room as his mingled with mine. I had not looked at him the entire time he screwed me, but he demanded, "Look at me!"

At first, I refused, but he demanded it again. "Look at me. Now!"

My eyes flew open. His gray ones glittered with lust and pleasure. His jaw clenched and he threw his head back as he rammed deep into my ass, pumping the condom full of his seed. The feel of his cock pulsing inside me triggered my own orgasm and I cried out as I spilled over my belly. He collapsed on top of me, breathing heavily, and lay there for several long moments before pulling away and out of me. He stood up, grabbed his clothes, and left me there, not saying a word.

I curled into a ball of misery, feeling used and sore. I felt tears prick at my eyes but I held them back, swearing I wouldn't let the bastard make me cry. I lost myself in my misery until I fell into a deep sleep just before dawn.

I only slept for an hour, and when I woke up, I knew my sister was going to sleep in late since it was Sunday. So I rolled wearily out of bed, took a very hasty hot shower and pulled on a pair of jeans and a heavy sweatshirt. I walked quietly downstairs, jammed my feet into my boots and grabbed my dad's heavy fleece jacket before stepping out onto the back porch. Stopping in my tracks, I was struck anew by the beauty of the thick layer of snow coating the world in its icy grasp. This was one thing I did miss in New York. There was nothing like the clean, fresh smell and sight of new snow. My feet sank deep into the blanket of whiteness and I shivered as the coldness invaded my toes. Despite the brief flash of awe, I couldn't quite bring myself to feel anything else except a heavy depression. Wading through the freezing snow, I tromped out to feed the chickens. They were all huddled down together in their nests. I threw the chicken feed around the ground of the coop, and went towards the barn to take care of the cows and horses.

It was slightly warmer in the barn and I sighed with relief to get out of the cold. "Hey, guys," I called out in greeting. I grabbed the stool for milking and the pails, settling down at the first cow and making my way through the other three. I took the pails to the storage area and then grabbed their feed, tossing it into the troughs inside their pens.

Oscar and Delilah. What a pair of names, but my mother had named her horses. Oscar was a striking black gelding with a white blaze across his face and Delilah was a beautiful white mare with a darker off-white mane. She reminded me of a unicorn. They both let out little whickers of greeting and I rubbed their muzzles one at a time, before dumping the food into their bins. As they munched away, I leaned against the stall door and just stared, lost in thought. It was only four days until Christmas and my dad was still in the hospital. Because of his accident, he hadn't been able to get a tree as usual, so I decided once Oscar was finished with his feed, I would travel out into the woods to get one.

I grabbed an axe, some rope, and the shotgun my father kept for emergencies and when foxes raided the chicken coop. This time of year, the woods were thick with wolves looking for food. I didn't believe in killing them, because they were only doing what came naturally to them, but I'm not stupid enough to trust they wouldn't hurt me. After Oscar was finished eating, I saddled him, and strapped the gun to the saddle along with the axe and rope. I led him out into the deep snow, and stopped to stare around me once again, struck by the stark white snow glistening in the already rising sun. It looked like tiny diamonds littering the ground. Oscar nudged me with his nose as though to say, 'What gives,' and I laughed, turning to rub his muzzle and pat the side of his neck.

My skin prickled with awareness. I knew someone was watching me. I turned my gaze to the house, but I couldn't see anyone. I shrugged and swung myself into the saddle, grimacing when my ass protested. I clicked my tongue and urged Oscar with my heels to head towards the trees. The only sounds were my breathing and the horse's heavy steps in the crunching snow.

Maybe I should have stayed here. Maybe I never should

have thought I could survive in a city as large as New York. After all, I had lived in a small town my entire life. But the thought of staying here chafed my sense of freedom and I knew even if I hadn't moved to New York, I would have had to move somewhere else. Oscar snorted in the cold air, white shafts of steam puffing out, and I felt him shift nervously. I comforted him with a pat on the neck. "Easy, boy."

We stopped quite a ways into the forest, where I found the perfect tree. I jumped down, my feet sinking into the snow, and I shivered again as the cold seeped into my boots and socks. I grabbed the axe and made my way to the tree. The thwack of the axe hitting the wood soothed my shattered nerves and I imagined every one of my problems being eaten away by the blade. The cracking sound as the trunk gave way was satisfying, almost as satisfying as the tree slamming into the ground. I grabbed the rope, strapped up the trunk, and led Oscar around the back end, tying it tightly to the saddle. Making sure it wasn't going to come loose on the trip home, I tugged on it hard. Just as I swung back up into the saddle, a low growl came from my left. I tensed, gripping the reins and saddle horn. Oscar shied to the right, and suddenly, several wolves leaped from behind the trees to form a circle around us.

Oscar whinnied in fear and reared up on his hind hooves, almost unseating me, but I managed to hang on as his front hooves lashed out at the nearest wolf, sending it flying with a loud yelp. I winced and watched as the other wolves tensed up to attack. Oscar struck off for the trees, racing blindly back towards the farm. Branches ripped at my clothing and face. I could feel the tiny scratches and the blood seeping up to trickle down my cheeks. I leaned as close to Oscar's neck as possible. I could hear the wolves crashing through the trees behind us. I took a moment to look back only to find to my horror that one of the wolves had leapt onto the tree, struggling to reach me. I tightened my knees, sitting up slightly to grab the shotgun. I hated to think of hurting it, but I couldn't risk the wolf reaching us.

I half-turned around, took aim with the gun and pulled the trigger. The first shot missed, and I could only pray the second would hit the target. I struggled to hold onto the saddle as I twisted my body around once more and brought the shotgun up. My eyes closed as the bullet slammed into the wolf's body, tossing the animal away from the tree. I grabbed hold of Oscar's mane as we broke out into the open field behind the house and I brought him to a stop, looking back over my shoulder to see the wolves still racing towards us. I lifted the shotgun into the air and fired off another round, watching as the wolves came to a stop. They froze for a moment, then retreated back the way they'd come.

I heard the back door slam open as I slid from the saddle. My knees gave way as I sank to the ground. The adrenaline racing through me faded away and with it went my consciousness.

I woke to find myself in my bedroom. It was several hours later, if the dim twilight outside was any indication, and I shakily pushed myself up from the bed. I stood there for a moment to try and gather my wits. I carefully made my way to the bathroom across the hall and found my face had been cleaned up and some of the deeper scratches bandaged. Sometimes, I wonder why I have never contemplated suicide. The person in the mirror didn't look like me, yet he did. There was a haunted look in my eyes and I wondered why it had been deemed for me to have such a difficult life. Yeah, I had a lot of good things going for me in some ways, but it seems love wasn't meant to be mine. Sighing, I pushed back from the sink, used the bathroom, and washed my hands, studying myself again in the medicine chest mirror.

Xavier was leaning against the wall next to my bedroom door when I exited the bathroom and I stopped short.

"What the hell were you thinking?" he demanded angrily.

I didn't even bother to reply, just went downstairs to the kitchen, Xavier following me closely. "Why did you go out into the woods on your own if you knew there was a possibility of danger?"

I had suddenly had enough and I whirled around to glare at him. "In order to get away from you for a while, Xav. Not that it's any of your business what I do outside of the bedroom, now is it?"

I didn't bother to wait for an answer, just headed over to grab a mug and fill it with coffee. I stared out the back window and wondered where Rayne was. But I would rather bite off my tongue before I'd ask him for anything. I could feel his presence behind me still, but I did not acknowledge him. Once I had finished the cup of coffee, I rinsed the mug out, placed it in the dishwasher and turned around to leave, only to find him in my way, blocking me.

"If you ever do anything that dangerous again, you won't just be facing the wolves out there, you'll be facing one in here," he stated silkily, yanking me against him and kissing me hard before abruptly stepping back and leaving the room.

I touched my bruised lips and sighed, wishing I was back in New York or somewhere far away from the man who had done nothing but hurt me from the moment he met me. The snowplows wouldn't be getting to our road until tomorrow, which meant I would be stuck here in the house with him the whole day. I decided to go into my father's study and read for a little while. It might make me forget everything that had happened the last few days. I wandered into the room, sniffing at the scent of the pipe tobacco that reminded me of my father. I suddenly missed him, even with all his disappointment and anger at me. He should be here, with his family for Christmas, not lying in some hospital bed. I picked up the phone and dialed the hospital, listening to the ringing on the other end.

"Memorial Hospital."

"Yes, room 212, please."

The nurse transferred me immediately. "Hello?"

I almost started crying when I heard my father's voice. "Hey, Dad. How are you feeling?" I leaned back in his chair.

"Like I want to get the hell out of here. You know since your mother died, I can't stand hospitals."

"I know, Dad. But hopefully, once they clear the roads, they'll let you go home and we can all be together for Christmas."

"That would be nice, son. Is your... friend still there?" He hesitated at the friend bit and I bit my lip.

"Yes. He's still here." I paused for a moment and then opened my mouth, "Dad?"

"Hmm?" I could hear the TV in the background as well as the beeping noises from the monitors in the room.

"Do you sometimes wish your life was different? That you could change something and make it either better or disappear?" I asked.

"Of course. Who doesn't wish for the opportunity to go back and change something? But, unfortunately, we have to live with the hand we're dealt and find ways to adapt to it. You sound like something is bothering you. Has something happened?" he asked his voice alert.

"No. No. I just... never mind. It's nothing. Get some rest, okay? The snowplows should be coming through tomorrow, so we'll be out to pick you up for Christmas. I'll talk to you later." I hung up and stared up at the ceiling, wondering why

I just couldn't bring myself to tell him the truth. It's not like I haven't disappointed him before.

'Dad... um... there's something I need to tell you. I'm gay.'
'Dad, I'm moving to New York City with Trinity.'
'Dad, I don't like farming, and I don't want to inherit the farm. I think you should leave it to Rayne. She loves this place.'
'Dad, I want to be an artist.'

The list went on and on. I can still see his expression every time: the hurt, the disappointment, the anger, and the sadness. I stood up to build a fire in the fireplace and as soon as it was crackling, I grabbed a book off the shelf and settled down on the floor by the fire to read. Soon I was immersed in the story of a young man who was forced to choose between his family and his love. I found myself so drawn into the story that I barely even noticed Rayne peek her head inside the door to check on me. The tale struck a chord inside me and I had to find out what the man decided to do. It even had me smiling and shaking my head at certain places because it sounded so much like my life. It turned out the man persevered until he got what he wanted, both his family and his love.

12

I sat up once I was finished and saw it had grown dark outside. I doused the fire and headed out to the kitchen to find Rayne standing at the stove cooking dinner.

"I'm glad you weren't seriously injured, but you're an idiot for going out there on your own," she reprimanded, shaking a fork at me.

I grinned, and hugged her. "I'm fine. It just occurred to me this morning that we didn't have a tree, with dad in the hospital and all, so I wanted to get one. By the way, where did you guys put it?"

"It's in the living room, leaning against the wall. I had Xavier bring it inside after he carried you upstairs. You know, I think he'll be good for you, Fagan. He cares about you, a lot."

I snorted, and just shook my head.

"It's the truth," she insisted and looked at me, her eyes boring into mine. "He was really upset when he saw you were covered in blood and I thought he'd jump out of his skin when he heard the gunshot."

"Look, Rayne, just leave it alone. I can't explain the situation to you right now but I will. I promise. Later. Anyway, Dad should be able to come home tomorrow. I spoke to him on the phone. He's chomping at the bit to get out of there." I grimaced. "I don't blame him. Since Mom died, none of us have been able to stand hospitals."

Sadness washed over me as I remembered her laugh. "I really miss her, Ray. She totally would have understood everything, unlike Dad. He's never got me." I laughed humorlessly. "Do you remember the moment I told him I wasn't interested in being a farmer? That I wanted to be an artist? I thought he was going to get his old twelve-gauge and shoot me right then. I still remember the disappointment and hurt on his face. Sometimes, I wish I could take it back, but I know it wouldn't change who I am. I know I wouldn't be happy being a farmer."

"Dad understands, Fagan. And yeah, he was upset at first because you're his only son and he wanted you to want the same thing as him. But he got over it, and he's glad to see you happy."

"Maybe, but I can see the way he looks at me. He's not proud of me. Ah, it doesn't matter. Listen to me, being so depressing. So what are you making for dinner?" I asked, peering into the pot on the stove.

"Spaghetti with meat sauce and garlic bread. Why don't you go set the table?" she asked.

I grabbed three plates, three sets of silverware, and three glasses, turning around and coming to an abrupt halt at seeing him standing in the door way. How much had he heard? I didn't say anything to him about eavesdropping. Deciding it was just better to ignore him when we weren't having sex, I walked over to the table and placed each setting at our chairs. "I'm going to go check on the animals before dinner," I stated, needing to get away from his presence for at least a few moments.

"Oh, I already fed them, Fagan," Rayne called after me. I pretended not to hear.

Depression threatened to swamp me on my way to the barn. I shook it off, desperately clinging to the hope Xavier was treating me this way because he didn't know how to express himself any other way. Oscar was fine, munching away on some hay, and Delilah looked up at me, before returning to her own. The rest of the animals were also eating their dinner and barely stirred at my appearance. I took a deep breath to fortify myself for the return to the house. My eyes widened when I saw him standing hesitantly in the barn door. "What are you doing here?" I asked, my voice harsher than I intended.

His mouth tightened, little strain lines forming at the corners. "I wanted to see if you were okay or if you needed any help."

I jerked in surprise. "That's a first. Are you saying you actually care about me, Xav?" I asked sarcastically, holding my breath in the hopes he'd admit it.

"No. Your sister sent me out here. I can see you're fine, so I'll head back."

"Tomorrow, I'm going into town to get my father. I hope you go home and let me enjoy the rest of my vacation in peace, but I guess that's too much to ask for." I shoved past him and stumbled through the snow to the house, hanging my jacket on the door and kicking off my wet boots. He wasn't too far behind me. I felt him staring at me occasionally as we ate dinner.

Rayne and Xavier had an easy camaraderie and were chatting back and forth. I just let it flow around me while I pushed my food around on my plate, but stopped the twirling of my fork when I heard him laugh. It was the first time I'd heard it. It was deep, husky, and it rolled down my spine like hot, lustful fingers stoking the fires of passion. My hand clenched briefly around my fork before I dropped it, letting it clatter against the plate as I shoved away from the table. "I'm done."

I dumped what was left on my plate in the garbage, rinsed it off, shoved it into the dishwasher, and stalked out of the room.

How could he be so comfortable with my sister but so harsh to me? Was it because of the escort job? Or was there something else about me that he hated? Did he hate me so much because he liked to screw me? And he'd never been interested in men before? Was it because someone had hurt him before? My head ached from all of the questions spinning around and around.

I decided to watch a movie to forget for a little while and settled down into the family room, popping in a comedy. One of my favorite comedies is Lake Placid. The pure sarcasm that drips off their tongues is amazing. Oh, and the language the little white-haired lady from Golden Girls uses trips me out. I would never expect her to use such foul language. My sister and Xavier wandered into the room about twenty minutes into the movie. She settled down into the easy chair and he sat on the couch beside me. I immediately tensed, but eventually relaxed as I lost myself in the comedy once more. I didn't even notice he kept glancing at me. There was one part where I couldn't help it, I threw my head back and started laughing so hard, holding my stomach as it became painful. "God, I love this movie!" I exclaimed, grinning as I glanced at him.

"I've never seen it before." His voice was husky and I looked at him shock.

"Never? You don't know what you've been missing." I launched into an explanation of the beginning he missed and pointed out the best parts.

When the movie ended, I put in another one, called

Tremors. "This one is a combination of comedy and seriousness. It's pretty cool. Do you remember when we saw this one, Rayne? It was right before mom..." I let the words trail off, and looked back at the TV screen.

"Yeah, I remember," she said, her voice low with remembered pain.

That had been right before mom had gone into the hospital for the first time, only for us to discover she had leukemia. It had been the most painful thing I'd ever experienced until the day she passed away. "Yeah."

I fell silent, and became engrossed in the movie, only brought back to awareness when Xavier laughed. I peeked out of the corner of my eye to see him actually grinning. My heart lurched and I couldn't believe how beautiful his smile was. "You should smile and laugh more often," I stated calmly, still keeping my eyes on the movie.

I felt him look at me, but he didn't respond. Out of the corner of my eye, I could see Xavier study me for a few moments before turning his attention back to the television. As the movie neared the end, I knew it was close to bedtime, and he was going to want what he'd had last night. Me.

After the movie was over, I turned it off and stood up quickly. I murmured a hasty good night and raced upstairs. It was more out of fear than anticipation. Even though I found him more beautiful than a sunset over the beach, I still didn't wish to be emotionally blackmailed into a sex-only relationship. I grabbed my sweatpants off my bed and went across the hallway to take a shower. The steam started to fill the small bathroom as the water warmed up, and I stripped off my clothes, stepping under the hot spray with a deep, contented sigh, ignoring the sting of the small cuts. The pounding stream of water pouring over me was soothing to my chilled flesh. I didn't hear the bathroom door open and close, or the sounds of clothing hitting the floor. It wasn't until the curtain was pulled aside and he stepped in behind me that I was aware of his presence. I tensed, not looking at him, and asked in a tight voice, "What are you doing?"

"What do you think?" he parried, stepping closer to me, pressing the front of his body against my back.

I closed my eyes and tried to ignore the heat building in my belly at the feelings he evoked in me. "Can I at least take a shower in peace?" I snapped.

His hands settled on my shoulders and he started to massage my tight muscles. I groaned, bending my head forward, relishing the feeling of his fingers digging into my muscles. His lips settled against the base of my neck and I jerked in surprise. "Don't," I said quietly.

He ignored me yet again, and I clenched my fists when his tongue darted out to lap at the droplets of water clinging to my skin. His hands slid down my body, running over my skin and almost searing the flesh with his heat. I felt his cock hardening against my ass and I squeezed my eyes shut tighter as my body responded to the feeling. I could feel the head of his shaft pressing into the cleft of my cheeks and he pushed his hips forward slightly, eliciting a gasp from me. His hand reached past me to grab the bar of soap sitting on the little shelf and he ran it over my back, lathering it along my skin. His hand dipped lower, pressing it against my entrance. My hips involuntarily pressed backward and I bit my lip in shame. My body betrayed my every sinful desire, and I groaned quietly when I felt his index finger pressing inside me, pushing in deep and hard.

The soap-slicked finger pulled back out and became two, pushing deeper inside of me. I felt his mouth nuzzling my neck again as he continued to stretch me in preparation for himself. I felt empty when he pulled those digits away and then he tugged my hips back against his pelvic bone, pushing the head of his stiff prick against my tight entrance. I heard a low growl come from his chest and then he was burrowing into me, drilling deeper with each inch of his shaft. The slight friction between my body and his assured me he wore a condom, but the question of when he'd put it on slipped my mind as his fingers dug into my waist, his nails creating half-moon furrows in my skin. I could feel his body trembling from the overload of sensations, and I felt a heady sense of power at being able to affect this icy man so deeply. I deliberately clenched my muscles deep inside and he grunted, thrusting his hips forward, hard. His hands held me in place for his driving plunges, yanking me into each one.

I felt his soapy hand enclose my own aching staff and start to tug on it with each of his desperate invasions. My legs shook with the strain of holding myself upright, my arms tensed, and my hands resting against the tiled wall curled into fists. I brought one hand to my mouth, biting down on it, hard, to stifle my mewls of pleasure. Tiny surges of electricity raced up my spine as he buried his cock inside me over and over again. His mouth closed hotly over the edge of my shoulder, and he sucked deeply, pulling my skin into his mouth. The water still sluiced over us, drenching his long hair, causing it to stick to our heated skin. Little curls of steam rose off our bodies as the slowly cooling water hit us.

His hand felt wonderful against my stiff flesh, and I wondered what it would be like if our positions were reversed. I almost laughed, but it turned into a small cry when he hit that sweet spot deep in my ass. I felt my orgasm approaching and hunched my body farther back into his. My release hit as his slammed through him, his teeth sinking into my shoulder, and the slight pain triggered the hard spurts of my semen. I could feel him pulsing inside me, the heat flooding the sheath over his cock. His legs shuddered with the effort of holding us both up, as I had lost all control my muscles. My fluids spilled over his fingers and when I was done, I felt his hand leave my member and I saw him raise it up past me. I could hear his mouth sucking on his fingers and almost moaned at the pure sexiness of the sound and what he was doing.

After we rested, him pressed close to me while I leaned against the wall, he slowly slid out of my body and stepped back, grabbing a towel off the rack and stepping out of the shower to dry off. Again, like last night, he didn't say a word, just left the bathroom and I couldn't believe he could be so heartless. I sank to my knees in the shower and just wrapped my arms around my aching middle. "Why?" I whispered but my voice was drowned out by the pounding water.

I dragged myself out of the shower, and dried off, pulling my clothes on and walked wearily across the hallway to my room. I slipped in between the covers and fell into a deep sleep, dreaming he was chasing me, trying to force my submission, but not offering his own. I whimpered when I felt his hands biting into my arms, and pushed at him, trying to keep him away. Each twist and turn of the dream became worse and worse. True fear ran through my veins and brought me upright in the bed, gasping and panting for breath. After I was able to breathe normally, I turned my head and saw it was six in the morning. I sighed because I knew there was no way I was going to be able to get back to sleep. I stood up and pulled on a sweatshirt, stepping out my room while in the process of pulling it on. The house was quiet as I headed downstairs.

It was almost time to bring Dad home. I'm not sure which was worse, facing Xavier or facing my father. Did you ever feel like you were trapped no matter where you went? I felt like one of those rats in a maze or a hamster on a wheel. No matter how fast or how hard I ran, it's like I'm right back where I started.

I looked out the front window and saw the snowplow had

come through in the last hour. The roads were clear and I decided to head into town early. I turned and went back upstairs, exchanging the sweatpants for a pair of jeans before pulling on a pair of heavy socks. I grabbed my wallet and keys, quietly making my way downstairs again, stopping to jam my feet into my boots. Rayne was still sleeping and I had no idea if Xavier was too. I left a short note for them, stating I had gone into town early to do some errands before going to get Dad.

My truck started up with a low growl and I backed up, expertly maneuvering it around the other car in the driveway. I glared at the snow-covered Toyota Rav4 in anger. I pulled out onto the main road and drove slowly towards town, my hands gripping the wheel tightly. You never know you hit a patch of ice until it was too late. I pulled up to the gas station, hopping out and grinning with pleasure when I saw Tony Delpino, one of my good friends from high school, standing in the window talking with the cashier. I started the pump and jogged towards the door. "You know, Tony, you shouldn't hassle Greta. Her dad's likely to pull a shotgun on your ass." I leaned against the counter next to him.

"Fagan! When did you get back?" he cried, hugging me and pounding me on the back.

"I'm only back for Christmas. I came back earlier than expected because Dad's in the hospital."

"Yeah, I heard about him. Is he doing better?" He slipped his credit card across the counter to Greta.

"He's coming home today. He was unconscious for a day so they had him under observation to make sure everything is okay. He also broke his arm and fractured a couple of his ribs. Sucks. I'll be here at least a few days more until everything is situated at home." I grimaced and smiled at Greta, handing her my own credit card, indicating the truck with a jerk of my thumb. "I just wanted to come into town early to get a couple of last-minute things for Christmas."

"That's great. Hey, we're having a Christmas Eve party at my house tonight. Want to join us?"

"I'd really like to, but with Dad coming home tonight it probably won't happen. But I'll try. Maybe, if only for a couple of hours. He can't stay up all night. Right?" I grinned at him, gripping his forearm with my hand in a warm goodbye, then trudged back outside.

It was almost eight by the time I'd reached the mall. I hadn't even realized I intended to go there. I found myself standing in front of the large building and sighed. I almost turned back around, but tomorrow was Christmas and since Xavier intended to stay apparently, I felt the need to buy him a gift. Aside from whether he deserved it or not, no one should be without something to open on Christmas. So I wandered through the mall, studying item after item. Nothing seemed good enough until I came across a beautiful silver watch with a deep blue face that reminded me of how his hair shone in the right kind of light. Even though it cost over a hundred dollars, I bought it anyway. I stopped in a smaller store to grab a stocking and several goofy items to stick in it. I had the watch gift-wrapped before putting together the stocking really quickly, to be able to hang it when I got back to the house. The tree would be decorated tonight and the presents put underneath.

Heading over to the hospital to pick up my dad, I found him fidgeting in the wheelchair just inside the lobby. "Let's go," he said impatiently, wheeling himself towards the front door.

I waved to the nurse and grabbed the handles of the chair, pushing him out to the truck waiting at the curb. "Do you need help?" I asked, reaching out to steady him, but he stopped me with a cold look.

"I'm fine. I'm not crippled," he snapped and slid up into the passenger seat.

Sighing, I made my way around the hood after returning the chair and climbed into the driver's side. "Rayne will be happy to see you in such fine spirits, Dad," I said as I pulled away from the curb and made a U-turn to head back towards the farm.

"Yeah, yeah," he ground out.

I knew he would feel better once he was home so I concentrated on the driving. When we pulled into the driveway, I frowned, a shaft of shock and hurt flaring through me when I saw the Toyota Rav4 was gone. Rayne was waiting on the steps and squealed with excitement when she saw our father. I decided if the bastard wanted to leave, so be it. Let him leave. I don't need him here. I don't want him here. Yes, you do. Shut up! I snapped at my inner voice, and stomped up the steps behind my dad and sister.

13

My sister and I settled Dad into the easy chair in the living room and together we put up the Christmas tree. I started to feel slightly melancholy as I remembered how Mom used to hand-craft a new ornament every year. As I pulled them out of the box, I studied each one until I came to the first one I ever helped her make. I smiled softly and ran a finger down the length of the clothespin reindeer. Who hasn't made one of those though, right? I turned it over and felt my eyes water at her elegant initialing of my name. I carefully hooked it onto the tree and turned back to the box. I almost dropped an ornament in shock when I saw Xavier standing in the doorway, staring at us. I couldn't help but stare back. His gray eyes glittered with some undefined emotion and he wandered farther into the room, sitting on the couch, closest to where I was kneeling. I couldn't believe he hadn't left. He didn't leave, my inner voice cried joyfully.

Dad turned and started talking to him, asking him questions. I tensed when he asked how we had met, but Xavier smoothed it over by stating I worked for his cousin and he'd met me at the office. I sighed in relief and gave him a quick, grateful look before turning back to finish hanging the ornaments. But the next question my dad asked almost had me passing out with the rush of blood from my head. "So Xavier, how long do you intend on using my son?"

"What?" I whirled around in horror. "Dad!" I frowned at my father. "Leave him alone."

"It's okay, Fagan." That brought me to a halt because it was the first time the bastard had used my name without sounding sarcastic. "Mr. Swift, I don't know why you think so, but I am not using your son."

I guess Xavier was a better actor than I thought because a few seconds later, my dad nodded and turned back to watch us finish the tree. I glanced at Xavier, rolling my eyes at him. I thought I saw him wince as I went to turn back around, but I shook my head, as if he would feel anything with a heart as cold as his. Rayne was smiling and that was all that mattered. Christmas had been a solemn affair most of the time. Each year was the same: put up the tree, exchange gifts, eat dinner, take down the tree, and then it was, blessedly so, over.

I pulled a bar stool over beside the tree and climbed up onto it, stretching to put the star on the top of the tree. It wobbled as I pulled back and my eyes widened as I felt the stool start to fall. Rayne's loud gasp and my father's small sound of distress barely reached my ears, drowned out by the frantic beating of my own heart. Just as I started to topple backwards, I was suddenly caught up in Xavier's arms and cradled against him. "I don't know how you managed to stay alive all these bloody years without breaking your damned neck!" he exclaimed gruffly and slowly set me down.

I flushed with embarrassment, but wouldn't let him intimidate me enough to make me look away. Finally, he moved away and I looked over at Rayne and my father to see them studying us with knowing looks on their faces. The flush on my cheeks deepened. If they only knew I was nothing but a hole for him to screw. Sighing, I walked out of the room to grab the bags I'd dumped in my room as well as the packages from my suitcases. Xavier had left the room by the time I came back. I settled all of the packages beneath the tree and walked over to the fireplace to hang the three stockings. One was for Rayne, one was for Dad, and one was for the man who would haunt me for the rest of my life. Rayne had made one for me, and I smiled at her. "Can we open the stockings tonight like we used to with Mom?" I asked softly, wanting to feel close to her again.

"Why not?" Rayne said, slipping an arm around Dad's shoulders.

We put the finishing touches on the tree and started cleaning up the ornament packaging, putting it back into the boxes to store until the next day. I teasingly tossed a handful of tinsel on Rayne's head, laughing at the picture she made. "Do you remember the time you and Jared tried to make spaghetti?" Rayne grinned at me.

I winced. Even now we couldn't explain to my father how it came to be all over the kitchen floor and us. It'd started out as a minor food fight that exploded into an all-out war, which ended in us rolling around on the floor kissing one another. The memory reminded me of Tony's party. "Hey, Dad, would you be up to going to a Christmas Eve party tonight?" I asked hesitantly. "I met Tony at the gas station on Main Street and he invited us to go."

"You three go. I'm too tired. I'll just get to bed early then. Rayne, how're the animals?" He launched into a conversation with my sister, pretty much ignoring me like he always did.

I sighed and started to leave the room, but stopped when I looked up, because Xavier was standing in the doorway. His eyes were locked on the fireplace where his stocking hung with the others. There were four stockings on the mantel altogether, so I'm pretty sure he could guess the one without a name was for him. I wondered if he'd think Rayne made it for him. A twinge of jealousy over how well the two of them got along hit me square in the chest. I stopped at his side. "There's a party tonight at a friend's house. If you want, you can go with us." I brushed past him to enter the kitchen.

I started to make everyone sandwiches for lunch. I heard him enter behind me and sit at the table. At first, I was uncomfortable, but I forced myself to continue slathering mayonnaise on the bread. My hands stilled at his next question though. "How long has your father treated you like that?"

Hesitating, I thought back to the exact day I'd crushed his hopes for me. "Since I was fifteen," I stated softly and slowly continued to construct the sandwiches.

"Why then?" he asked curiously.

I wasn't sure I wanted to reveal the exact reason why, because then he might believe I truly enjoyed the acts he submitted me to. And also, then he would know I hadn't had sex with any of those women. I took a deep breath and revealed my secret in a whisper. "Because I told him I was gay."

There wasn't a sound behind me, but when I finally worked up the courage to turn my head, there was a look of absolute rage in his eyes. I raised my eyebrows in surprise.

"What? Did I shatter all your precious misconceptions about me?" I asked bitterly, slamming the plate of sandwiches down on the kitchen table in front of him.

I stalked from the room to get my father and sister. I poked my head into the living room to let them know lunch was on the table, but I didn't return to the kitchen. Instead I grabbed my heavy jacket and went out to the porch to sit on the swing to think. It creaked as I settled down and I pushed off with my foot, setting it to swinging slightly. I leaned my head back to look at up the clouded gray sky. I heard the front door open and sighed with frustration. My eyes rolled to the side to see who was standing there, and I saw Xavier holding a plate and a glass of milk. He sat next to me and shoved the glass into my hand along with one of the sandwiches. He picked up the other and started eating, not saying a word. "You know, I truly don't get you," I told him sadly, turning back to look up at the sky again.

"Why didn't you tell me that from the beginning?" he asked, hunching over with his elbows on his knees.

"Because you immediately believed what you wanted about me. And I was over trying to please everyone. It's enough attempting to make my dad happy, let alone a stranger I had just met."

"You still should have told me," he accused, turning his head to pierce me with those gray eyes of his.

"So does this mean I'm out of our deal?" I asked hopefully.

"No." He stood up, still pinning me with his gaze. "It means what I want you for will increase." He left me sitting there staring after him in horror.

I stepped out of the car in front of Tony's house, my breath crystallizing as it hit the air. My eyes strayed to the tree house we'd played in when we were younger. I wondered if Jared was going to be here tonight. I heard Rayne's door and then the back door of the car shut. It had been a long, strained afternoon and it had given me a slight headache. The urge for a drink hit me, but then I remembered what had happened the last time I'd drank. I shuddered and ignored Xavier as I strode towards the house. The music was already blaring and light streamed from the Christmas decorations along the eaves. Even the lights inside the house shone brightly. I knocked on the door and it was jerked open.

"Fagan!" Tony cried boisterously. "You came. Come in."

He stepped back to let the three of us inside and I immediately became lost in the crowd, searching for the one face I wanted to see.

Jared stood against the wall talking with a pretty redheaded girl and I walked over, smiling. Even though it hadn't been the easiest of partings, at least not for me, we still had remained on speaking terms. "Jared." I greeted him over the music.

His blue eyes lit up and he grinned, giving me a backslapping hug. "Fagan! I heard you headed over to the Big Apple. How's it going out there?"

Returning the hug, I replied, "Great. I enrolled into some art classes and I've got a great job."

"At least one of us got out of this place. This is Megan, Megan this is Fagan, my best friend since we were kids."

I smiled at her, shaking her hand and dropping a light kiss over her knuckles, but my lips had barely left her skin when I was yanked backward, to the side of the man who had become a thorn in my own. I glared at him and gritted my teeth in frustration.

"Who's this?" Jared asked over the music.

"His lover." Xavier's voice was dark with what I knew to be anger.

What the hell did I do now? My shoulders slumped and I grinned weakly at Jared when his eyes widened a little, taking in the muscular man beside me. His eyes communicated his approval and I bit my lip. "This is Xavier. We work at the same company."

"Nice to meet you. I'm Jared." They shook hands and I swear I thought I saw Xavier's hand tighten slightly on Jared's. The obvious jealousy he was displaying baffled me, but then again, I guess if I became interested in someone else, then he'd lose his toy.

The thought depressed me once again and I glanced sadly at Jared. "I need to get something to drink." I pulled away from Xavier and walked over to the makeshift bar in the opposite area of the house.

Tony was mixing some drinks and I requested a Jack and Coke.

"So how's your Dad doing? I know he got home from the hospital today, right?" he shouted as he poured the whiskey and then the soda.

"Yeah. He's fine. He stayed home to rest." I grabbed the drink, slugged it back and held it out for more. "How are your parents and your sister? Is Mary pregnant again?"

"They've been trying, but she hasn't been able to yet. My parents are great. They're in Hawaii right now, retirement vacation." Tony refilled my glass again before mixing an apple martini for a woman I didn't recognize who stood nearby.

After talking with Tony for a few minutes, I glanced around and saw Xavier talking with my sister and a couple of other people. I figured I could take a cigarette break outside and be able to relax. I picked up my drink and wandered out the back door to sit on the wooden swing Tony and his sister had hung from the tree. The tree house we'd all built together with Tony's dad was still standing and looked in pretty good shape. I pulled out my pack and lit one up, blowing the smoke up into the moonlit night.

"Those are bad for you."

I heard the voice come out of the dark and turned my head to see Jared walking towards me, his hands inside his jacket pockets.

"I know. Maybe they'll kill me sooner rather than later," I replied bitterly, without really looking at him.

"Is something going on? You seem really unhappy." Jared grabbed a hold of one of the ropes and pulled it, causing the swing to shift.

I didn't say anything just shook my head. "Come on, Fagan. I saw the look you gave me inside. Something's not right between you and that guy in there. Xavier was his name, right? Is he hurting you?" Jared demanded.

"Not physically." My voice was low and I dragged on the cigarette again, taking the smoke deep inside my lungs and then released it.

I saw his hand tighten on the rope and looked up at him. "It's nothing, Jared. Just forget it. Eventually I'll have outgrown my usefulness and he'll throw me away like everyone else does."

Shock flared in Jared's eyes. "You think that's what I did?"

"Didn't you?" I asked, not accusing, just stating a simple question.

"No!" he protested. "I can't believe you actually think I would do that to you. I loved you, but I wasn't *in* love with you. You understand?"

I couldn't stop the melancholy swamping me and I looked at him with feelings of sadness etched in my heart. To my absolute horror, I could feel my eyes getting wet and I blinked like crazy, turning my head away from him. "I just want to be who I am and everyone around me wants me to be someone else. To make them happy or to satisfy what they want." My voice trembled and I ran a shaky hand through my hair, brushing the annoying strands back from my face.

"You need to stop worrying about pleasing others before you please yourself, Fagan," Jared insisted and he leaned closer, his lips next to my ear. "And if you truly want that man you brought with you, you should grab on and not let go. I can tell you care for him, but you aren't happy." He pulled back slightly and stared into my eyes. "If you aren't happy, you should find someone who does make you happy."

"Like who? You?" I tensed when I heard Xavier's voice and almost groaned. Not now.

Jared was jerked away from me and Xavier grabbed the front of his jacket, lifting him slightly off the ground.

"What the hell do you think you're doing?" I demanded, standing up and grabbing Xavier's arm, trying to pull him away from my friend.

"Protecting what's mine," he ground out, his eyes locked with Jared's.

"I am not yours!" I shouted, ready to stamp my feet like a five-year-old who didn't get his way. "God damn it, Xav. You may have control over what we do in the bedroom, but who I talk to and who I spend time with is none of your business. He doesn't want me. He never did. So let him go before I get really fucking pissed off and beat the shit out of you!" My breathing was heavy, and I panted, my breath clear in the freezing temperature.

Xavier looked over at me, a cocky smirk on his face. "You think you could take me?"

I just glared at him, my arms folded across my chest. "Let him go."

Xavier pulled his hands back, smoothing the jacket back down Jared's chest. "Stay away from him," he growled, grabbing my hand and tugging me back towards the house.

I jerked away and demanded, "What the hell is wrong with you? Acting like a jealous boyfriend. You aren't my boyfriend, remember? I'm nothing but a warm body for you to screw. If you want anything else then you need to ask for it, because I will not act like a boyfriend without some kind of reciprocation." I slammed past him, stalking through the crush of bodies and out the front door to the car.

The engine turned over nicely, and I flipped on the heater

after a couple of minutes, breathing into my hands to fight off the cold. Soft music played out of the speakers, and I closed my eyes wearily. He acted like he was jealous, and I suppose he was because he was afraid he wouldn't have me at his beck and call whenever he was horny, but it pained me to know the only reason he acted jealous was because of our deal. The warmth from the heater barely penetrated the chill invading my body, because it wasn't only physical. I felt cold all the way to my soul.

Rayne and Xavier left the house a few moments later. None of us said a word on the drive home. The headlights cut a swath through the flurry of snow kicked up by the tires, and I concentrated hard, not just to be able to get home in one piece, but also because I didn't want to think about him.

14

We entered the house quietly so as not to wake Dad. Rayne went straight upstairs to her room and I walked towards the living room to turn off the Christmas lights Dad had left on. Xavier followed me, but I just ignored him as I pulled the plug. I walked around the couch on the far side opposite where he stood so I could leave without stepping near him. But he moved like lightning and suddenly he was beside me, grabbing my arm and yanking me against him. I went to protest, but before I could, he brought his lips down on mine. Expecting a punishing kiss, I was surprised to find his mouth hesitant and sweet. Unable to resist the temptation of kindness from him, I pressed up against him and responded in kind, lightly moving my lips against his. It was like a sweet caress from a lover, from someone who cared about me.

I felt his hand reach up and it settled against the back of my neck, pressing my mouth tighter against his. His other arm looped around my waist and gripped me firmly. My head whirled. With so many conflicting emotions running through me, I just lost myself in the tenderness he seemed to be offering. Confusion and desire both raced through me. Did my words have an impact on him? Did they make him realize that being with him, not just being used by him, was what I wanted? He pulled back to look into my eyes and I flushed, tilting my head down slightly. A small laugh came from him and I peeked through my eyelashes to see him smile. "You really are the most beautiful when you smile," I admitted in a low voice.

His fingers, which had been playing gently with the hair at the nape of my neck, stilled.

"You think I'm beautiful?" he asked in a rough voice.

I lifted my head up in surprise. "You know you are! Why would you need me to confirm it?"

"Because it doesn't matter to me what others think. Only what you do." A slight red color stained the high cheekbones of his sculpted face and I could only stare, flabbergasted.

Before I could respond, his mouth was on mine again, his tongue pressing against my lips for entrance, which I allowed willingly. The hot flesh flowed over my own and I groaned, sucking on it lustily. I heard a low growl and realized it had come from him. I drew on his tongue again with my mouth, my cheeks hollowing out as I dragged it deeper inside. My body raged with desire and I prayed this would last forever. Without breaking the kiss, he pulled me around the arm of the sofa and down onto it, pressing me deep into the cushions with his body. My legs opened instinctively and he sank between them, fitting like a perfect puzzle piece. A moan escaped my throat when his stiff erection came into contact with mine, and he pushed his hips forward, grinding it against me. He trailed his lips down to my throat, his tongue laving the indentation at the base, and then moved to the side, sucking and biting gently at the flesh there.

I slid my fingers into his hair, yanking the leather cord out and tossing it aside, watching as the long strands slipped around his shoulders to pool on my chest and arms. I felt his teeth rake the sensitive skin over my pulse and I cried out, arching my back. His hand quickly slipped over my mouth, stifling the sound before it could pass completely from my lips.

"You have to be quiet," he commanded huskily before going back to feasting on my neck.

"You try being quiet... ah... when someone is... mmm... sucking on your neck!" I replied in a heated whisper, groaning in between words because his tongue and mouth felt so good.

Suddenly, I flipped us so he was under me, and I smirked at the shock in his eyes. Instead of saying anything, I lowered my head to his neck, sliding the tip of my tongue from his Adam's apple down to the pulse beating just beneath the surface. Then I closed my lips over it, and sucked the flesh there into my hot, wet mouth. I felt him shudder and his hands gripped the shirt that covered my back. A heady sense of power filled me at having the ability to make him weak with pleasure. I slid my hand between us and underneath his shirt to run my fingers teasingly over his chest and belly. His breathing became erratic and heavy. Just as my thumb and forefinger closed over his nipple, I sank my teeth gently into his neck, causing his body to jerk. He let out a cry of rapture, which I quickly muffled with my other hand. I grinned wickedly at him. "You have to be quiet," I mocked, rolling his nipple between my fingers.

He grunted and arched his back, pressing up against me. My legs straddled him and I pressed down lightly, rubbing our hard flesh together through our clothing. I sat up partway and looked down at him. His gray eyes glittered with lust and his dark hair was splayed out around him. "We should go upstairs before we get caught," I suggested, moving to stand up, but his hands locked around my waist and held me in place.

"They're both sleeping. Besides, it would take too long for me to feel your skin against mine," he ground out, yanking my shirt up over my head.

His hands moved to the fastening of my jeans, which he swiftly unbuttoned and unzipped. "Take them off," he demanded.

I stood up and slid the fabric down my legs, letting it pool at my feet, and then slipped my boxers down as well, releasing my already stiff and throbbing length. I could feel a blush stealing over my body as his eyes locked on me and roved downward towards my erection. He stood up as well, and I watched in fascination as he removed his shirt and then his pants, letting them drop to the floor with mine. It felt like I couldn't see enough of him. My eyes wandered over his body. I noticed for the first time, even though we had been intimate before, he had a small birthmark in the shape of a heart just on the inside of his thigh. "What's that?" I asked, dropping to my knees in front of him.

Before he could answer, my lips settled over it in a kiss. I swiped at the mark with my tongue and I felt his hands grip my shoulders. His fingers dug in as I continued to assault the birthmark and sucked it into my mouth. I trailed tiny kisses up the inside of his leg and higher still until I reached the patch of hair surrounding his shaft. I leaned back slightly, staring up at him as I trailed my tongue over the head. He tilted his head back in pleasure, the long hair streaming down his back. I really love his hair. I love the feel of it on my skin, the way it caresses my flesh as he rocks against me.

I've had very little practice at this, since I'd only had one lover before, but I swirled my tongue over and around the dark pink head, my hand grasping the base firmly while I closed my mouth over the end, and slid him inside. I heard a moan rumble deep in his chest and one of his hands moved from my shoulder to the back of my head, pulling me closer to him, pushing his cock in deeper. I could feel him jerk inside my mouth as I swallowed convulsively and I did it again, his fingers tightening in my hair to guide my head as I continued to suckle him.

I felt him getting closer to the edge, but he pushed me away. I looked at him in disappointment, and he said softly, "I want to come inside you."

Lust blazed through me at his words and he pushed me down onto my back on the thick carpet, lowering his body on top of mine. It was mostly dark except for the fire slowly dying in the hearth, and it cast shadows over his face as he stared down at me, brushing a lock of my hair back from my forehead. I actually felt like he cared about me as I lay there, watching the dim light flicker across his features. I went to speak but he placed a single finger across my lips and shook his head. "If we do this here, we have to be quiet or we'll wake your family. I don't relish the idea of your dad coming downstairs with a shotgun, only to find my naked ass in the air," Xavier teased, mirth dancing in his gaze.

I nodded in agreement and he lowered his head to press his lips to mine. I heard him fumbling blindly before he backed away enough to rip open a condom package with his teeth. Apparently he'd been carrying one in his pants' pocket. I raised an eyebrow at him and he had a sheepish look on his face as he rolled it down the length of his cock. Instead of the usual quick launch into it, Xavier slid two fingers along the seam of my lips. "Suck them," he murmured huskily.

Slowly, I parted my lips, letting my tongue meet the salty flesh of his fingers. His eyes darkened even further, if that were possible, as he watched me. The sound of his breathing deepened and he wrenched his fingers away, slipping his hand between my thighs. I felt the tip of one slick digit caress the sensitive skin around the entrance to my body and shivered in anticipation. My breath caught in my throat when he slowly pushed into me, sending flickers of electricity along my spine. He slid in and out, touching further each time. I couldn't stop the toss of my head when his finger grazed my prostate or the groan at how good it felt. "Shh," Xavier whispered.

Biting my lip to stifle the next moan threatening to burst forth, I thrust my hips down, trying to force him deeper still. Xavier tugged his finger free, but my dismay was short-lived as he thrust two inside me this time. Unable to stop it, I gave a small cry, arching my back from the floor. He covered my mouth with his, muffling the sound quickly. Affectionate consternation glimmered at me in the dim light and, embarrassed, I looked at him. "I'm sorry," I breathed, "but it feels so good."

Smirking, Xavier nuzzled at my throat as he scissored his fingers, stretching me and preparing me to take him. He ran his palm along the expanse of my thigh, opening my legs wider and seating himself between them. The fat, spongy tip of his cock nudged against me, slowly entering me and tunneling inside, inch after inch. Once buried deep in my ass, he remained there for several breaths and then began the sensual mating dance, thrusting his hips back and forth. My legs locked around his waist and I rocked up towards him, meeting each of his deep plunges. Our fingers entwined and he continued to seal my lips with his, his tongue rubbing over the sides of my mouth. It felt as though my body was spiraling through outer space and this was a dream, a beautiful, sweet dream. I never wanted it to end. I wanted to feel cherished like this for the rest of my life. Pleasure soared through my veins and I moaned against his mouth. His hard flesh impaled me over and over again, and he angled his hips just so, causing the head to slam against my sweet spot each time. It sent me over the edge rapidly and my hot fluids were spilling between our thrusting bodies in a matter of minutes. My cries of completion were swallowed by his mouth.

I felt him tense before the heavy warmth of his come filled the condom and I knew he had reached his own peak, spilling into me. His eyes were shut and he threw his head back. His teeth bit hard on his bottom lip, and I watched in fascination as he finished, collapsing on top of me. We were both breathing heavily, our bodies still giving occasional shudders from the absolute ecstasy we had achieved.

The log in the fireplace crackled as we tried to catch our breath and relax. I could feel the stickiness against our bellies. What a mess I had made! I knew the tenderness he had just shown was temporary. Even so, I couldn't help but hope it was more than that. I held it deep inside my heart to get me through those moments when his actions would make me feel like my soul had been buried in a deep, dark cellar and would never be released.

After a few moments, I shuddered when I felt him slide out of my body, and he stood, helping me to stand on shaky legs. We slipped on our pants, grabbed the rest of our clothes, and walked up the steps to take a quick shower. We washed each other off, our hands touching each other with no words exchanged, for fear it would shatter the peace we'd achieved. I expected him to head back to his room when we were done, but he followed me into my bedroom, slipping into the bed next to me and gathering me close.

As I heard his breathing deepen and even out, I knew he was asleep, and tears stung my eyes. Forgive my pessimism, but nothing in my past had given me reason to believe his affection would last beyond tonight. Maybe it was because it was Christmas Eve and he was feeling the urge to be kind. I didn't know, but as I lay there, locked in his arms, my head resting on the pillow next to his, I prayed to God He would hear my words and grant my wish for this to last forever. From the moment he had kissed me in the living room tonight, I knew I had fallen in love with him.

As hard as I tried to deny it, it had happened, and if he reverted to his former self, it would destroy me.

The following morning, I woke up to an empty bed and I sighed, not wanting to let go of the beautiful dream last night had been. I swallowed and went to sit up, only to stop in shock. Xavier stood in the doorway, holding a tray with food on it. He stepped inside and shut the door with his foot. I couldn't help but stare as he walked towards me. "What?" he asked, his eyes revealing uncertainty.

"You brought me breakfast in bed?" I squeaked.

A flush spread over his cheeks and he set it down across my lap. "I brought my own to eat with you. What? No one has ever brought you breakfast in bed before?"

"Not since I was five and sick with the chicken pox. My mom brought me chicken noodle soup," I replied as I picked up the cup of coffee, breathing in deep. I couldn't live without coffee in the morning.

He settled on to the bed next to me, his back against the headboard, and he reached for the second cup of coffee on the tray. I watched as he raised it to his lips. "Merry Christmas, Xav." I grinned at him, turning back to my food, picking up my fork.

I almost dropped the fork when I heard his voice next to my ear. "Merry Christmas, Fagan." I shivered when his breath passed over the edge of my ear and I tilted my head slightly to be able to see him.

"I don't know what's gotten into you, Xav, but I sure hope

it lasts," I admitted before stuffing a forkful of eggs into my mouth.

His hand reached past mine to grab a slice of toast and he settled back again, munching away. "So what do you guys usually do for Christmas?" he asked me.

"Well, we usually get up whenever we feel like it, and once we're all awake, we open presents. Rayne and I make Christmas dinner. After that, it's over," I said in a monotone.

"You guys don't do anything else?" He seemed amazed by the fact we didn't do more celebrating.

"It's more of a depressing holiday for us. My mother passed away right after Christmas, and it used to be such a big event for her. We just lost our spirit after she died." I kept eating, not looking at him, trying to hold the memories at bay. "We spent Christmas morning in her hospital room that year. I still remember the smells and sounds."

"How did she die?" he asked, his hand coming to rest on my arm in sympathy.

"Leukemia. They tried to find a match in one of us, but neither my sister nor I were a good match so we couldn't save her." I still blamed myself, but I'd never let anyone in on my shame.

His next words annihilated me. "And you blame yourself, don't you?"

I swung my head around to stare at him. I couldn't believe he'd been able to see what I had hid from everyone else for years. "What?"

"You think because you weren't a match, you're to blame for not being able to save your mom," he stated gently, ensnaring my eyes with his intense gaze.

"I... I... how? How did you know? I never told anyone," I whispered, still unable to look away from him.

"Sometimes you speak without using words, Fagan. I would feel the same way if I was in your shoes." Xavier had floored me, completely and utterly. How could he possibly have guessed?

I finished eating without saying anything and then I heard my sister's door open and close down the hall. "I think my sister is awake. Do you want to head downstairs to open gifts?" I glanced over at him, sipping the last bit of coffee from my mug.

"In a minute," he whispered huskily, reaching out to snag the back of my neck and yank me towards him, crushing his lips down on mine.

"Mmm, I could get used to having my coffee this way every morning," he said, rolling out of the bed and grabbing the tray to walk towards the door.

He stopped and tossed over his shoulder. "You coming?"

15

As the four of us settled down to open gifts, I remembered we hadn't opened the stockings last night. I grabbed those and handed them out before sitting by the tree on the floor to go through mine from my sister. Laughter spilled out when I saw the first thing I had pulled out. It was a miniature version of the Red Ryder BB gun from A Christmas Story. It had always been one of my favorite movies, and I'd watched it so much I had ruined our VHS tape. "Where did you find this?" I crowed, a huge grin on my face.

Rayne smiled. "They released the movie on DVD and they started releasing toys and stuff for it. I found it in that gag store, Spencer's Gifts. You remember the place?"

I nodded and pulled out each item one at a time. I enjoyed opening the stocking because it was always silly stuff we gave each other. Xavier hadn't said anything and I looked over to see him staring at a small item. I frowned, walking a little closer on my knees. It was the sketch I had done of him, smiling. I had written in the corner, 'This is what it looks like when you smile.' I had been meaning it to be a tease about him not smiling, but it looked like he was shocked. "Are you okay?" I asked, concerned.

He looked up at me and my breath caught at the utter awe in his gray eyes. "You drew this?"

"Yeah." I frowned. "Why?"

"This is beautiful. You have a great talent for drawing. Why don't you try to advance yourself in the field of art?" he demanded.

I laughed because his words showed how little he knew me, which actually was kind of sad and my laughter faded away as I looked away from him. "I am. I've been taking art classes since just after getting the job at… Temptation."

He didn't respond and I moved back over to open the rest of my gifts, the shine of the morning dissipating. Rayne gave me a questioning look but I shook my head. I didn't want to talk to her about it, because then I would have to reveal where I worked. I knew she wouldn't judge me or tell my father, but I just didn't feel up to telling her. I opened the gift from my Dad and stopped in surprise when I saw it. My eyebrows went up and I looked up at him to find him flushed with embarrassment. "You bought this for me?" I picked up the book of artwork and touched the cover reverently. He had never bought me something like this before.

"I knew you were taking the classes and thought you might like it. It's no big deal," he said gruffly.

I grinned at him, and wondered if maybe my Dad was beginning to accept who I was and, in his own way, showing he supported me. I placed the book carefully aside before picking up the gift from Rayne. She had given me an oil paint set with very expensive-looking brushes. I looked up at her and smiled. "Thanks, Ray!"

There was another gift under the tree and I looked at it, puzzled. I picked it up and my eyes widened when I saw it was for me, but the real kicker was that it was from Xavier. I wondered what he had bought me since he didn't know me all that well. My eyes connected with his and I saw an almost childlike anticipation in them. Pleasure at seeing him actually happy flooded me, and I smiled softly. "When did you get this?"

"The other morning. Open it," he urged.

Shaking my head, I started pulling the paper apart and looked down in amazement at what I saw. Somehow he'd known I collected carved wolf figures from a special store in town. I didn't know how he'd even know where to get them. I looked up at him. "How did you know?"

"I saw them in your room the other night. And I just asked around until I found the right place. Do you like it?" he asked with uncertainty in his voice.

I nodded eagerly, and looked back down at the white wood the wolf had been carved from, tracing the deep lines of its elegant face. The artist had given the wolf a serene yet regal look and it stood with all four legs on the ground, holding stiff, as though waiting for something. I knew that no matter what happened between us, I would treasure this gift forever.

"It reminded me of you," he pointed out.

I snorted with laughter. "I'm regal and elegant?"

"When you want to be, and yet you keep yourself elusive from others around," Xavier stated quietly.

Rayne helped my Dad stand and they left the room, as though they knew we needed a few moments alone. Xavier moved off the couch to lower himself down next to me. He reached up with his hand and turned my face towards him. Feathering his lips over mine, his hand caressed the skin of my cheek lightly. When he pulled back, I felt such hope balloon inside my chest. I prayed the balloon didn't pop. This was too good to be true. It had to be. Nothing like this had ever happened to me before. Even when I was with Jared, it had never been like this. "Thank you," I whispered before moving to stand.

He stood with me, and helped me clean up the wrapping paper and bows. I carried the items I'd received upstairs to my room, placing them near my bags so I wouldn't forget them tomorrow when it was time to leave. The rest of the day was a blast. Xavier laughed more than I'd heard in the six months I'd known him. Things had turned out in a way I hadn't expected, and I had to admit this was the best Christmas I'd had since my mother passed away. It felt like a fragile dream just waiting to be shattered. And unbeknownst to me at that time, it would shatter into a million pieces just like it had all those years ago.

As I was turning off the Christmas lights, I noticed something shining from beneath the tree and realized Xavier had never opened his real gift. I crawled beneath the tree, grabbed it and backed out, wiggling as I went to avoid hitting the hanging ornaments. Sitting up, I looked over my shoulder to see Xavier standing in the doorway, his arms crossed over his chest with an amused expression on his face.

"Lose something?" he asked, pushing away from the doorjamb to approach where I knelt.

"Yep. You didn't get your main gift from me. It must have been knocked to the back when we were passing things out." I handed it up to him and smoothly stood up, pushing him towards the couch to have a seat.

"Your drawing was enough. You didn't need to get me anything else," he protested, trying to give it back to me.

I refused to take it and forced him to sit down. "Open it."

He slowly removed the wrapping paper and stopped short when he saw the watch I had purchased for him. "Do you like it?" I asked eagerly, moving closer to his side.

Before I knew it, I was in his lap and he was kissing me, passionately. I tasted something salty, as though he were crying. I tried to pull back to look at him, but he held me tightly, cupping the back of my head. I soon lost all thought but the kiss, our tongues pushing against each other. I felt his hand drift beneath my shirt and his fingers tenderly caressing my stomach. It didn't go beyond that. It stayed tender and sweet. Soon he stood up, without looking at me, and pulled me with him upstairs to my bedroom. Once there, he slowly undressed me, carefully, as though I would break. It confused me when he left my boxers on and took his own clothes off, but left his briefs on. He pulled the covers back and pushed me into the bed before sliding in next to me and pulling me against him. "I just want to hold you tonight," he said quietly and closed his eyes.

Delight raged through me and I snuggled in closer, shutting my eyes and relaxing. Within a few moments, I was out. If I had known how the next day was going to go, I probably would have enjoyed those moments a lot more before falling asleep.

The next morning, I woke to find him already up, and I pouted in disappointment, but rose to dress for the trip back to New York City. I didn't know if I wanted to go back to being an escort but it might be the only job I could do for now. Hopefully, Xavier believed me now that I didn't sleep with my clients. Rayne and my father were out in the barn taking care of the animals when I headed downstairs, and Xavier dropped a kiss on my shoulder as he passed by. "I'm going to pack up for the trip. I'll be back in a few," he explained as he continued up the stairs.

Excitement at having Xavier all to myself on the flight back made me grin, and I was heading towards the kitchen when I heard a knock on the door. Opening it, I was surprised to find Jared there. I stepped out onto the porch, pulling the door closed behind me. I knew Xavier wouldn't be happy to find him here. "What are you doing here, Jared? Xavier's going to be really angry if he sees you."

"I wanted to see my best friend before he flies off to New York again."

"We just managed to reach an easy truce, and I don't want anything to shatter it," I protested, glancing around furtively.

Unexpectedly Jared pinned me against the side of the house and held me there. "Come on, Fagan. I know you aren't happy with him, and I know you were happy when I was the one holding you. Let me be that one again. I've missed you. Last night when I saw you, it made me realize just how much."

Suddenly he was kissing me. I struggled to get away, pushing at him. He grabbed my hands and forced them back against the house. I tried to bring my knee up, but he blocked that as well. He kept mashing his lips against mine, trying to thrust his tongue inside. Stubbornly, I kept my mouth closed. Abruptly he was gone, tossed off the porch into the snow. I glanced gratefully at Xavier, but he didn't look at me as he glared down at Jared. "I told you to keep your hands off what was mine. Get out of here before I kill you."

Jared scrambled out of the snow and stumbled to his car, jumping into the seat and skidding across the icy driveway as he backed out frantically. I moved to Xavier's side and watched, reaching out to put my hand on his arm except he jerked away, glaring at me. "You can't believe I wanted him!" I exclaimed, staring at him in horror as I saw the condemnation in his eyes.

"You want to act like a slut then I'll treat you like one," he ground out, grabbing my arm and dragging me into the house.

I struggled to get away but his anger made him stronger, and a few moments later, he had me in my bedroom, his back against the door and he shoved me to my knees. Once again, I tried to explain, but he just gave me this look that was a combination of anger, hurt, and disillusionment. At that very moment, I knew someone in his past had hurt him, a lot. Except it was me getting the punishment that person deserved. I watched in dread as he undid his pants and lifted out his semi-hard cock.

"Suck me," he demanded, gripping the back of my head in a hard, punishing grip.

Shaking my head, I tried to back away, but he tightened his hold, causing me to wince in pain and I hesitantly opened my mouth. He filled it with one thrust, ramming it almost to the back of my throat, making me gag. He leaned his head back against the door, and I slowly started to pleasure him with my mouth and tongue. I felt tears burning behind my eyes. They started to overflow, trickling down my cheeks in tiny streams. I ran my tongue along the underside of his shaft, sucking hard at the head, and closed my eyes, pushing forward again to the base. I continued this for several long moments. When he flooded my mouth with his semen, I gagged as I swallowed it all. He pushed me away, and I fell back onto the floor, still crying silently. I refused to look at him while he shoved himself back into his pants and zipped them up. "Get your things together. We're going to the airport now."

I couldn't believe how deeply I was hurting. To know the man I loved had just used me like a common whore was almost more than I could stand. My heart felt like it had been smashed and then ground up in a blender to leave nothing behind. I carefully dragged myself up, afraid my body would break too, and I stumbled across the hall into the bathroom to brush my teeth and rinse my mouth out. I didn't want the taste in my mouth, because knowing how it had come to be there repulsed me more than anything.

Making sure I had everything together, I slowly took my things downstairs, trying to keep myself together long enough to say goodbye to my family. I was no longer excited to be going back or to be alone with him on the long flight. He didn't even look at me as we said goodbye to my family, and he got into the car as I hugged my sister, tightly. "I'm going to miss you, Ray."

"Is something wrong, Fagan?" she asked me, pulling back, her eyes searching mine as though she could see the pain in their depths.

"No, not at all. I'm just sad to be leaving my family again, that's all." I turned and hugged my Dad before racing to the car and climbing into the passenger seat.

The ride to the airport was made in silence, as was the flight home. He kept his eyes closed most of the time, but as we neared New York City, he lifted his head from the seat to pin me with a severe gaze. "You will be moving in with me when we get back so I can have you any time I want."

"I can't leave Trinity!" I protested, digging my heels in on this one, not wanting to live with a man who despised me because of someone else.

"You can and you will." He settled his head back against the seat again as though his word was law.

Once back on the ground, he grabbed our suitcases and walked away, expecting me to follow. "We will be stopping by your place to get your things, and then we'll go to my apartment."

I tried to protest again but he didn't listen and I finally gave up, knowing it wasn't going to work. Once in his Camaro, we shot off into the city and arrived at my apartment a half-hour later. Trinity wasn't home when we got there, and he followed me upstairs to stand guard as I slowly packed my things. He started carrying them downstairs. "You can leave the bed and furniture. I have my own."

I sat down to write a note to Trinity, telling her I would call and explain later. I left it propped on the kitchen table, and reluctantly followed Xavier out, locking the door for the last time. Again, the ride to his apartment was made in silence. I felt as though I was a prisoner and my chest hurt so badly. It almost felt like I was having a heart attack with how much it hurt. Cars flew past us in the opposite direction and I wished I was in one of them instead of sitting here. He pulled up into the parking garage of a huge apartment building and got out of the vehicle. He grabbed several suitcases, taking them to the elevator to set them there and then came back to get more. It took a couple of trips, but we got them all onto the elevator and once upstairs on his floor, he pushed the stop button and we unloaded everything into his apartment.

When it was all inside, he led me to the room he was going to give me. "I don't want you sleeping in the same room as me since you're here as nothing more than my whore. You'll sleep in here unless I want you."

He said this so harshly and I felt numb, like this wasn't really happening to me but to someone else.

He left me there to bring everything in myself. When I was done, I sat down on the edge of the bed and just looked around me at my new room. The bed was really nice, a four-poster with a plush mattress. It had blue carpet and white walls. I felt so fragile, as though one more thing would put me over the edge and I would splinter. I slowly put my things into the dresser and closet. I had several sketches I'd done of various people I knew and even Hercules, Victor's dog, and I put those on the walls around the room. I put a picture frame of Trinity and me from last year at Disney World on one nightstand, and the picture of my Dad, Rayne, and me on the other nightstand. I trailed my finger along the frame, and suddenly wished I was back home, and that I'd never come to this city.

I didn't hear him enter the room or notice that he stood there watching me, his lips in a tight line. I jumped when he started speaking.

"I'm going to work. Victor needs some things completed in bookkeeping before the New Year. You can do what you want but no one is allowed to touch you. Understand?" he demanded.

Without looking at him, I nodded and breathed a sigh of relief when he was gone. I wrapped my arms around my waist and sank to the edge of the bed, finally letting the tears I'd been holding at bay come. I hated to cry. Crying was useless, but I just couldn't stop them. I curled up on the bed and buried my face in the pillow, trying to keep from making any sound. My throat felt raw by the time I was done and I sat up, dragging myself into the bathroom nearby to wash my face. My eyes, as well as my nose, were bright red.

16

I heard my cell phone ringing in the other room and listlessly went to answer it. It was Trinity. "Fagan, what the hell is going on?" she demanded. "I came home to find a note that you're now living with that guy from your work?"

I explained in short what happened and she was stunned. "Just tell your father the truth! That's a very unhealthy way to live! Fagan, please. Just tell your father the truth and come home," she pleaded.

My eyes started to water again and I choked out, "I can't. If I tell him what I've been doing, it could kill him, Trin. Can you understand?"

"That son-of-a-bitch!" she screamed, taking me by surprise. "I'm going to kill him. Tear him limb from limb!"

"It's okay, Trinity. I'll be all right. I just have to wait until he gets bored with me. That's all. Then I can just go back to living my life like I was."

"How long do you think it'll go on, Fagan? He could use you for two months, a year, three years? You'll wither away and die inside. I know you, Fagan. That kind of cage will destroy you."

"I know, babe. I know. I just have to try and get through this. But… Trin… I… I love him," I whispered, squeezing my eyes shut. I prayed he would tire of me quickly.

She was silent for a long time, and then said, "Oh, baby, I'm so sorry. You know if you ever need anything, I will be by your side in seconds."

"I know. I will never stop being friends with you, no matter what he says." We spoke for a little while longer and then disconnected the call.

He didn't touch me that night, and I was grateful for it. I didn't think I could bear it. I reported to work the next day with dark circles beneath my eyes, which most people attributed to my father's accident. However, Winston sensed something else. He kept nagging me about what was wrong and before long I had broken down and told him the whole story. He could only stare at me in shock. "What a bastard! I knew he was a prick, but I never thought he'd go this far."

His use of those words brought me up short in my agony and I grinned sadly. "You actually swore."

"Hey, I'm not a complete nerd!" he protested.

"So how goes things with Trinity?" I asked, curiously.

"Great! She's a great lady. I really like her. We have a lot in common, although you wouldn't think it by outside appearances," he stated, handing me a cup of coffee.

"That's great. I hope you guys work out. Trinity deserves someone to make her happy. Just know if you hurt her, I'll kill you," I threatened mockingly.

"You just be careful with this explosive situation you're in. It's very unhealthy for you, mentally, physically, and emotionally."

I nodded, grateful he cared about me. "Any new assignments for me?"

"No. Not yet. There should be one tomorrow night, but I won't know until Victor confirms it. You should get some rest. You look like shit."

I grimaced. "Yeah. I'm sure I do." I stood up and hugged him. "Thanks for listening to me whine. I hate it, but I needed someone to talk to."

"Anytime." He grinned and we spoke for a bit longer before I decided to head out.

As I was leaving Winston's room, Xavier was walking out of the elevator. When he caught sight of me, he glared at me for a moment and then beckoned for me to follow him. I shuddered and started down the hallway towards him, wondering what he wanted. The room he led me into was his office. I could tell from the organized neatness and the way he comfortably settled down into the chair behind the desk. I didn't look at him, just stood there, staring at a spot on the wall.

"Come here in front of me, and sit on the desk," he demanded.

Biting my lip, I complied and sat my bottom down on the edge of the desk in front of him. He pulled his chair forward, and reached out his hands, opening my pants. I closed my eyes, dying a little more inside. To be touched like this without thought, without care, killed something inside me and it became a mechanical thing. I let him take my swiftly hardening flesh into his mouth and he pleasured me with his hot, wet lips, running his tongue along my length. I shuddered, clenching my fingers in his hair, disgusted with myself for enjoying this senseless act of lust. But I couldn't deny him and soon flooded his mouth with my fluids, throwing my head back and grunting with ecstasy.

He stood up abruptly, pulling me off the desk and turning me around to bend me over it, yanking my jeans down around my ankles. I heard him open a drawer and the next thing I felt was a cold, wet finger pressing against my tight entrance. I groaned as he forced it inside me, quickly changing it to two fingers and then three, thrusting them deep inside and twisting them. I felt him pressing against my prostate. It sent blood rushing to my cock, which swelled beneath me. His fingers were suddenly gone and I could hear his zipper being lowered. The belt buckle tinkled as it hit the floor. I knew what was next just before I felt the tip of his stiff prick pressing hard into me. He didn't stop, didn't give me even a second to adjust to him, just pushing deep and hard into me. I could hear his breathing getting heavier as he moved inside me. My own breathy moans filled his office and I could feel my hips starting to thrust back, much to my dismay.

His fingers gripped my hips tightly, digging roughly into my flesh with each slapping thrust. My hands clenched on the surface of the desk, and I could feel my orgasm rising, pushing me towards that moment of intense pleasure. I felt his cock swelling inside me and knew he was going to burst soon. He gave a strangled cry and rammed inside me again, spilling his warm spunk. The pulsing of his shaft triggered my own release. I cried out, my eyes shut tight, my fluids drenching the desk underneath me. He collapsed against my back, his body heaving with exertion. My cheek lay against the smooth surface of the desk as I waited for him to remove himself from my body.

Finally, a few moments later, he slid out of me. I could feel his fluids trickle out and start to drip down my legs. I hurriedly pulled my pants and boxers up, looking at him from the corner of my eye as he smirked with amusement.

"Get out," he stated, fixing his own clothes and settling down to work again.

Feeling used, I slowly walked out of his office. Things were quickly deteriorating and I didn't know how to break free from this torture. I didn't understand how I could love someone who could use me so callously, without thought for my feelings.

The next two months proved to be the most difficult time I have ever endured. He would take me whenever and wherever he wanted me, brutally and quickly, until he'd satisfied himself. It was especially bad whenever I returned from an assignment, as though it would remove any lingering thoughts of the woman I had escorted. I started to lose weight, so much so that people began to notice.

Winston, Trinity, and even Professor Klein, my art teacher, approached me about it.

"Are you ill?" he asked one day, after class, just as I was leaving.

"No. Why do you ask?"

"Because you've lost about thirty pounds in the last two months," he stated sarcastically. "And you have bags under your eyes deeper than my grandmother's."

I laughed weakly. "Yeah. I just haven't been sleeping well."

He stepped closer to me. "Your technique has definitely improved these last two months, but you're leaning towards a darker overtone. Something's wrong. Is it your boyfriend?"

I looked at him in surprise and he laughed. "I'm not blind. I knew you had someone in your life."

"He's not my boyfriend," I whispered, not looking at him, fiddling with the strap of my backpack. "In order for someone to be a boyfriend, they have to actually care about you."

"Do you want to go get some coffee and talk about it?" he asked.

Suddenly needing someone who seemed to care about me to understand, I nodded. He grabbed his things and locked up the art room, and we walked to a nearby cafe.

"So tell me what's going on?" he asked as we sat down.

Everything just spilled out in a rush of words. It was like a dam I hadn't even been aware of had been building up inside of me and it suddenly burst open. I told him what my job was, how I had come to work there, about Xavier, and everything he had done to me. He had a sympathetic but angry look on his face when I was done.

"He sounds like a real bastard. But you care about him still, don't you?"

I nodded bleakly, and stared down into the brown liquid in my cup. "Yes. That's the sad part." I laughed humorlessly.

"You are in a very unhealthy relationship. You need to get out. Even if it's not physical abuse, it's still abuse. I can see you aren't happy." He pointed out, taking a sip of his coffee. "You need to tell your father. I think he's stronger than you give him credit for. And it's been several months since his accident, so he should be able to hear it now without adverse effects. It's the only way out of this situation you're in."

"Things just snowballed so fast. One minute he seemed like he actually cared about me and suddenly, I was being treated like I was nothing but a whore." I flushed at my revelation and couldn't meet his gaze.

His hand came to rest on mine, and I looked up at him gratefully. "You know, it's too bad you rejected me all those months ago," he teased, sighing dramatically, tilting his head to the side and flashing me a grin. "You could have had me and I would have never treated you like that."

For the first time in months, I felt like laughing, really laughing. I threw my head back and started to crack up. Deep peals of laughter spilled from my lips, and I felt something give inside me, something good. "You know, I wish I could have felt that way about you back then because you are a truly beautiful person," I told him once I'd managed to stop laughing.

We finished our coffee and I left to head back towards Xavier's apartment. I didn't consider it home. It was more like my jail cell. I thought back on the conversation with Trace as the elevator started up. Maybe if I had met him before I'd met Xavier, things could have been different. Trace was the complete opposite of Xavier. He was kind, sweet, and beautiful. But it wasn't meant to be, or I would have met him first.

Xavier was sitting on the leather sofa when I entered the apartment, and I could feel pure rage radiating from him. I sighed and dropped my bag beside the front door. "What did I do now?"

"You should know what you did." His voice was silky but there was searing lava behind it. "Where were you?"

"Out, with my art teacher for coffee. He wanted to talk to me about my work," I lied.

"What did I tell you when we came back here two months ago?" He stood up and stalked towards me slowly as though he were a lion stalking its prey.

"There's a lot you told me. I don't know which one you mean."

He grabbed me by my hair, pulling me close so we were nose to nose. "I told you that you can do whatever you want, but no one, no one was to touch you. You let that teacher touch you."

"What?" I asked in shock.

"I saw you in the cafe with that man. He touched you."

"Are you following me now?" I demanded, wincing when his fingers tightened on my scalp.

"I was actually driving past on my way home. Luckily the

street light turned red or I may have missed it. I saw his hand on yours."

"It's not like that!" I cried, but he cut me off with a bruising, punishing kiss, forcing me backwards towards his bedroom.

I struggled, trying to get away. Finally, I couldn't take it anymore and I snapped. I brought my knee up, hard. I felt it connect with his groin and he grunted in pain, dropping to his knees. I couldn't do it anymore. This was the final straw. I ran, snatching up my backpack that was by the door as I left. I didn't even wait for the elevator. I took the stairs two at a time in my desperate rush to get away from the pain, the agony that tore through me every day. His harsh words, his cruel treatment, and the way he used me chased me like the hounds of hell. I didn't know where to go. Anywhere I went, he'd find me. I couldn't go home to Iowa, nor could I return to Trinity.

I ran until my lungs felt as though they were going to burst, and I stopped in an alley, bending at the waist to catch my breath. When I could finally breathe normally, I pulled out my cell. "Hello?" a deep voice answered.

"Victor. It's Fagan."

"Fagan! How are you?"

"I'm not going to be returning to work."

"What? Why?" he demanded.

"I can't bear it any longer. I am leaving the city. I can't tell you where, either, for reasons I can't explain. Just know I am grateful to you for giving me the job when I needed it. Tell Winston I'll be in touch with him and Trinity soon."

"Fagan, wait! What's going on?"

"I am finally breaking out of a situation I can't bear any longer. If you truly wish to know, you need to ask your cousin." Without giving him the chance to say another word, I disconnected the call.

I cleaned out my bank account. I had built up quite a bit of money since I hadn't had to pay rent, and now I would need it. I decided on Boston. I could live off my savings until I found something. I called Trinity and left her a voicemail, omitting any mention of where I was headed. Then I bought a one way ticket on the Greyhound. I would need to buy essentials when I got there. My heart felt heavy at having hurt him, even though he'd hurt me enough to last four lifetimes. I prayed he would be happy. Maybe he'd be able to find someone he could trust eventually, but as much as the thought caused my heart to ache even further, I would never be that person.

A voice came over the loudspeaker, calling my bus departure and I stood up. I walked towards the bus with the weight of the world on my shoulders. I could feel my heart telling me to turn around and go find him, but my brain argued he would just continue to hurt me. It was chilly on the bus and I settled into one of the seats towards the back. Thirty minutes later, we were out of New York City and on the way to Boston. I slept for the first half of the ride. The second half, I just stared out the window, watching the trees and towns flashing by.

17

It was late when the bus arrived, and I found a small motel for the night, paying cash so I didn't have to give my real name. I used the key and pushed the door open, looking around bleakly at the shabby room. I dropped my bag on the floor and collapsed on the bed, and fell into sleep, only to be chased by the demons in my nightmares. My cell woke me up the next morning, and I grabbed it, staring blearily at the number on the screen.

"'Lo?"

"Fagan! Where the hell are you?" Trinity's voice blared over the cell and I pulled it away from my ear.

"I'm sorry, Trin. I can't tell you because I don't want him to find me," I stated calmly.

"What the hell did he do to you?" she shrieked.

I could hear Winston in the background behind her. His voice came over the phone and I smiled wearily at the protective tone.

"Where are you, Fagan? You shouldn't be alone right now."

"Why? You think I'll kill myself, Winston? I can't lie. The thought has crossed my mind," I stated wearily.

"Don't talk like that!" he demanded.

"Things just got progressively worse. No matter what I did, he hurt me." I started to cry. I thought I was all cried out, but the tears just spilled over again. "I just want the pain to stop, Winston. I couldn't take it anymore."

"Jesus," he breathed. "Fagan, please, tell me where you are. I swear, I won't tell him. In fact, I'll go over there and make sure the bastard stays away from you."

The picture of Winston standing up to Xavier popped into my head and I started to laugh softly. "He'd kick your ass, Winston."

"Nah. I'd just bring Trinity with me."

I laughed harder and swiped at my cheeks. "I still would rather not reveal where I am right now. When the time is right, I'll tell you. I just needed to get away, and I couldn't do that by going back to the farm or Trinity's apartment because he'd find me. I need to call my dad to tell him the truth, before Xavier can do it."

"I think you should have done that from the moment he started blackmailing you," Winston pointed out.

"Yeah, I know, but I didn't want to disappoint my dad, yet again."

I finished my conversation with the two of them. I felt lonely afterwards and placed a quick call to Trace, telling him what happened after we'd parted. He was angry and threatened to hurt Xavier, but I told him not to bother. I would heal, with time. I gave him my cell number and told him to keep in touch with me. He promised to hold the painting for me, and he would call me with details about the art show in May. Once I finished with him, I placed the call to my father. My dad answered the phone on the second ring.

"Hey, Dad. It's me."

"Fagan. How are you?" I heard the rustle of sheets and knew I'd caught him in bed for the night. "Are you okay?"

"I'm good. Listen, has Xavier been in touch?" I held my breath.

"No. Why? Is he supposed to be?"

My breath almost wheezed out of me in a whoosh of relief. At least I'd gotten to be able to tell my father before the son of a bitch could have the satisfaction. "No, no. I just wondered. I'm actually calling because there is something I need to tell you."

"Okay. What is it?"

"Um… it's kind of hard for me to tell you this because I… don't want to disappoint you any more than I already have."

"Fagan, you're my son, and I love you. I know we haven't exactly been on the best of terms the last few years, but almost losing my life has shown me my family is important to me. I'm sorry for the way I've treated you, son. It was wrong. Can you forgive your stubborn, pig-headed father for being so stupid?"

I was shocked into silence for a moment and my eyes burned even more. The words I'd been longing to hear for so long had come at a time when my heart hurt the most. "I love you too, Dad," I whispered. "Of course I forgive you. You're my dad."

I heard him give a sigh of relief. "So what is it you needed to tell me?"

Swallowing hard, I gathered my courage to tell him. I had to be honest with him, especially after everything he'd just said. "For the last year I've been living in New York, I've been working at an escort agency, escorting women to different functions." I held my breath as I waited for him to blow up.

"I know."

I felt my mouth open and shut several times, like a fish out of water. "You what? How? When?"

"I may be a backwoods farmer, son, but I do know how to read. I've seen the pictures of you in the paper and you also mentioned the name of your company when you were out here. I researched it online. I've known for some time now."

I was flabbergasted, to say the least. "I see. Why didn't you say anything?"

"Because I wanted you to feel you could tell me yourself."

Suddenly, my world felt like it had fallen even further apart. All these months and I could have been saved the pain and anguish. I started laughing and the sound quickly grew hysterical. My dad was shouting over the phone, wanting to know what was going on. I couldn't speak, only shake my head and continue to laugh. Eventually, I grew weak and my laughter slowed. I lay there, staring up at the ceiling, and said, "Dad, I love you. I'll talk to you later okay?"

"Wait—"

But I didn't let him finish, I disconnected the call and just lay there, lost in the senseless events of the past four months.

Nothing made sense anymore. After disposing of my cell phone and getting a prepaid one, I spent the next week looking for a job where I could work under the table and finally found one working with a photographer. He paid me cash and I would help him whenever he needed me. He gave me a place to stay as well. I started to sleep a little bit and eat more. I gained back about fifteen of the thirty pounds I lost, and started to fill out my clothes so they fit better. I continued to draw and paint, using it as an outlet for my emotions. Trinity would call me once a week and ask how I was doing. She told me Xavier had been around looking for me, but she'd demanded he get lost. My heart lurched when she said his name and I bit my lip as she related how he was constantly hounding Winston at the office for information about me. All he would give Xavier is that I was fine and doing better without him. The weeks blended into one another and it was soon the middle of April. I still hadn't revealed to anyone where I was staying, but they'd stopped asking long ago. Trace called one day to talk to me about the art show.

"You should come," he urged. "You can get your painting and see your sketch. I plan to include it in the show."

"I can't. If he finds out I'm there, he will try to see me. And I can't face him right now." I pleaded for him to understand.

"How will he find out?" Trace demanded. "I won't be telling the bastard and no one else has to know you're there. Please just come, Fagan."

"I'll think about it," I promised, but I was trying to convince myself it would be a bad idea to go.

I finally decided against going to the show just a few days before it was being held. I called Trace to let him know. "I just can't stand the thought of being close to him right now. I'm still too weak inside. One more moment of the agony I suffered and I may not come back from it this time," I said quietly.

"I guess I can understand, Fagan. At least tell me where you are so I can come visit you afterward and give you your painting. And, of course, return your sketch to you," Trace asked.

I hesitated for a moment. I knew I could trust him. "I'm in Boston. I work at a photographer's studio called Mirage of Dreams. He lets me work for cash and gives me a place to stay."

"Did you tell him why you're in hiding?"

I laughed and remembered William's expression when I'd told him everything. "He wanted Xavier's name so he could go to New York and kick his ass. He understands and is supporting me fully. I know hiding like this is being a coward, but I'm so weak when it comes to him. I even almost turned back as I was boarding the bus to come here. And I lie in bed awake at night sometimes, thinking about returning to him. I'm sick. Aren't I?" I couldn't hide the bitterness in my voice.

"No. You aren't sick. When you love someone, it's hard to break away from them. Believe me, I know. I've been through a similar situation, but I managed to stay strong and here I am. From everything you've told me about him, it sounds like something really bad happened to him in his past."

"I had that suspicion as well, but it doesn't give him the right to treat me that way. Trinity told me he keeps pushing Winston to tell him where I am and he keeps asking questions about me. You're the only one who knows where I am right now. I didn't tell Winston for the very reason that Xavier's been asking him where I am. He has plausible deniability now, you know?"

"All right, well I'll call you when I'm on my way up there to see you. Okay?"

"Sure. I look forward to seeing a familiar face. I'm actually feeling kind of lonely, but William does keep me company sometimes. He's a great guy, but straight. I seem to find the good ones, but they're all straight." I sighed dramatically.

Trace laughed huskily. "I'm a good one and I'm not straight. When you finally find yourself getting over him, maybe you can let me know. I still find you attractive."

I didn't speak for a brief second, and then began, "It's not that I don't think you're attractive, Trace. I just... don't feel attracted to you. Maybe that will change, who knows. I don't want to say no entirely. I still love him and maybe I will always have a tiny piece of my heart locked away for him, but right now, I just need to be alone."

We finished our call and I got back to the studio, where William was posing a little girl for a portrait. I kept laughing at the antics he used to get the little girl to smile. He'd been teaching me about photography and I'd shown him some of my paintings and sketches. He'd raved over them and even took some of them to display on the walls of the studio. I glanced at one now, a painting I had made from a sketch of Xavier. It had been soothing to paint him that way, a beautiful smile curving his lips and a happy light shining from his eyes. I could only hope he was able to find his peace and live his life without reserve, without pain. I just wanted him to be happy.

William closed up the studio and suggested we go get some Japanese food. I agreed eagerly, and we talked as we walked. I could actually smile again, though sometimes it would turn sad as something triggered a memory of Xavier. Even though it hadn't been a long relationship, we had done things together. Whenever an aching memory rose up in my mind, I would remember those precious hours on the farm at Christmas before Xavier allowed the pain of his past to destroy the fragile bond we'd begun to build between us.

The morning of the art show I called Trace to wish him good luck. We'd talked on the phone at least twice a week since I had 'run away'. I felt uncomfortable at the lack of maturity in that thought, but it was the truth. I had run away, but I didn't feel I had any other choice to be able to save myself. The first two weeks I was here, I'd had non-stop thoughts of suicide, but I'd beaten them, not letting those thoughts persuade me to do something stupid because it would mean being an even bigger coward than I already was. I wouldn't let myself succumb to such weakness.

The day went by slowly, with only a handful of customers coming in to have their pictures or their children's pictures taken. I was in the back room when I heard the bell over the door chime, and William began talking to someone. It was silent for a few moments and then the bell chimed again as the door opened and shut. I wandered out and questioned William about the short visit, but he said it was just someone looking for directions. I shrugged and spent the rest of the day organizing the film trays and packaging up completed photos.

It was eight when we closed up. I walked out of the front door and tossed my goodbyes over my shoulder. "I'll see you at home, William." When I turned back around, I froze in place like a deer caught in headlights. No, No. This couldn't be happening.

"Fagan."

The deep husky voice I loved swallowed me whole and my knees almost gave out. I was swamped by a fresh pain so agonizing I didn't know how I remained standing.

18

"No," I whispered, backing away and reaching behind me to blindly search for the door handle, but it was locked already. I yanked on it, desperately.

I saw him wince and anguish splashed across his features.

"Fagan, wait. Please. Can we just talk?"

"Why? So you can fuck with me again?" I exclaimed, losing my calm and pressing harder against the smooth glass surface.

"No!" he protested, stepping closer, but he stopped when I flinched away from him. "Please, just let me explain."

"Why should I let you?" I demanded, glaring at him as I remembered those moments of shame and hurt.

"Because I love you," he stated simply, as though it were an irrefutable fact.

I started laughing harshly. It was loud even to my own ears. My hand covered my mouth and I shook my head. When I could finally speak, I looked at him with skepticism. "I'm supposed to just believe that you love me? When did that happen? When you were using me like a common whore?

When you kept hurting me because someone else hurt you in your past?" I saw his eyes widen slightly at my words. "Oh, I figured that one out a long time ago. I waited and waited for you to realize I wasn't that person. I wanted you to realize it more than anything. I finally got tired of being abused. Just go away, Xavier. Please," I begged wearily, looking away from him.

"Please, give me a chance to explain and apologize. Let me take you out for coffee and we can talk," he begged.

I studied him for a moment before giving an abrupt nod. He motioned for me to precede him and when he went to touch me, I jerked away, glaring at him. "Don't."

He held his hands up and backed away slightly, letting me lead the way towards a nearby diner. We chose a booth in a corner, and he sat across from me. I ordered a cup of coffee and he did the same. "How did you find me?" I asked.

"I went to see your teacher today. At the art festival. He told me where to find you."

Shock and anger flooded me. I'd been betrayed. "I see."

"Don't be upset with him. I forced him to tell me."

"Unless you held him down and threatened him with a gun, there is no other way you could have made him tell you," I stated sarcastically.

He studied me for several long moments and I flushed, looking away from him. I felt angry he could still make me feel anything for him at all. "You were right when you said I had been hurt. Will you listen with an open mind? Please?"

His gray eyes were sad and I felt a sharp tug in the region of my heart. I rubbed at my chest, trying to ease the pain. I gave a small nod and he started to tell me how he came to be so hurtful.

"I was just out of college, fresh-faced and ready to take on the world with a gung-ho passion. I had only ever been in one other relationship, with my college roommate, and we broke up, mutually, a few months before graduating. I started working at an accounting firm, and one day, at a party given by the firm, I met this man I thought was the most beautiful person I had ever seen. He started flirting with me, and almost immediately we hit it off. I thought we had the perfect relationship and I had found the man I was going to spend the rest of my life with." He paused, staring down at his coffee cup in remembrance.

"After about six months, I confessed I was in love with him and we moved in together. I started to notice things as time went on. He would disappear for hours and never tell me where he went. He would go out at night and come home reeking of perfume. I began to get suspicious and followed him one night when he left. I discovered he was an escort, for both men and women. I confronted him that night when he got home and he admitted it. He also admitted he had sex with them for an added bonus. I was disgusted and I gagged at the thought of him being with so many other people. I was devastated to know the person I loved more than anything in the world had cheated on me, over and over again." He took a breath and looked up at me, his eyes meeting mine.

"I started working at Temptation to remind myself of everything my ex put me through and to remind myself why I wouldn't get involved with someone like him again. When I first saw you in Victor's office, I felt an immediate attraction to you. I knew you were there for an escort job, and it disgusted me I could feel any desire for you at all. It was a knee-jerk reaction to treat you so cruelly. I had no respect for anyone who could have sex for money. But as time went by and we interacted, I found these little things you did that made me start to like you as a person. You know, the way you spoke to the security guard at the front, the easy friendship you built with Winston, your smile, the kind way you treated everyone around you. It didn't fit who I had decided you were from the beginning." He stopped to take a sip of his coffee.

I just watched him, not saying a word as I waited for him to continue. That's when I noticed he truly did look awful. He'd lost weight and there were dark smudges beneath his eyes. He looked tired. Sympathy for his past flooded me, but I couldn't let it justify what he'd done to me and how he'd used me. He took a long time before he continued.

"The night of the Christmas party, I knew you were drunk when you started coming on to me. I used it as an excuse for my behavior that night, but the next morning, you ran. I felt upset and angry you would leave without saying anything to me. So I followed you to Iowa because I couldn't leave it where it was. I saw an opening, and I used it to my advantage when it was obvious you wouldn't want your father to know about your job. That way I could have you without having to open myself up to the same uncertainty and pain."

His tone was bitter and I could see he wasn't really seeing me, but what he had done as he spoke.

"Then I saw a side of you those few days I couldn't ignore any longer. When you yelled at me at the party and said you wouldn't act like a boyfriend without it being reciprocated, I thought you wanted to actually be with me. I decided to take a chance that you truly wanted me. When we made love, the way you touched me gave me hope. It made me realize how much I loved you."

My breath caught in my throat at his confession and I swallowed painfully. His lips twisted bitterly as he continued with the chain of events leading us to here.

"When I found you and Jared kissing on the front porch, it felt like I'd been betrayed all over again. Jealousy, anger, and pain became this big ball that seemed to lodge itself inside my chest. Before I could stop, I found myself doing things I was ashamed of but, as time went on, I didn't know how to get myself out of it. It just kept getting worse and worse. I could see you were suffering, and losing weight because of my stupidity and fear."

Xavier's jaw clenched as he continued. "I hated myself for what I was doing to you but I couldn't stop. When I saw you sitting in the café, I saw him touch your hand and you started laughing. This beautiful smile broke out over your face and I was so angry I couldn't make you smile that way." His breath hitched and I looked up to see him fighting tears. "You were actually laughing, but not with me, with someone else, another man. I lost it. When you got home that night, I couldn't see anything but the anger and hurt I was feeling. Angry at myself for treating you just like you said, like you were nothing but a common whore. Hurt that you couldn't love me the way I wanted you to. You were right to do what you did. You should have done it sooner. In fact, you should have kicked my ass the morning at your father's home."

His fingers tightened on the coffee cup, and he looked me straight in the eyes when he continued. "I know what I did was unforgivable, and it will take a long time for you to trust me again, but I beg of you to find it in your heart to give me one more chance. To show you who I am and to show you how much I love you."

I sat there, stunned. Everything he'd told me whirled around in my brain and I looked down at my hands, twisting my fingers together. After a moment, I looked up, and I said honestly, "I did want to be with you. More than you could imagine, and it confused me, to desire to be with someone who could treat me like you did. I don't know if I can forgive you or forget. So much has happened between us. I tried to stay with you as long as I could because I truly loved you." I saw him stiffen when I used the past tense.

"But I can't be with someone who could use me the way

you did. Who could treat me so coldly and never once think of what I would feel. I'm sorry, but right now, I just need you to leave me alone." I moved to stand but he grabbed my hand, his eyes pleading.

"I know you still love me, Fagan. If you didn't you wouldn't have drawn me the way you did. I saw the sketch at the art show and the painting in the studio. No one has ever seen me the way you do. I don't know if anyone else will ever be able to. Please, just think about it. Sleep on it for a few days and I'll be in touch. Please."

His words stabbed deep inside me. I was still in love with him, but my fear remained. Once I was back with him, he could revert back to being the same cruel person he had been, and it kept me from saying yes. "I don't know. I'll think about it. Please let go of my hand," I said softly.

Reluctantly, he released it, and I walked out of the diner without looking behind me to see if he was still sitting there.

It was late by the time I got home and William was already asleep. I quietly entered the house and went through to the garage just off the kitchen. He'd had it converted to a small apartment just before I arrived that he could rent out and make a little money on the side. I sighed with relief as I kicked off my sneakers and socks, my toes sinking into the plush carpeting. I dropped onto the edge of the bed wearily and took off my watch before setting the alarm for the next day.

Picking up my cell, I dialed Trace's number and listened to it ring until his answering machine picked up. I let him have it. "God damn it, Trace. How could you tell that son of a bitch where I was? He came here tonight and he actually told me he loves me. He's put me through enough already! I trusted you and you betrayed my trust. I thought you were my friend." I disconnected the call and tossed my phone onto the nightstand, angry again.

I quickly undressed and slung on a pair of sweatpants, going over to the small fridge and grabbing up a beer. Turning on the TV, I settled down on to the couch to watch for a while, knowing I would not be able to sleep anyway. The beer tasted great. So great, I was tempted to chug it down and grab a couple more, but getting drunk wasn't the answer. In fact, getting drunk was what started this whole fiasco in the first place. The beer didn't taste so good then, and I set it down on the coffee table. Some fat guy on TV was spouting off about how this invention works great and it's only nineteen ninety-five. That shit makes me laugh. Late night infomercials, how many people actually watch them? I mean besides losers like me who can't sleep because of some bullshit going on. Finally, I found a great movie, Unleashed starring Jet Li. He's one of the greatest martial artists of this millennium. I love his movies. Most of the movies I own had been left behind at Trinity's when Xavier had forced me to move out. My fingers clenched the sofa cushions and I tried to blank my mind out, not wanting thoughts of him in my head.

Finally, I managed to fall asleep around two in the morning. I groaned wearily when the alarm went off at six. Yawning, I dragged myself up, took a quick shower, dressed, and grabbed a bowl of cereal before meeting up with William out front. "Mornin', William."

"I see you didn't sleep well last night. Did something happen with your ex?"

I stopped walking to stare at him. "What?"

"He came into the studio yesterday afternoon. I recognized him immediately from the painting on the wall of the studio. How did he find you?"

"Trace told him. Can you believe that? I thought he was my friend," I said bitterly, once again disillusioned by someone I cared about.

"Maybe he had a reason to tell him," William stated in a low voice, and I glared at him.

"No. Nothing would be a good enough reason to tell him where I was. I refuse to run again. I am not going to be a coward any longer, and I like living here. It's peaceful and quiet. And of course, there's also the fact I love working for you."

William slung an arm around my shoulders. "Well, that's always good to hear. I like having you work for me too, Fagan. And I think it's a great thing you intend to stay instead of running. Standing your ground is the best way to handle this kind of situation."

I smiled gratefully and he pulled away to open the door, letting us inside. The morning passed uneventfully, but at lunchtime, I was in the back room again, sorting through photos booked the previous week, when I heard the front bell chime. William was in the darkroom and I rushed out to greet the customer, stopping in my tracks when I saw Xavier standing there. "What are you doing here?" I demanded.

"I came to have my picture taken."

"You promised to stay away for a few days," I accused.

"I promised to give you a few days to think about it. I didn't come here to discuss it. I just came to have my portrait taken," he stated simply.

I was stunned into silence at his insistence and turned abruptly away to buzz William in the darkroom. He came out a few moments later and I disappeared into the back room again. This was ridiculous! I couldn't believe he was here today. I clenched my hands into fists, my nails digging crescent moons into my palms. Fine, he wanted to play it that way, then I'd play my role to the hilt as well. I picked up my cell and phoned the only other friend I had made since coming to Boston. "Mark, it's Fagan. Listen, I need a favor."

About twenty minutes later, I grinned wickedly as I heard

the front door open and the bell above it rang again. Anticipation at revenge ran through me, and I looked up as Mark entered the back room. "Hey, baby," he boomed, winking at me since his back was to Xavier. "I've missed you."

He stepped into the back room, shutting the door, and I couldn't help but grin as he came towards me. "So that's him, huh?" he whispered, ruffling my hair, unbuttoning a couple of his own shirt buttons, and I mussed his hair up a little bit, giving the impression we'd been passionately kissing.

"Yeah," I whispered back. "He got here last night. Thanks for doing this, Mark. Tell Karen I'm glad she loaned you to me for the day."

Mark and I had met one day when he and his wife had brought their baby in for her first photos. We'd hit it off immediately, talking about the sketches I did and the paintings on the studio wall. His wife was a great person, beautiful, inside and out. Their baby girl, Marisa, had Mark's eyes, and Karen's beautiful smile. She was going to be a true heartbreaker. I'd been over to their home numerous occasions just to talk, eat dinner, and hang out. I eventually told Mark what had happened to me because he could tell there was a lot of pain in my past.

"Should I go out there and kick his ass?" he asked me.

"No. It's okay. I'll deal with it in my own way. He begged me for forgiveness yesterday, but I don't know if I have it in me to forgive him," I replied softly.

"He's got a lot of balls asking you to forgive him. I just hope you know what you're doing," Mark stated, reaching out to open the door as he plastered a sexy grin on his face. "That's the best greeting I've had all year."

I stepped from the back room and saw Xavier's eyes narrow and anger flash through them, but then it was gone, only to be replaced by a haunting sadness. Guilt shafted through me, and I felt angry at myself for letting him get to me. "I'll see you tonight, Mark."

"Sure thing, baby. I'll make sure I don't overdo it this time." He winked and left.

I almost laughed, but stifled it and turned around to find Xavier looking at me, hurt reflected in his dark gray eyes. My breath caught in my throat and I turned away quickly. I wanted nothing more than to run over to him and hold him, kiss him, comfort him. But I had to be strong. I couldn't give him the chance to destroy me. I busily tidied up the front desk, hearing William directing Xavier how to stand and everything. When he was done, William handed me the necessary paperwork and I processed it, totaling his bill. "Three seventy-five, please," I stated, not looking at him.

"Who was that earlier?" he questioned softly, his voice soft with a strange emotion buried in it.

"No one. Three seventy-five."

I almost gasped when his hand reached out and two of his fingers settled underneath my chin to gently lift my gaze to his. "Please don't lie to me. Is he your new lover? Just tell me if I even have a chance. If I don't, then I'll leave and not come back."

I felt guilty again and my eyes shifted away. "I..." I couldn't tell him he didn't have a chance because the thought of never seeing him again caused my heart to drop and I swallowed with difficulty. "He's not my lover," I confessed quietly.

Xavier closed his eyes for a brief second in relief and pulled his hand away from my chin. I felt bereft of his touch and I almost wanted to cry. He handed me his credit card, which I processed mechanically and handed back to him. His fingers brushed mine when he took it. My skin tingled from the brief contact. I wanted to give in to him so badly; my entire body ached with need. The fear of being devastated again kept me strong. "Thank you, and I hope you keep Mirage of Dreams in mind the next time you need portraits," I said by rote, not really thinking.

"I'll be staying in town for a few days. At the Regency Hotel on Charles Street, room 315. If you need to talk, I mean. I'll see you around, Fagan." He smiled sadly and walked out, leaving me to stare after him.

19

For two days I agonized over whether I should contact him or not. I would pick up the phone and drop it back into its cradle. Finally, three days after Xavier's visit to the studio, I picked up and called the Regency Hotel asking for him. The receptionist transferred me to his room and I held my breath as it rang. That husky voice answered and I closed my eyes, almost ready to cry. "Hello?"

I almost couldn't answer. "Xavier, it's Fagan."

"Fagan. I… I'm glad that you decided to call me." I could hear his beautiful voice deepening with happiness and I bit my lip.

"I called because… because…" I stuttered, unable to continue.

"Because?" he queried in a low tone. I heard the ruffling sound of sheets and almost groaned at the thought of him in bed. My body became alert and sensitive.

"Because I thought about what you said," I started slowly. "And if you truly want to be with me again, without the anger, then you need to prove it."

"Prove it? What do you want me to do?"

"I don't think I should have to tell you. You need to figure it out on your own. But if you do want me to believe you really love me then I want you to prove it." I know asking someone who loves you to prove it is probably ridiculous, but there was no way in hell I was just going to say okay and accept it all at face value. Not when all I could see was the hard look in his eyes each time he'd taken me all those months ago.

He was quiet for a moment, and then came back with, "All right. I'll do whatever it takes."

"I'm going to sleep now. Goodnight," I told him.

"Goodnight, Fagan," he countered. I disconnected the call and lay there, wondering if I had made an even bigger mistake than before.

I woke to my cell phone ringing the next morning, and I groggily reached for it, peering at the caller ID. My eyes widened and I was completely and utterly awake as I answered the phone. "You have a lot of nerve calling me after what you did!"

"I knew you were going to be mad. I'm sorry, Fagan, but I felt he had the right to know," Trace argued.

"Who are you to make that decision, Trace? Why would you open me up to that kind of pain again? I trusted you!"

"I spoke to him for a long time at the art festival, Fagan. Even going so far as to show him the sketch you had done the first week of class. I could see he was honestly sorry for what he had done and he really does love you," Trace explained softly. "I just thought maybe it was time you both worked it out, no matter what the outcome was. Because I know you're strong enough now to stand against him if you truly don't want him in your life."

"Trace, damn it! I should come back to New York and kick your ass," I replied heatedly, my fingers clenching on my cell phone.

"Have you talked to him yet?"

"Yes. He came out here immediately after the festival and hasn't left. He told me he loves me and he wants me to give him one more chance to prove it."

"And are you?" he asked.

"I don't know. I told him if he truly wants to be with me then he needs to prove it. He wanted me to tell him how to do so, but I told him he needs to figure it out on his own."

Trace laughed into the phone and then came back with, "So what do you think he needs to do to prove it?"

I thought about it for several long moments and it was hard to decide what would be enough to prove it. "I don't know. This may sound cheesy and old fashioned, but I want to be courted. Truly courted. Does that sound corny, or what?" I laughed sarcastically. "But I want it more than anything. I doubt he has it in him to do it."

"I see. Well, I hope you at least give him the chance, because when he saw that first sketch, he very nearly started crying in the middle of the festival. Call me if you need anything, okay, Fagan? I've got to run to class now so I'll talk to you later." Trace disconnected the phone call before I could say another word, and I leaned back against the headboard.

I was stunned. Xavier had almost started crying? Over me? I stared at the phone, desperately wanting to call him, but knowing I shouldn't. I dropped the phone on the night stand and stumbled out of bed. No. I wouldn't give in to it. I had to be strong. If I grew weak again, I would wind up back in the same situation. There is an upside and a downside to giving him another chance. The upside, having what we had at Christmas in Iowa. The downside, always having the fear he'd start treating me the same way again. I don't know if the benefits would outweigh the consequences, or if trusting him again would be a mistake. I would just have to wait and see. No promises from me. Hey, I know that's pretty harsh, but how else can I deal with it?

I reported to work as usual and around noon Xavier made his first choice at proving his intentions. I walked out of the studio to go to lunch when I saw him standing outside, leaning against a lamppost and holding a perfect red rose. I have to admit, my heart jumped, but hey, who wouldn't react that way? He smiled at me and I wanted to melt right there, but I stiffened my spine and gave him a tight smile instead. He pushed away from the post and strode towards me, stopping in front of me to give me the rose.

"I came to take you to lunch. If you're willing, that is."

To give myself a moment to think, and also to make him sweat a little, I lifted the rose to my nose and sniffed at its sweet fragrance. The petals had just begun to open and it was a beautiful, ruby red color. Finally, I lifted my eyes to his and gave a small nod in agreement. A bright grin broke out on his lips and I blinked at the sheer happiness he showed at just being able to take me to lunch. I still didn't want him touching me, mostly because of the fear I had of my own weakness. I walked a few feet away from him along the sidewalk. "How's Victor doing?" I asked as we were seated by the hostess. We had gone to a small Italian place a couple of streets over.

"He's doing well. He hasn't really spoken to me much since…" He trailed off, and I realized he was talking about when I had run off.

I grimaced at the memory and I smiled sadly. "I'm sorry. I hope he doesn't stay mad for long."

"You have nothing to be sorry for," he said angrily. "I'm the one at fault. My stupidity and blindness caused everything that's happened and I have to atone for it in some way. Whether it's losing my cousin or more."

I stayed silent and looked down at the checkered pattern of the table cover. A moment later, he spoke again.

"I'm sorry. I shouldn't have gotten angry but do not apologize to me for something you had no control over. It deepens the pain and guilt I feel over how I've made such a mess of things."

"I'm sorry, but could we possibly talk about something else?" I whispered, almost pleading, not wanting to think about those things again right now.

"Of course. I actually have something for you in my car back at the studio. Trace gave it to me to give to you."

Excitement raced through me and I looked up at him. "Is it the painting he promised me?" Xavier nodded. "Awesome! I can hardly wait to see it again."

"How long have you wanted to be an artist?" he asked me, folding his arms on the table.

"Ummm... since I got into high school and started hanging out in the art room during lunch. I wasn't exactly the most popular guy in my school." I began to regale him with tales of the cheerleaders and their jock boyfriends out in Tyson's Point. I also told him how the head cheerleader had tried to get me in bed just to see how far she could get me to go since everyone knew I was gay.

The food came sometime during the story and we started to eat. Xavier told me about his own small town and the trouble he used to get into. "I got hauled to the county jail for a night because I was drinking with some friends and got into a fender-bender on the way home. Needless to say, my father wasn't happy."

He'd had a much better childhood than I had. I didn't

understand how he could have let one relationship that had gone sour affect him so badly. I didn't say anything about my insight, just continued to eat and chat with him. I hadn't known much of anything about him those few months ago, only how he'd grown up in a small town, was Victor's cousin, and Christmas was something to be celebrated in his home. By the time lunch was over, I felt I knew a little bit more about him than I had previously. He walked me back to the studio, and left me with a casual goodbye. "I'll see you again later."

I still held the rose when I returned through the studio door. William raised a questioning eyebrow at me, but I just shrugged and went into the back room to get a small glass container to put the rose in. It felt like the room was a little brighter with the rose, and I hugged the feeling to myself. I prayed this wasn't just a joke, and Xavier didn't go back to his former self.

When I got home from work that night, there was a tall box sitting in front of William's doorway. I thought it was for him, but when I picked it up it had my own name on it. I frowned and brought it inside to my own small apartment. The box felt slightly heavy and I placed it on the dinette table before grabbing a knife and cutting the twine that held the cardboard in place. A gasp left my lips as the wrapping fell away to reveal the painting of the moonlit lake, the small mountain cottage in the distance. I trailed my finger along the elegantly etched frame that had been added and I lifted it up. I saw a small white piece of paper flutter to the ground and stooped to pick it up.

Fagan, I hope you can forgive me for revealing where you are to your 'demon'. Please understand my own past has left me to suffer the fate of the faceless man in the painting and I care deeply for you. I do not wish to see you end up like the occupant of the cabin, alone with only wild animals for company. Enjoy your painting, my friend, and I hope you can find forgiveness in your heart. Your Friend Always, Trace.

I glanced back at the painting and stared hard at the cabin. There was a single shadow in the window of the cabin, a faceless man. It screamed loneliness. It also made me realize something terrible had happened in Trace's past. I couldn't help but wonder what it was that would make him feel like he had no hope left. I felt guilty for screaming at him over the phone and after hanging the painting above the sofa in the small living area, I grabbed my phone and curled up on the couch to call him.

"Hey. It's me. I got the painting... and your note," I said softly.

"Ah. Well I hope you enjoy the painting, Fagan. You deserve it." His voice was quiet and I could hear his loneliness.

"So when are you going to come visit me?" I teased. Trace was quiet for a moment.

"I didn't think you'd want me around after I told Xavier where you were."

"I know you did it for a reason, Trace. I understand something has left you feeling as though you have no hope for the future. I'm sorry I yelled at you and I want you to know I will always be there for you, no matter what happens. You don't have to feel lonely anymore." I felt my heart swell with emotions for Trace, and sighed inwardly. I wish I could have fallen in love with him. It would have made it a whole lot easier for me.

He was so quiet I thought he'd hung up on me, but then I heard him breathe and I grinned. "For once, the incredible Trace Klein is speechless?" I laughed.

I heard him laugh on the other end. "You better enjoy it because it won't last," he growled and I started laughing again.

I told him about lunch with Xavier and how I had finally started to get to know some things about him. We talked about planning to get together soon. I truly missed his witty conversation. He could come out with some real jewels sometimes. It was late by the time we ended the call. Just before he hung up, he almost brought me to tears. "And, Fagan, thank you." I heard a tone of peace in his voice and I was happy to know I had made him happy.

"You're welcome, Trace. Anytime."

After I hung up, I lay there thinking about all the things that had happened to me in the last year or so. It was amazing how quickly everything could change. I thought I had made the right decision to move to New York, and if I hadn't, then things would have turned out differently. I wouldn't have suffered the things I did. On the other hand, if I had never moved to the city then I would never have met Xavier. Sighing into the dark, I rolled to my stomach and thought of him. I had seen a side of him today that was surprising. He had seemed almost gentle, and it pained me to remember the cruel way he'd treated me. I was so confused. I didn't like having to deal with this situation. I love Xavier, sick as that may seem with the way he has treated me, but I do. My heart aches at the thought of never seeing him again while my brain screams at me to run away again or demand he leave me alone.

I fell into a fitful sleep and dreamt of a life without him. Dark, cold bleakness surrounded me, and I saw him off in the distance, walking away from me. His long black hair swung back and forth like a horse's tail. I tried calling out to him, my hand stretched towards him. I screamed his name and shot up in bed, gasping for breath. Sweat dripped down my bare chest, and the sheet had become entangled in my legs. Light was just beginning to show into my room as I glanced at the clock. It was only fifteen minutes before I was due to get up so I turned off the alarm and went to take a shower, letting the water rain down on me as I tried to process the dream I had just woken from.

My cell phone was ringing when I stepped from the shower. I hastily wrapped a towel around my waist and raced to answer it. It was Xavier. "Good morning, Fagan," he bid me as I picked it up.

"Xavier. Good morning," I said breathlessly.

"Did you run to catch the phone or are you just out of breath from talking to me?" he teased.

I laughed, losing what little breath I had gained back. "I was just getting out of the shower when the phone rang," I gasped.

He went silent and I frowned after a few seconds. "Is something wrong?" I asked.

"No." His voice had deepened and taken on the husky sound I loved so much. "I was just trying to keep from picturing you standing there in nothing but a towel with water dripping down your body."

I flushed and felt heat race through my veins. My body responded and I bit my lip. "Did you need something?"

"I wanted to ask you to go out with me tonight."

"I have to work until my normal time." I fingered the edge of my towel. Elation that he wanted to spend time with me overcame me. My throat worked slightly as I swallowed roughly.

"That's all right. I'll pick you up at work at eight."

"All right. I have to finish getting ready for work. I'll see you tonight, then."

"Until tonight." He disconnected the call and I reached down to adjust myself slightly.

My cock had hardened at the desire in his voice and I didn't have time to relieve the tension since I had taken so long in the shower. I quickly got dressed and headed out the front door. William was waiting for me. "I thought we could walk to work together," he said.

I grinned and nodded. We chatted easily as we walked. I told him about Trace and Xavier. I also told him about the painting. He asked me to show it to him later. About halfway through the day, a delivery man walked through the door, holding a package. I was amazed to find it was for me. I signed for it, confused as to what it could be. It was a good-sized box and I opened the top to peer inside. Inside was a vase, but instead of flowers, fruits of all kinds were arranged as a bouquet. There was also a note inside.

I can't wait for tonight. To spend time with you and just be with you is more than I could ever ask for. Love, Xavier.

I felt tingles race through my body and I plucked a strawberry off the bouquet to pop in my mouth as I studied the bold signature on the bottom. It reflected a lot about the man who'd written it. The heavy curves indicated his strong personality and the passion I knew he was capable of. I was suddenly looking forward to tonight's outing very much. I wondered where he intended to take me.

20

Anticipation is the most evil emotion sometimes. It makes the clock slow down to a crawl. I kept glancing at it as I waited for eight o'clock to roll around. I admit I was really looking forward to it. There, I said it. I was dying to be with him, to spend time with him and get to know the real Xavier. William could sense I was antsy and kept smiling amusedly whenever he saw me. I pulled a childish move and stuck my tongue out at him one time. He just laughed and shook his head, continuing into his darkroom to develop some of the pictures from the morning. I entered the billing information for each customer along with the type of payment they had made. My eyes kept straying to the painting of Xavier on the far wall, and finally, I gave up trying to work and propped my elbow on the desk, chin on my hand, and just stared thoughtfully at the painting. Those gray eyes jumped out at me and I wished to see a contented look on his face for real.

Finally, it was time to go and I rushed out of the studio with a hurried good night to William. I stopped short when I saw Xavier standing just outside, in front of a stretch limo.

He was absolutely gorgeous in a pair of black slacks with a stormy gray button shirt. His long hair was tied back once again. My eyes widened and I looked at him questioningly. The driver opened the door for me and Xavier motioned me in. I stepped inside, sliding over to let Xavier sit beside me. The driver shut the door, closing us off from the world. "What is all this?" I asked, looking around in amazement.

His voice was directly at my ear, causing me to jump in surprise. "I wanted to treat you to a night view of the city before taking you to dinner."

I turned my head to find his face dangerously close to my own and I swallowed hard. I wanted nothing more than to lean forward and press my lips against his, but I turned my head back around to gaze out the window. "This is great!" I exclaimed as the driver drove through the streets of Boston. "This is such a beautiful city. I'm glad I've had the chance to see it."

I reached up and opened the small window at the top of the limo before standing up to stick my upper body out. I gazed around me in fascination. "You should see this!" I called back into the window, and a moment later, Xavier rose up beside me. I couldn't help but give him a goofy smile.

I pointed out a particularly beautiful building that caught my eye, a church which seemed to glow with a heavenly aura. The stained-glass windows, with breath- taking designs etched into the glass, shone brightly from the lights inside. "Wow."

He barely glanced at the church, just kept looking at me with an almost indulgent smile. I blushed and turned my head away to gaze out over the bay as we passed the church. After another ten minutes of standing and looking around, I moved back down into the limo and settled onto the seat. Xavier came back inside as well. "So...where are we going to eat?" I asked curiously, suddenly starving.

"Do you like sushi?"

"I've never tried it," I admitted.

"If you wouldn't mind being a little adventurous, there is this great place not too far from here where I want to take you." I nodded eagerly, resting back against the seat. He reached up and hit a button, speaking into the intercom to direct the driver where to go. "Are you having a good time?"

"Oh, yeah. This is great! I haven't really taken the time to fully explore the city yet. But I really like living here. There is so much history in this place, and it's not as busy as New York can be." I chatted happily, almost like a little boy who'd found his favorite toy. "I might think about staying here permanently. There's an awesome art school not far from the studio and I've checked it out a couple of times. Their courses seem really challenging. Trace said I should think about taking a couple, to expand on what he was teaching me."

Xavier's voice sounded strange as he replied, "Sounds like a good opportunity. I think you should go for it."

"Really? But you haven't seen any of my paintings, so how do you know I'm good enough?" I questioned.

"I have seen some of your paintings. The ones you have hanging in the studio. Even if I hadn't, I know the passion you have for art and if you have that kind of passion usually you have the talent to succeed," he replied with certainty.

Awed at his faith in me, I was a little unsettled and glanced away again. The limo pulled up in front of the restaurant a moment later and the driver got out to open the door for us. I would have liked to have taken Xavier's hand, but it was a little too soon. He opened the door of the restaurant for me and motioned me inside, following closely behind. Japanese artwork covered the walls and I stared around me in fascination. "This is beautiful."

I felt his hand come to rest on my lower back as the hostess led us to our table and a shiver ran down my spine.

It was the first contact we'd had since the other night. My stomach fluttered at the brief touch. He helped me into my seat and I smiled in thanks as he sat across from me. "Would you like me to order for you?" he asked, his gray eyes seemingly caressing my features.

"That would be great. I don't know what I would enjoy."

"Do you like seafood? Crab? Fish? Anything specific?"

"I've eaten fish before, no crab, but I wouldn't mind trying it."

He smiled up at the waitress and before I knew it, he was speaking perfect Japanese to the lady and I could do nothing but stare. Turning back to me, he looked at me quizzically. "Is something wrong?"

"You speak Japanese?" I asked with surprise.

Xavier laughed slightly, and nodded. "Yes. I may only be a couple of years older than you but I spent three years in Japan. Right after the disaster my life became when I found out about my ex's job." He took a deep breath. "But Japan… it's definitely an experience everyone should have at least once in their life. The culture and the history there is amazing. So many beautiful buildings and traditions."

"I would love to go there someday! What did you do while you were over there?" I asked excitedly.

"Mostly sight-seeing and wandering around the country. I didn't want to see just what the tourists see. I wanted to see what the Japanese see on a regular day. To experience everything to its fullest. The hot springs over there are the best. I went to one almost every day. And the museums, you would love those."

I listened, amazed with everything he had experienced, and seeing his eyes sparkling with happiness made my heart beat faster. He spoke so animatedly about it, and I knew he truly had enjoyed that time even though it had been after a terrible experience. I hoped someday he would take me there and share it with me. I pulled myself up short at the thought, and shifted in my seat the moment I realized I had thought of a future with him. I didn't want to let myself get that far ahead. I wanted nothing more than to enjoy my time with him. I roughly shoved those negative thoughts from my mind and concentrated on just laughing and having a good time.

The sushi was really great. Tasty and not overly fishy. I was surprised. I had expected it to have a strong fish taste. My eyes watered when I tried the wasabi. I drank long and deep of my soda, trying to rid myself of the spicy taste. He laughed and teased me about it. I just grinned, and popped another roll in my mouth. When I couldn't eat another bite, I leaned back against the chair and sighed contentedly.

"Full?" he asked me, raising his cup of hot tea to his lips.

"Yeah. That was great. Thank you for taking me here. I enjoyed it a lot."

"I'm glad. I hoped you would," Xavier replied softly.

"Xav, can I ask you something?" He nodded and I continued. "Why me? What is it that makes me special enough to go through all of this trouble for me?"

At first he didn't respond, but after a moment, he looked up at me and I saw so much emotion shining in his eyes that my heart skipped a beat.

"Even though I didn't see it at first, you're a kind and loving person. You treat people with respect and care. I think you're extremely smart, funny, and intuitive. You have a very strong will and when you set your mind to something, you do it." He paused and reached with the tips of his fingers to touch the back of my hand. "And even when someone treats you in a way you should never be subjected to, you still find it in you to care for that person, and endure their censure and cruelty. You deserve to be cherished and loved and I hope I can be the one who has the right to give you that."

I was speechless as he pulled his hand away and beckoned for the waitress to bring the check. I didn't know what to say and his words swirled around in my mind, over and over. I slowly followed him from the restaurant back to the limo out front, and was silent on the way home. When we pulled up in front of William's house, the driver let us out and Xavier walked me to the door.

"Did what I said at the restaurant upset you?" he questioned quietly, his hands in his pockets.

I shook my head no and leaned forward to press my lips against his cheek. I pulled back with a small smile and let myself into the house, whispering goodnight as I turned to close the door.

"Good night," I heard him reply before he strode back towards the limo.

Shutting the door, I leaned back against it and took a deep breath, then let it out on a long sigh. My lips tingled from the touch of his smooth skin, and I trailed my fingers over my bottom lip. It felt so good to be treated like a true person in a relationship. I couldn't help but wonder how much longer I could hold out against him. I pushed away from the door and carefully walked through the darkened house to my apartment. Some things were best left up to fate, I suppose.

The next three weeks were the happiest I had ever been. He was constantly surprising me by sending me little gifts, taking me out to lunch and dinner. He took me to a museum, an art gallery, a play, and even to casual places such as the movies and miniature golf. I even talked him into getting on the swan boats across the Charles River. It was a great time. The miniature golf was a lot of fun. I won, of course! I had enjoyed the ride on the swan boat, but the art gallery had been my favorite. Though I would think that would be obvious to anyone who has been listening to me ramble the last few hours. There had been so many great paintings by amazing artists in the gallery: Van Gogh—one of my personal favorites—da Vinci, Matisse, Monet, Renoir, and many others.

He had been so indulgent and sweet. There had been several moments where I had been close to kissing him but I forced myself to back away. I was getting frustrated. I wanted nothing more than to hold him, touch him. I would catch glimpses of longing in his eyes and he would rush to hide it when he realized I was watching him. I knew he was waiting for me to take the initiative. But I was scared, too scared to actually think about being vulnerable to him.

It was Saturday, a day off for me, and I was up early, getting ready for an outing he'd said was a surprise. He told me to dress comfortably so I pulled on a pair of tight blue jeans that hugged my ass just right, and I grinned wickedly, hoping it would tease him to frustration. I also pulled on a tight forest green tank top and a white, short- sleeved button-down shirt which I left open. I slid my feet into my sneakers, tying them tightly.

I heard a car pull up out front and grabbed my wallet, keys, and cell, stuffing them in my pockets, before racing out front to meet him at the walkway. "Hi." I smiled at him, and his gray eyes softened upon seeing me.

"Hi, yourself," he replied. As he turned to walk with me back down towards his car, our shoulders brushed lightly.

"So where are we going today?" I asked, eager to know.

"You'll have to wait and see. Here, put this on." He handed me a blindfold and I looked at him skeptically. "Please?"

Sighing, I took it and tied it over my eyes and around my head.

"No peeking," he said sternly.

I could smell his cologne in the small confines of the car. It sent a piercing arrow of arousal straight to my groin and I almost groaned. The desire I had for him had gotten deeper and more intense these past three weeks. My control was spreading thinner with each passing day. Despite everything, I still lusted for the man like he was the last drop of water in a barren desert.

The drive was quite long and I was getting really curious about where he was taking me. "Please tell me where we're going," I begged.

"No. I promise you'll like it," he teased.

My fingers itched to pull the blindfold off, but I kept them tightly clasped to keep from giving in to the urge. It was obvious he was enjoying himself and I didn't want to take that away from him. Finally, we pulled off the road and he brought the car to a stop. As soon as he opened the door for me I could smell salt; the ocean! I could hear the waves against the shore and anticipation soared through me. "No looking yet," he warned, helping me out of the car as he led me down a set of stairs. Finally, he brought me to a stop and said, "Shut your eyes."

I did as he asked and he pulled the blindfold off. "Okay, open them," he said after a few seconds of impatience on my part.

My eyes flew open eagerly and I stared in astonishment. Before me stood a man holding the reins of two beautiful horses, a blood bay mare and a slightly larger black-and-gray gelding. "I've been dying to ride with you since the farm," he admitted as I looked at him.

I grinned and said, "Come on then!" I strode excitedly

towards the horses. I had never ridden on horseback on the beach before!

Taking the reins from the man with a smile, I swung up onto the mare and Xavier took the gelding's, elegantly mounting the horse with ease. As he sat astride the horse, I couldn't help but admire the striking image he made: his long hair trailing down his back to pool around his rear, his body erect in the saddle, and his long, lean hands holding the reins lightly.

"You ready?" he asked, looking over his shoulder at me.

I nodded enthusiastically and we set off at a sedate pace down the beach. After a matter of minutes, we urged the horses to go faster, trotting and eventually galloping. I could hear their hooves splashing through the waves and feel the salty sea-spray splashing up against my jeans. He raced beside me, keeping pace with the smaller mare. Joy at being able to experience this with him spread through me and I knew I couldn't let him go. There was no way I could let him go now. I would tell him tonight when we returned home. But for now, I would just enjoy our ride together. I nudged the horse to run faster and the sand sprayed up behind us. Hoof prints in the wet sand were quickly eaten away by the lapping water. "This is fantastic!" I shouted over the wind. I suddenly had the desire to see his hair flying out behind him. "Take out the tie," I demanded.

He looked at me with a questioning glance but did as I bade and took it out. His long hair instantly flew out behind him, like a banner in the wind. I grinned happily and tossed my head back, reveling in the wind on my face. We eventually took the horses down to a slow walk, just listening to the hooves clomping through the sand while the seagulls screamed above us. My head was turned towards his and I didn't see the dog barreling down the grassy slope towards us until it was too late.

The mare was spooked and reared back, catching me unaware. I didn't even have time to tighten my hold on the reins. My body came away from the saddle and I was airborne for just a second before slamming into the hard sand. The wind was knocked from my lungs, leaving me breathless. From a distance, I heard Xavier screaming my name and then he was beside me, his hands running over my body, looking for broken bones.

I choked for air, trying to pull it into my lungs. I could see the utter fear and concern in his eyes. He was terrified I was hurt. Even in my pained condition right then, the love I felt for him swelled up inside me and tears formed in my eyes.

"Fagan! Are you okay?" he demanded. His voice became pleading. "Please answer me."

"I... I'm... f-fine," I gasped out. "J-just... winded." He reached a shaky hand out to brush a lock of my hair back from my face and I reached out my own hand to grab his, holding on tightly. I closed my eyes and just lay there, pulling air into my lungs. When I could finally breathe easier, I opened my eyes to find him almost in tears. "Xavier?" I questioned softly.

"I... I thought you were hurt. I was terrified when I saw the horse... and... and you falling towards the ground. I thought I would lose you," he choked out.

I reached up and touched his cheek. "You'll never lose me," I whispered, my heart aching at the anguish in his eyes.

His eyes searched mine at my words, and then he groaned, hauling me up against his chest. "God, I love you so much, Fagan."

I wrapped my arms around his neck and held on tightly. "I love you too, Xav."

I felt a shudder run through his body, then another and another. I pulled back to see tears flowing like little rivers down his face. I exclaimed in surprise. "What's wrong? Why are you crying?"

"I didn't think you'd ever say it. I didn't think you'd ever find it in you to be able to forgive me after all the hateful things I have done to you." His voice was shaky, and I hugged him tighter, my arms still around his neck.

"I've never stopped loving you, Xavier," I whispered into his throat. "I just couldn't take being treated that way anymore. I'm still scared, petrified even. I don't know if that feeling will ever go away, but I do know I don't ever want to be without you."

He pulled away slightly to look down at me. "I swear to God with everything I am, Fagan, I will never, ever treat you that way again. I'm begging you just for a chance to prove it. I regret every terrible thing I have ever said or done to you. I have to live with those thoughts, night after night."

"We'll build something far greater on top of the rubble, Xav. We just have to try to trust one another." I leaned up, tentatively brushing my lips over his.

His arms tightened around me as he responded, keeping his own kiss gentle, his lips moving sweetly against mine. My hands twisted into his hair, running through the long black strands and relishing the feel of the silky mass underneath my fingers. "I love your hair," I whispered against his lips, and slid the tip of my tongue to the outline his bottom lip.

He parted his lips slightly, offering his mouth to my questing tongue. I pushed inside, moaning deep in my chest at the taste of him. The smooth, wet glide of my tongue over his drove me crazy, and I pressed against him harder. His lips traveled from mine to blaze a trail of hot, wet kisses down to my throat. I gasped as his mouth latched onto my skin, sucking hard. His hands roamed over my body, gripping my ass and pulling me into a straddling position, my knees digging into the sand on either side of his legs. I whimpered with pleasure as I felt his stiff length pressing hotly against mine. I could feel my cock pulsing inside my jeans, pressing hard against the zipper, aching for release.

This was going way too fast for me, and I pulled away, panting for breath. I scooted away from him, and settled on the sand again, flopping backward. I could hear his breath racing in and out of his lungs. He was as turned on as I was. After I had regained most of my composure, I sat up, looking at him with all seriousness. "I don't want to be a tease, but I'm not ready for sex yet."

"I understand." His voice was low. He looked over at me. "I'm content at just hearing you say you love me."

I blushed and looked away, but he put his finger underneath my chin, turning my head back towards him. Our eyes locked on each other for the longest moment. Sometime later, we were on the road to return home, the sun hanging low in the sky. I sighed in pleasure, and settled against the seat, my eyes drifting closed as the car lulled me into a warm, contented sleep. I felt him pick up my hand in his as I slipped away. It was dark when he woke me, leaning over me and whispering my name into my ear. My eyes sleepily opened and he was looking down at me, leaning over from his seat. I looked up at him and reached up to hook my hand behind his neck, pulling him down to me to kiss him again, sweetly. Our lips touched, moving slowly, languidly over each other's. "Stay with me tonight," I whispered. "Just to hold me."

His eyes locked with mine, and he whispered back, "Are you sure? I don't want to rush things. I want to make sure you're comfortable before we progress further."

"I'm sure." I held out my hand for his once we were out on the sidewalk and he grasped it lightly.

I led the way up to the house, indicating to be quiet when I unlocked the door and we stepped inside. He followed behind me to the garage apartment, and I opened the door, motioning him to enter before me. I smiled tiredly as he looked around, studying the way I had decorated the small place and made it mine. His eyes locked on the painting from Trace, and I walked up to stand beside him. "That's what Trace gave me. I had admired it at the first art show he had."

"It's beautiful. Lonely," he said quietly, studying the cabin and the surrounding woods.

"That's what I thought as well. He has something very tragic in his past. I'm almost sure of it." I took his hand and pulled him towards the bed. "Let's go to sleep."

He nodded, and I grabbed a pair of sweatpants to change into, tossing him a pair as well. They were a teeny bit long on him since he was an inch or two shorter than me, but I thought it made him look adorable. We climbed onto the bed and I settled my back against his chest, sighing with pleasure at the feel of his skin against mine. "Goodnight, Xav."

His right arm slid under my pillow, and his other arm hooked around my waist, pulling me tighter against him. "Goodnight, Fagan. I love you."

I don't know if anyone could ever get tired of hearing that phrase from the person they love. "I love you back," I whispered into the darkness, feeling his lips press against my neck, sparking a shiver that ran through me. I think I fell asleep first, but I don't know for sure.

21

I woke to a heavy weight across my stomach and I frowned without opening my eyes. What the hell? Then I realized what it was and my eyes flew open to find a beautiful, tan arm pinning me in place. Carefully, I turned my head and studied Xavier in his sleep. He looked so peaceful, a lock of hair having come loose from his ponytail to lie across his cheek. I reached out and gently brushed it back, listening to his deep, even breathing. I couldn't believe everything that had happened yesterday. I was so afraid to believe it was real, to hope he truly did love me and would care for me for the rest of our lives. I wanted to believe it so badly, but I didn't know if I could let myself.

The strong lines of his face were relaxed in sleep and his arm tightened unconsciously, bringing me closer to him. My breath whispered from me as his hard, lean body came into contact with my own. It felt so good to feel him against me again, his warm skin against mine, his arm around my waist. His movement had brought his face closer to mine. I tugged at my bottom lip with my teeth. The urge to lean forward and kiss him awake raged through me, strong as a pit-bull that'd sunk its teeth into the mailman's leg and wouldn't let go. Deciding to go with it, I moved my head those scant inches, settling my lips upon his, just a gentle meeting of mouths. I felt him stir, and he responded tentatively, caressing my lips with his. His hand rose from my waist to cup the back of my head, holding me in place as he adjusted the intensity of the kiss, slanting his lips over mine and completely dominating me. I gave a breathy moan against his mouth and moved my free hand up to his shoulder to clutch at him.

"Fagan," I heard him whisper, and he slid his wet, slippery tongue into my mouth, rubbing against mine, moving over and around it. He ran it over the sides of my mouth, pulling out to trace the outline of my lips before darting back inside to continue the ravaging kiss.

He pressed against my side, his hard-on digging into my upper thigh, and I reluctantly pulled back. His gray eyes caught mine, searching for an answer to his silent question. I just smiled faintly and moved away from him, off the bed. My own flesh was straining at the front of my sweatpants, but I couldn't do this right now. I yawned and stretched, completely aware of his gaze on me. He had propped his head up on his elbow and was just watching me. "I'm going to go take a shower really quick. Then we can go get some breakfast, okay? The studio is closed on Sundays so I have the whole day." I grabbed some clothes from the small closet and entered the bathroom, pushing the door closed behind me, not noticing it didn't shut completely.

I started the water, letting it heat up as I brushed my teeth and once it was at a good temperature, I took off the sweatpants and stepped underneath the spray, sighing with pleasure. I closed my eyes and just enjoyed the feeling of the water hitting me. My eyes flew open when I heard the shower curtain open and close. I felt his naked body press up against me and I groaned. "Xav, please, I…" I trailed off as his lips settled against the side of my neck.

I leaned my head back, electricity zipping down my spine. I reached up behind me and locked my arms around his neck, while his own slipped around my waist. "I just want to hold you," he whispered between kisses he trailed up to my ear.

I gasped as his teeth nipped lightly at my earlobe, and I felt one of his hands leave my waist. It reached past me for the shampoo bottle. I almost whimpered when he pulled away slightly to squirt some of the shampoo into his hand. Then his hands were in my hair, massaging my scalp, and soaping my hair. "I want to do this with yours," I moaned and my eyes closed as I enjoyed his careful ministrations.

"Whatever you want to do," he replied, turning me around to face him, his gray eyes intent. He slowly moved me back until just my head was under the spray, washing all of the soap from my hair.

When the shampoo was gone, I forced him to switch places with me, our bodies rubbing against each other as we shifted in the small tub. His fingers tightened on my hips at the feel of our slick flesh sliding past each other. I helped him wet his hair and then I turned him to face the wall, putting a generous amount of shampoo in my hands. I started at the top of his hair, lathering it as I moved down to the bottom, where it rested against his delicious rear. I grinned wickedly, and pinched him, eliciting a yelp from him and a mock glare thrown over his shoulder. I gave him an innocent look, and he laughed, shaking his head slightly. "I wish I had hair like this," I sighed as I helped rinse the soap out.

"You're perfect the way you are."

My skin tingled with his words as he turned towards me, lifting the soap from my grasp.

His hands traveled over my body, running the bar of soap

over my skin. I closed my eyes, leaning my head back against the wall. I quivered when his hands brushed over my cock and balls, which had begun to soften, but instantly became hard again. His fingers lingered there, trailing over the head and back down around the base. He pulled away reluctantly and continued to wash my body. When his turn came, I teased him in retribution. I ran the bar of soap over his broad chest and abs. Lathering up his arms and shoulders as well before traveling farther down, I reached around him to grip his bottom, which caused him to jerk in surprise. His eyes widened slightly and then narrowed. Ignoring his look with a saucy smile, I brought my hands around to his front, soaping his already stiffened length.

My lips curved up in a smirk as I saw him bite his lip to stifle a moan. My fingers danced over his flesh, the soap providing a slick feeling between my palm and his silken staff.

"If you don't cut that out, I won't be able to stop myself from taking you right where you stand," he ground out. I casually pulled my hands away from his stiff prick when all I really wanted to do was drop to my knees and savor the hard column with my mouth and tongue.

He rinsed the soap from his body and turned off the water while I reached for two towels, tossing one at him. I stepped from the tub, rubbing the terry cloth over my skin.

I strung the towel around my neck once I was done and strolled casually from the bathroom, completely nude. I could feel his eyes on my ass and I laughed. Even though I already had clothes in the bathroom, I couldn't stop from teasing him. Was I being mean? Should I have put him out of his misery? Eh. Maybe later! I was having too much fun like this. Besides, I didn't know if I was ready to give it up willingly yet. And I certainly didn't want our first time together since we'd told each other how we felt to be a quickie in the shower. Although, what a hot quickie that would have been! I grabbed a fresh set of clothes from my closet, and pulled on jeans and a tight, black t-shirt.

"Do you want to go back to your hotel room to change before we get breakfast?" I called out, my voice muffled as I dug around under my bed for my lost sneaker.

I was totally unaware of the sight I made, my ass sticking up in the air, wiggling around as I struggled to reach underneath. I gave a triumphant cry as I found my other shoe, and wiggled back out from under the bed.

"No rush. I'm just enjoying the view."

Glancing behind me, I saw him leaning against the doorjamb, smirking at me. I suddenly became aware of what he meant and flushed bright red, mumbling something about needing to brush my hair as I raced past him into the bathroom again. As I shut the door, I heard him give a deep laugh that rolled out of his chest. I smiled even though I knew my cheeks were hot with embarrassment. I loved to hear his laughter. It meant he was happy. Even if just for that split second he was laughing, he was happy. In my heart, I truly believe when the person you love is happy, it makes your happiness seem brighter and stronger. The one thing a person has is the ability to make someone laugh and smile. Somehow, some way, be it on purpose or by accident.

After I brushed my hair and my cheeks had returned to normal, I walked back out of the bathroom and sat on the edge of the bed to slip on my sneakers. He was sitting at the small dinette table, a cup of steaming coffee in front of him. His hair hung around the back of the chair, still damp from the shower. He had yet to tie it back. I grabbed a mug and poured more of the coffee into it, and sat down across from him. "Did you want to go change before we go?"

"That's all right. I have a change of clothes in the car. I

always carry them with me. You never know when you might need them."

I nodded and sipped at the brown caffeine-filled liquid while deeply breathing in the aroma. My eyes closed in pleasure. The smell of coffee is truly intoxicating and it stirred memories of my mother every time I smelled it. She loved coffee, and every day she had at least three or four cups. If she didn't get her coffee in the morning, she would be grouchy the entire day.

"Fagan?" I heard Xavier say quietly.

"Hmm?" I questioned, not opening my eyes, just reveling in the coffee and being able to enjoy it with him across from me.

"About what happened in the shower—"

I cut him off. "It's all right. I shouldn't have pushed you like that. It was mean of me. I'm sorry." I opened my eyes to show him my sincerity.

I saw a flash of emotion in his eyes and then it was gone.

"What would you like to do today?" he asked, leaning his chin on his hand.

"How about we just relax? Maybe walk around the city a little, do some shopping, and we can get a picnic and take it to the park close by here for lunch. I just want to spend the day with you. It doesn't matter what we do."

"That sounds good." His voice hitched and I frowned at him, wondering if I had said something to upset him.

I was about to ask when my cell phone went off. I walked over to the coffee table, picking it up and saw it was Trinity. "Hey, babe. What's up?" I returned to my seat across from Xavier.

"Fagan! Winston told me Xavier disappeared and no one knows where. He's been gone for almost three weeks now." Her voice was panicked.

I grinned broadly, staring across the table at the man she

was shrieking about. "Really? And I should care about this because?"

"Because he knows where you are!" she shrieked.

I decided to string her along a little further. "What?! What do you mean?" I injected just enough panic in my voice to make it seem plausible.

Xavier gave me a questioning look. I just smiled and shook my head. I mouthed I would explain later and continued to listen to Trinity's hysterical ranting on the phone.

"Victor told Winston that Xavier called him the other day and told him he was going to go see you. Are you all right? Have you seen him? Has he tried to contact you? Fagan, you need to leave before he finds you!"

I couldn't stifle my laughter any longer, and I started laughing hysterically, deep, stomach-paining laughs.

"What the hell is so funny, Fagan?" she demanded. "This is serious!"

"I… I can't… he-help… it… babe," I gasped out between laughs. After I had managed to calm down enough to talk, I decided to tell her the truth. "Listen, it's all right. He's actually sitting across the table from me right now."

"Wait a minute! What? Are you okay?"

"I'm fine! Jeez, you act like he's going to attack me or something." I saw Xavier's head come up at my words. I covered the mouth piece to whisper. "It's Trinity. She found out you know where I am."

He winced and nodded as I took my hand away from the phone to continue talking. "Trin, it's okay, babe. I promise I'm fine. We've done a lot of talking, and things have been going really good." I locked my gaze with his. "In fact, things are going great. We've been taking it slow and it seems like everything is going to work out between us."

His eyes widened at my words and hope shone from

them, stealing my breath away at how uncertain he must be about me.

"If that son of a bitch hurts you again, Fagan, I'm going to personally beat the shit out of him! I swear it on everything I am!" she shouted.

"Relax, Trinity." I rolled my eyes at Xavier as I tried to get her to calm down. "Everything is fine. We've been getting to know each other better. In fact, I got to ride a horse on the beach yesterday! That was great. Oh, and I got to see some of the most beautiful art in the world!" I launched into detail about where we had gone on our dates and the new experiences I had with him.

I saw him listening with an indulgent expression as I continued through everything that we had done the last three weeks.

"Have you had sex?" she asked.

I almost choked and had to cough several times before I could speak. "Trin!"

"Well, that gives a person a certain hold over you, and I want to know if you're thinking with your big head or your little one!"

"No. No, we have not," I stated quickly.

"Good. Hold strong, Fagan. Don't do it until you are absolutely certain of him. Please. As your life-long friend, I am begging you."

"I know, Trin. I miss you. How's Winston doing?"

"Great. He's got this new escort he says is a lot like you. The man's been frustrating him to no end."

"Tell old Winnie I said hi, and if you see or talk to Victor, tell him I said hi as well. I'm going to go. We're going out for breakfast." We said our goodbyes, and when I hung up, I saw Xavier studying me.

"What?" I asked suspiciously.

He didn't say anything for a moment, just continued to

stare at me and I shifted uncomfortably. Then he spoke, "You told your friend it looks like everything is going to be okay with us. Is it true? Do you really believe that?"

I was a little surprised at his words, but I nodded. "I believe things will work out between us. The last few weeks have shown me a side of you I've never seen before." I stopped for a moment, lost in thought, a small smile lurking around the corners of my mouth. "You know, I would swear to God you had my phone tapped the other day. I spoke with Trace, and he asked me what I thought you needed to do to prove you were telling the truth. I told him as old fashioned and cheesy as it may sound, I wanted to be courted. I wanted to have the whole knight-in- shining-armor thing, to be treated like I was worthy of being in a relationship and not just some fuck toy."

He grimaced at my words and hung his head. I continued on. "You started doing just that. Showering me with gifts, but don't think that's what I was looking for," I came back quickly. "I don't need gifts, but you did start courting me; taking me out to dinner, spending time with me, and allowing us to get to know each other. It's been a truly amazing time and I can't promise I am ready for sex, but I do know I love you, and I want to be with you more than anything else in the world."

There. I was done. I'd spilled my guts and could only wait to see if he would return my feelings or turn his back on me. I held my breath, waiting for him to respond. He stood up and hurt speared through me when I thought he was going to leave, but instead of walking out the door, he moved to my side, and kneeled down to look up at me.

"I know it's going to take time for the memories of what I did to you to fade. But I want you to know I will do whatever it takes to gain your trust again. I know it's possible to love someone but not trust them, and I know I don't have your trust yet. I love you, Fagan, with all my heart." He leaned his forehead against my chest and started speaking again. "I want you to trust me more than anything else."

I groaned, and I ran my fingers through his drying hair, spreading it over his shoulders, enjoying the feel of it against my skin. "When you say things like that, it makes me want to give in to my desire to ravish your body from head to toe, but I can't. Not yet. I do believe you love me, and I am starting to trust you, but I can't give myself to you wholeheartedly just yet."

"I do understand." He nodded against me and pulled back to look up again. "If you need me to, I will wait until we're old and gray with no sex drive left."

I cracked a laugh and framed his face with my hands. "Thank you." I leaned forward, placing a soft kiss on his lips. "Come on. Let's go get something to eat. I'm starving."

We stood up, and I followed him out to his car, my heart light and rejoicing from the conversation we'd just had. To know he supported me and understood what I was feeling made me feel so warm and fuzzy inside. Damn, being in love really does make you use words you wouldn't be caught dead saying on a normal day! Warm and fuzzy? Sheesh, I sound like a chick flick! I prayed this feeling would last though, and I could hold out against my lust to jump his bones!

22

Xavier took me to a small cafe that had an almost quaint feeling to it. I ordered coffee, and a cheese Danish, not entirely starving like I'd claimed, and he ordered coffee with a bagel and cream cheese. "What do you want to do after this?" I asked, taking a bite of my Danish.

"Anything is fine with me," Xavier told me distractedly.

I saw the preoccupied look in his eyes and felt a little upset. "Are you bored?"

"Huh?" He looked up at me in confusion.

"Well, you looked a little like you weren't happy to be here." With me, I added silently.

"Of course, I'm happy to be here! Why would you think that? Haven't I told you I want to be with you?" he demanded.

I twitched in my seat and looked away, wondering how he knew what I had meant without me having to say it. "Never mind. Let's just forget it. Hey, Xav, let's go to a movie, okay?"

He didn't respond for a minute, just studied me as I sat there. Then he gave a slight nod and reached across to lightly touch my hand. "Fagan?" I looked down at our hands without saying anything. "I didn't mean to make it seem like I didn't want to be here. I just have some things back in New York that have been on my mind, that's all. I've been away for almost a month and I'm sure Victor is not taking care of them in my absence, as usual."

"You want to go home?" I asked my eyes still locked on our hands.

"It's not a matter of want, Fagan. It's a matter of when. Are you going to stay here permanently, or are you going to come home?" he asked quietly.

I didn't want to answer him because I knew it would ruin our day if I did. But I couldn't lie. I loved this place and I didn't want to leave. "I... I am home, Xav. I love it here. Truly."

His fingers trembled on top of my hand and he pulled away, putting his hand in his lap. I knew I had just hurt him, but I couldn't help it. I didn't want to go back to the city. Not only was New York filled with the horrible memories of my time with Xavier, but the city just felt so impersonal. It was the kind of city that contained no care or love. The people there were hard and cruel, and it didn't feel like home to me. "I'm sorry, Xav. I want to stay in Boston."

"I see," he said quietly.

"When do you need to return to the city?"

"Tuesday."

I sucked in a deep, pained breath. Two days and then he would be leaving me. My heart dropped to my feet and I felt my eyes burning, but I wouldn't let those tears come forth. No, I would not. "And then?"

"I don't know. You tell me." he asked, his gray eyes locking on mine.

Suddenly, I knew he wanted me to give him something to come back to. He was waiting to see if he would be welcomed back. I stood, dropped some cash on the table to cover our check and grabbed his hand, pulling him along behind me out of the cafe. I dragged him into the doorway of a business that hadn't opened yet for the day and pushed him against the wall.

"What—?"

Before he could finish, I claimed his lips with my own, kissing him frantically, desperately.

His arms wrapped around my waist and pulled me closer, his tongue snaking out to rub erotically against mine. I didn't want him to go, but it would have to be his choice to stay with me.

"Fagan?" he whispered questioningly.

I leaned my forehead against his shoulder and just breathed deeply. I couldn't speak for fear of begging him to stay with me. "Fagan?" he asked again, this time a little more forceful. "What's wrong?"

Suddenly, the words tumbled out of my mouth before I could stop them, and I buried my face in his neck, my arms tightening around him. "I don't want you to go, Xav. I want you to stay here, with me. I don't want to be without you anymore. Please. Stay here with me."

I felt more than heard his breath hitch in his chest and his arms crushed me tightly against him. "I'll come back, Fagan. I'll always come back for you. I wouldn't be able to leave you willingly." He brought his hand up to caress my hair. "I promise, baby, I'll come back. In fact, with how adamant you were about staying here, I was going to suggest I move here as well."

I reared back in shock and hope. His thumbs rubbed over my cheeks as his hands framed my face. "It's obvious you love it here. And I didn't bring it up in the cafe because I didn't want to scare you by moving too fast. I was going to wait, but… would you be okay if I moved here?"

"Yes! Yes. Would you really do that for me?" I breathed, hardly daring to believe he would give up his life in New York City for me.

"I have nothing tying me there. I can open my own accounting place here. In fact, there's a small office I was looking at the other day when I bought the tickets for the museum."

"I... I..." I was reeling from the shock and didn't know what to say. He wanted to move here just to be with me.

His thumbs continued to caress my cheeks and he searched my face for any uncertainty. "Would..." He paused and I looked at him questioningly. "Would you move in with me?" At my look of surprise, he hurried on. "We can get a two-bedroom apartment until you're comfortable, and then later turn the second bedroom into a computer room or a studio for you to paint in. I mean, if you want to, that is."

Something clicked, deep inside my mind, my heart, my soul, and I knew without a doubt he must truly love me to be willing to give up the life he'd known for the last several years to be near me, with me. Maybe it's only been a few weeks and maybe I'm giving in too fast but his words... the emotion reflected in his eyes. I couldn't help but give myself to him. I sent a short prayer to the heavens he wouldn't hurt me again, and I leaned forward, effectively silencing him with a hot, searing kiss.

When I broke away, his chest was heaving for breath, and he whispered, "Is that a yes?"

There was such a hopeful, puppy-dog look in his eyes that I couldn't tease him, but I couldn't speak past the huge lump in my throat, so I nodded.

"Thank God." He closed his eyes in relief and laid his head on my shoulder. "I promise, I won't try anything at all. You can choose when you're ready and it doesn't matter how long it takes for you to feel you're able to trust me," Xavier said fervently.

Unable to help myself, I ripped the leather binding from his hair and let it flow free. Yes, I have a hair fetish if you can't already tell, since I do nothing but free his hair and run my fingers through it. I pulled it around us like a cloak and just held him against me. I closed my eyes, wanting nothing more than to stay there forever, but a throat being cleared jolted us both and we turned in unison to see the owner of the store whose doorway we were standing in. He was waiting impatiently, but there was a knowing smile on his face. I don't know which of us blushed a brighter red, Xavier or me. I laughed suddenly, grabbed his hand and tugged him over to where we had parked the car. "Come on. Let's go hunting for an apartment, hmm?" I said eagerly.

We spent several hours looking around for the best apartment we could find. During the entire time, he constantly touched me, rubbing my shoulders, holding my hand, brushing my hair back from my face, and any other excuse he could come up with. By the time we found the perfect apartment, my entire body was on fire and I felt so aroused I wanted to jump on him the instant we were back in the car, but again I restrained myself. I was going to wait until our first night in the new apartment to ravish him, and this time I would be the one to do the ravishing, not him. I grinned in anticipation.

"What are you smiling about?" He eyed me suspiciously.

"Nothing," I said innocently. "I'm just happy we're going to be living together."

He must have accepted my answer, and turned his attention back to the road. I leaned my head back in the seat and breathed deeply, trying to calm my aching flesh.

"Will you come back with me to New York?" he asked

quietly as we pulled up in front of William's house. "To help me get everything done quicker?"

At first, fear at the thought of returning came over me, but I knew what he said was true, and I didn't want to be away from him for an extended period of time. "All right." I nodded.

"Really?" he asked in surprise, turning in his seat to look at me.

I linked my fingers with his and I smiled at him. "Yes. Really. I don't want to be apart from you that long."

"That's another reason I wanted you to come with me," he admitted, tightening his fingers around mine. "I can't bear the thought of leaving you for more than a night. I'm still afraid you'll realize I'm nothing but an asshole and leave me again."

"I told you I would give us a second chance and I believe we'll be okay. I've spent the last three weeks getting to see the real you, and those three days on the farm I saw the gentle, kind person you can be. If only for a second, I glimpsed into who you truly are in here." I placed my hand over his heart. "Call me an optimist, but I've always known you're a good person, just headed in the wrong direction because someone hurt you and led you astray from who you were meant to be."

He put his hand over the one on his chest, and held it there. "I'm astounded at the faith you've shown in me. I would have kicked my ass to the curb." He brought his hand up to cup my cheek and I closed my eyes, leaning into his touch. Then his lips were on mine in the sweetest kiss I'd ever experienced.

The tip of his tongue flitted along the edge of my bottom lip and I opened my mouth slightly, urging him to press inside, but he teased me by pushing forward and retreating. I whimpered in frustration and pressed against him, attempting to capture his tongue with my lips. I felt him laugh gently, and I pouted, moving to pull away, but he hauled me across the middle console and on to his lap. It was a tight fit with how long my legs were, but I didn't care. My body tingled with the feel of his hard thighs beneath my ass.

"I haven't necked in the car since I was a teenager," he whispered, pressing his lips in butterfly-light kisses along my jaw line and down my throat.

I arched my neck, moaning as I felt his lips lock on my skin, sucking it lightly into his mouth. "Ah! Xav… I… that feels really good. Mmm. Don't stop."

His fingers teased along the hemline of my t-shirt, slipping just underneath to trace along the skin just above my jeans. My determination to wait was waning and I gripped his shoulders tightly. Our heavy breathing had fogged up the windows and we didn't even care. My cock was straining at the front of my jeans, and I wanted nothing more than to rip them open, giving him free access. However, before we went further, he was placing me carefully back into the passenger seat as I gave a little mewl of disappointment. He gripped the steering wheel, his knuckles white as he clenched his fingers.

"I think it's time to say good night, Fagan. I'll come by tomorrow to take you to lunch and confirm another plane ticket for you."

I was disappointed, but I know he did it for me. So I nodded, and whispered, goodnight before sliding out of the car and shutting the door.

I had never felt more sexually frustrated in my entire twenty-five years. That's right, I forgot, my birthday was in March. Wow, does time fly. I hadn't even celebrated it. Oh well, I guess there's always next year. My nerves were on edge as I entered the darkened house and picked my way through to my apartment. After changing into my sweats, I lay down on the bed, my hands under my head, and just stared at the ceiling. I couldn't wait to move in with him.

Two days later, we were on a flight back to New York City. It was short, since Boston wasn't far from there. I felt restless and agitated. I really didn't want to return to the city. There were a lot of bad memories for me there. Trying to look on the bright side, I reminded myself I would get to see Winston, Trinity, Trace, and even Victor before I left. The first place we went was Temptation. Tom welcomed me back with a huge grin and a bear hug.

"Fagan! Hey! We've missed you around here! Are you coming back to work?"

Xavier reached out and grabbed my hand, pulling me against his side and shook his head vigorously. "No. He's not."

I blushed as I saw the realization that flashed through Tom's eyes and then he grinned. "Well, doesn't that beat all? I was wondering why you both disappeared. And why Mr. James here was wandering around like a grizzly with an injured paw. Congratulations, you two!" He clapped Xavier on the back in celebration and then turned to walk back to his desk. "I'll see you around, Fagan! Good luck." He winked at me over his shoulder and I grinned happily.

"Come on," Xavier said gruffly, pulling me towards the elevator.

Tyrone was coming out of the elevator as we approached and he smiled in surprise at seeing me. "Fagan! Hey, man, how's it going? Where've you been? Are you finally coming back to work?"

I laughed and shook my head. "I'm doing well. I've been in Boston all this time. I live there now. And no, I'm not coming back to work."

"That's great. This lifestyle isn't for someone like you. You're too kind-hearted to be here." He touched my chest over my heart and I felt Xavier's hand clench on mine almost painfully and I frowned at him.

"Yeah. I knew it wasn't going to be a permanent occupation for me. But it was great while it lasted!"

"Hey, listen, I'll see you around, Fagan. I need to get going. I have an assignment waiting." He winked and then hugged me quickly, before walking away.

Xavier was quiet as we stepped onto the elevator and I looked at him. "Are you okay?"

"There are way too many people hugging you," he growled jealously. I started laughing. "It's not funny!" he exclaimed.

I stepped closer to him, pressing him against the wall of the elevator. I slid the tip of my finger down his cheek in a caress, and said, "Xav, you have me. No one else matters. You have to believe that in your heart or else this isn't going to work. I understand jealousy, believe me, I do because I want to break the fingers of anyone who touches you, but I know you're mine." I leaned forward and kissed him lightly. "I don't want anyone else."

The elevator doors dinged as they opened and I pulled back to drag him out of the elevator. We stopped in to see Winston first. "Winnie!" I exclaimed as I walked in, catching him off guard.

He was holding a bunch of cuff links and dropped them in shock. "Fagan!" he cried happily and started to rush towards me to hug me, but came to an abrupt halt when he saw the man with me. "Xavier," he growled, anger glinting in his eyes.

"Relax, Winston. Everything has been worked out between us. There's no reason for you to be mad, especially since he's going to be in my life." I felt Xavier's fingers tighten on mine again, this time in a squeeze of affection.

Winston studied him for a moment and then looked at

me. "I may have to put up with him in your life, but I don't like him, especially after what he did to you, so don't expect us to be best friends, Fagan."

"I understand, Winston, but please just try to get along, for my sake. You're dating my best friend and you're my friend. I want us to be able to have a peaceful time when we're all together."

He gave a slight nod, and then asked, "So are you finally coming back?"

"No. I'm staying in Boston. We came back because Xavier is going to move there. He needs to get his things together so we can move into the apartment we found."

"Wow, that's pretty fast. Are you sure about this?" he asked, not caring that Xavier was standing beside me.

"Yes. I'm sure." I looked over at Xavier and smiled happily. "Things may not always be bright and cheerful between us, but I believe the worst is over. Everything we went through is over."

"Have you seen Trinity yet?" Winston asked, pushing his glasses up slightly.

"Not yet. We just got back into the city about an hour ago. We came straight here so he can talk to Victor. Xav, why don't you go talk with Victor while I spend some time with Winston? That way once you're done, I can see Victor and then we can go start working on getting your things packed." I nudged him in encouragement.

Xavier smiled softly and nodded. "All right. Sounds like a plan. I'll come back for you in a little while." He hugged me, tightly, before leaving the room.

As soon as Xav left, Winston started firing questions at me. I told him the events of the past few weeks and he asked again, "Are you sure about this, Fagan?"

"I would be lying if I said I was one hundred percent confident but... yes, I have faith things will work out. And I love him," I told him gently. "Please support me in this, Winston, because if it does go badly, I'll need you to be there for me."

"Of course I'll be there for you. No matter what."

We spoke for a bit longer, but a knock came at the door and a man about my age walked into the room, taking Winston's attention away. I decided to take one last cigarette break. I climbed the fire escape up to the roof and lit a smoke, taking a deep drag as I leaned against the ledge. That was one thing New York City had I would miss; the most beautiful, breathtaking skyline. No other city can compare. I felt the anxiety eating away at me. I was still unsure about Xav in so many ways. However, if you don't take chances in life, you'll miss out on living it. And I didn't want to miss out on the chance of loving him and being loved by him, even if there was pain later on. I know you're probably thinking I'm an idiot, or just plain naive to jump back into it so quickly, but how do you stop loving someone? Even if they hurt you?

23

A pair of strong arms slid around me and I jumped in surprise, so caught up in my thoughts I didn't even hear him approaching behind me. I breathed in his scent deeply, leaning back into him. He leaned his chin on my shoulder and just held me. "I had a feeling you'd be up here when I didn't find you in Winston's room," he said huskily.

"I just wanted to look out over the city again before we left," I explained distractedly, my mind still on Winston's words.

"Do you regret it?"

"What?" I asked with a frown.

"Do you regret giving me another chance?" I heard the fear and uncertainty in his voice, and I felt my heart swell. Maybe, just maybe, it hadn't been a bad decision to trust my heart to him again.

"No," I whispered. "I don't regret it."

Xavier's arms tightened briefly in response to my words. He was so unsure of me, it gave me greater hope he was being sincere. We stood there in silence for several long moments, and then I asked, "How did it go with Victor?"

"He's naturally upset that he's going to have to find a replacement for me, but he's happy that I'm happy. Actually, he wants you to go see him before we leave. Are you ready to go?"

Tossing the cigarette to the ground, I nodded and we turned together, and instead of taking the fire escape back, this time I followed him through the door leading to the stairs. "He's in his office. I'll be waiting down in the lobby for you, okay?" Xavier walked towards the elevators and smiled at me before stepping inside.

I knocked on Victor's door, waiting for him to answer. "Victor? You wanted to see me?"

Victor grinned broadly, and stood up, coming around to usher me into the office. "Fagan! I'm glad to see you're looking healthy. You were looking a little ill the last time I saw you."

"Thank you."

He indicated for me to have a seat, and I settled into the chair across his desk. "I actually wanted to see you today to tell you how grateful I am to you."

"Grateful?" I frowned, not sure I understand.

"Yes. I haven't seen Xavier as happy as he was just now in ten years. I want you to know when you left so suddenly, he was devastated. He told me what had happened and what he'd done to you. I was angry as hell at him. I couldn't believe he would do that to someone, especially a kind person such as you," he paused, looking out of his office window for a moment before continuing, "He had a rough time of it a few years ago. I'm sure he's told you about Chris."

"He didn't tell me the guy's name or anything, but he did tell me what had happened between him and his ex."

"Yes. He was hurt very badly by that experience. It's been

a long time since he's truly smiled, and I know after you came, he was a little brighter and a little happier. I saw a side of him I hadn't seen in a very long time. Then after you disappeared, he lost a lot of weight. I would find him here late at night, working. He pushed himself until he almost collapsed. I had to force him to go to the doctor."

I glanced at him in shock and surprise. "He never told me that!"

"I'm sure he didn't. He barely ate or slept, and he never wanted to go home to his apartment, said there were too many memories there. I'm telling you this because he told me you still don't trust him entirely and I wanted you to know he's telling the truth. He really does love you, Fagan."

I sat there in a daze. I couldn't believe what Victor had just told me. Xavier had been so upset at losing me he'd almost wound up in the hospital? "I'm glad you told me all of this, Victor. I hope you know I have always considered you a friend."

I stood and gave him a brief hug goodbye before going down to the lobby. Xavier was standing by Georgina's desk and I studied him for a very long moment, just watching his beautiful face and the peaceful calm he exuded. His eyes were sparkling and there was a certain happy glow around him. I felt warmth spread through me at being the one to give him that glow. Then Georgina noticed me and waved. "Fagan, hi! How are you?" she called across the lobby.

Xavier turned his head to where I was standing and gave me a look as though to ask if I was all right. I tipped my head in a small nod as I came up next to where he stood. His arm automatically encircled my shoulders and Georgina flashed a knowing smile. "So, Xavier tells me you two are going to be living together in Boston?"

My cheeks felt warm and I knew I was blushing, but I

grinned. "Yep. I'm tired of living here, and he's going to be moving there to be with me."

"That's great. I'm glad to hear things worked out between you two. Oops. I need to answer some phones, but good luck, you guys!" She went back to picking up calls.

We exited the building, waving goodbye to Tom on the way out, and got into Xavier's car. "That was great to be able to see everyone again." I sighed contentedly.

"I hope it's all right I told Georgina that we would be living together."

"Of course. Why wouldn't it be? I've never hidden the fact that I'm gay."

"I thought you might be mad or embarrassed."

I shook my head, letting out a small laugh because of his ridiculous thoughts. "I don't care if the entire world knows. I would never be embarrassed at living with someone I love. Besides, have I ever shown I care what other people think? Stop worrying so much."

The car pulled up in front of the apartment building and I breathed deeply, steeling myself to face the memories of things I didn't want to think about. This was going to be uncomfortable, to say the least. To my astonishment, the first thing that popped into my head the moment we walked into the apartment, was the night we had a bout of hot sex on the living room couch. As I glanced around, the small dining room area caught my eye and I remembered the night he'd taken me, bent over the table. My skin tingled at the thought of it and I shivered slightly as my body responded. He looked at me when I stayed by the front door and frowned.

"Are you all right?"

"I... I'm fine," I whispered. My eyes glazed over as the memory of the night he'd tied me to the bed and licked over every inch of my body roared through my mind. Oh boy, I felt my pants tightening, and then he was beside me, touching my arm.

"Fagan?" he asked roughly.

"I'm sorry... I just..." He pulled me against his chest.

"Are you thinking about the awful things I did to you?" he asked me, his voice strained. I nodded and then shook my head. I was thinking about those things, but not in the context he imagined. "Then what's wrong?"

I didn't want to admit it, and I cleared my throat, wondering what I could say to make him believe me. "I..." Then I just started laughing, and couldn't seem to stop. "I... I don't... mean... to laugh." I gasped out, breathless. "I actually was.... thinking about... the various... places and ways.... we had hot sex."

He stilled and pulled back to look down at me, speechless, which just sent me into even more peals of laughter. I suddenly couldn't stand anymore and dropped to my knees, my arms wrapped around my stomach, still laughing. When I was finished laughing, he helped me off the floor and led me to the couch. Sitting beside me, he faced me and took my hand in his, and rested his other hand on my cheek. "No matter how or where we were, I always considered it making love with you," he responded quietly.

My eyes widened as I looked at him with surprise. "You did?"

"Yes. I did. I—"

I cut him off, lunging at him and knocking him backwards against the leather sofa cushions, my lips sealing against his.

I shoved at his shirt, pushing it up his body to run my hands over his hard chest, relishing the feeling of his skin beneath my palms. I couldn't wait. I wanted to feel him inside me so badly. And I wanted to take memories of a better time away from this place. "I was going to wait," I admitted between kisses, sliding the tip of my tongue along the line of his throat.

"Wait for what?" he gasped out, a moan rumbling in his chest.

"For us to move into our apartment. To celebrate the event by ravishing you, but I want you so much. And when we leave here, I want to have a memory I can look back on and take pleasure in." My lips settled over the pulse beating at the base of his throat and I sucked it wetly, hotly into my mouth, his gasps of pleasure igniting my own desire for him and fanning the flame higher.

"F-Fagan, are you sure?" His hands held my waist, his fingers clenching and digging into my skin.

"More than anything." I slid down his chest, ripping the shirt off him, and swirling my tongue around first one nipple and then the other. His back arched from the couch.

My fingers made short work of the fastenings on his jeans. I nipped lightly at the small brown nub and squeezed him through his underwear then slipped my hand into the opening to cup his already throbbing hard cock. A groan tore from his throat and I felt him shudder with pleasure. His body jerked and I slid from the sofa to kneel in front of him, pulling his jeans and underwear down to release him from the restricting confines of his clothing.

"Fagan, wait… ah!" He cried out, sliding his fingers into my hair as my lips closed over the head of his shaft. My tongue swirled around the tip before I enveloped him in my mouth, sliding all the way to the base. I sucked hard as I pulled back up to the tip, tonguing the little indent underneath the head before plunging back down. He tasted wonderful and after so many months without him I wanted him to explode in my mouth, to taste him completely. It didn't take long for him—after all it had been quite some time for both of us— and within moments he was pushing at me, trying to get me to pull off before he came. I held on and closed my eyes as the first hard spurt flooded my mouth. I swallowed greedily as he continued to erupt inside my throat. After I ensured I had every drop, I cleaned him off and let him slip out of my mouth to rest on his belly. I grinned happily as I settled at his side again, leaning my head on his shoulder.

"Why did you do that?" he asked me, his cheek against the top of my head.

"I already explained to you. I wanted to." I sat up looking at him with all the sincerity I felt in my eyes. "I want to take a happy memory away from here."

I saw something click inside his head and he smiled. "I'm going to make love to you for hours to ensure you walk away with very happy memories." He stood up, pulling his pants back up to his waist and before I knew what had happened, he'd managed to pick me up.

"I'm too heavy for you!" I exclaimed, but he just laughed.

"You're perfect."

He carefully made his way to the bedroom. Even though I could feel his arms straining from my weight, he kept going, and once in the bedroom, he set me down on the bed.

I looked up at him as he stripped completely and climbed onto the bed next to me. He helped me remove my clothes and tossed them to the floor, not caring where they landed. I chuckled slightly and then he was next to me again, staring down at me, with one hand pushing a stubborn lock of my hair back from my forehead. His lips settled on mine and he started slowly kissing me before slipping his tongue between my lips, caressing the moist walls of my mouth. I slid my tongue over his, sighing at the slick feeling of flesh over flesh.

Xavier moved his lips from my mouth to travel down my body, dropping kisses over every bare inch. I was on fire by the time he had reached my feet. He turned back and was now making his way up to the inside of my thighs. His tongue traveled over the sensitive spot I had there and I gasped, arching up into his mouth. He moved up higher, until the warm breath flowing between his lips brushed over the head of my stiff length and I locked my eyes on the sight he made as his lips closed over the tip. I groaned and slid a hand into his hair, stripping the leather tie from it, and watching as it cascaded down around him.

One hand stayed in his hair while the other gripped the bed sheets tightly as he slowly took me down his throat, his tongue bathing the underside of my shaft. My eyes closed in ecstasy. "Please…" I begged, wanting him inside me.

He pulled off with a wet sucking sound and asked, "Please what, Fagan?"

"Please. I want you inside me," I pleaded, my eyes opening halfway to look down at him.

He smirked, and shook his head, sending his hair swirling around him. "We have plenty of time for that. Later, baby." And he lowered his mouth back over my rigid flesh.

I writhed on the sheets as he continued to lick and suck on my cock. I broke out in a fine sheen of sweat as my body temperature rose higher and higher. Everything felt so good, and the pleasure increased ten-fold as I felt his finger probing at the entrance to my body, slipping inside up to his knuckle. Moans were filling the room and I became aware they were my own. I felt my orgasm rising and tried to push weakly at his shoulders to warn him. My voice froze in my throat at that very moment. Then I screamed out his name in rapture, the sound torn from my soul as I came in heavy jets. My body shuddered as his throat contracted around my sensitive cock. He swallowed again and again, taking every drop of semen I had to give. It was one of the most erotic moments of my life and I hoped there would be more with him. I collapsed limply against the sheets, my body still shivering from the overload of sensations.

Then he was rising over me, reaching into the bedside table drawer for something, and seconds later I felt his fingers pressing against my entrance. Something cold and wet was on them. My body jerked at the sensation added to the many already crowding it. I moaned as he pressed deeper, curving them up to hit that spot inside and I gasped loudly. A moment later, his fingers were gone and a much larger object was pressing into my ass, but he stopped. I looked up at him, questioning with my eyes why he had stopped. He leaned over me, pressing his lips to mine in a sweet kiss, and pulled back to whisper, "I love you, Fagan."

Xavier shoved forward, pushing inside me, filling me. "Xavier!" I groaned, bringing my legs up to wrap around his body.

He withdrew until he was almost completely outside of my body before driving home again, emptying and filling me over and over. He would twist his hips and shove deeper, spearing me with his hard length. His breathing grew harsh and he reared up slightly, moving my legs to his shoulders to fuck me roughly. I cried out as the head of his cock pressed against my prostate and he groaned at my cry, throwing his head back, his hair sticking to the sweat building on his beautiful skin. I ran my hands over his chest and stomach. His hips slapped the back of my thighs with each downward plunge. I was barely aware of demanding more, harder and deeper. It became just our world, the two of us. My own prick had stiffened again and he brought his hand down to grasp it, tugging it in time with his thrusts. Only a moment later, my spunk was spilling out over my chest and belly. Cries of pleasure once again poured from my lips.

My hand slid down to rub my come into my skin and then he was grunting out his own release, pressing deep inside me, flooding me with hot pulses of cream. Spent, he collapsed on top of me, still buried inside. I embraced him tightly. "I love you too, Xav," I whispered against his ear.

His arms tightened around me and he pressed a kiss against the side of my neck, causing a shiver to run through me. We fell asleep, not caring about the sweat and fluids on us, entwined together as one.

24

Xavier kept waking me throughout the night to continue his personal mission to wear me out. I was so weak by the time he let me fall back asleep after the last time, I couldn't have moved even if my life depended on it. I could only hope there wouldn't be a fire or something. It was bright out when I finally woke, around ten in the morning. I was lying half on top of him, and I lifted my head to just watch him as he slept. His long black lashes rested against his cheeks, deep even breaths flowed from his lips, and his chest rose and fell slightly. I don't think I could ever tire of looking at him. He was so breathtakingly beautiful. It was frightening how strong my feelings were for him. If this turned out to be a dream and the nightmare became reality again, there was no way I could survive. I tilted my head up and gently pressed my lips to his. He stirred in his sleep, one hand coming up to rest on my arm, which lay across his chest, but he didn't wake as I slid carefully from the bed.

I was in desperate need of a shower, and I wrinkled my nose at the stickiness on my stomach where I had rubbed my come into my flesh. I have to say last night was the best sex I had ever had. Hot, hard, and intense could barely describe how I had gone up in flames, again and again. The second time we'd made love, I'd been astride him. As I turned on the hot water, a shiver at the memory of looking down into his glittering lust-filled eyes as I slowly lifted up and pushed back down onto his hard cock raced down my spine. I could still feel him inside me, and to my absolute astonishment, my flesh stiffened at the memory. Damn. I hadn't thought I'd be able to get it up again for at least twenty-four hours after the previous night's bout. I stepped under the spray and closed my eyes, warmth flooding me. I knew last night would be helpful in erasing all of the horrible memories I had of this apartment, and I smiled peacefully. I grabbed the soap and lathered it up between my hands, dragging my hands across my body to erase both our sweat and fluids.

The shower stall door opened and Xavier stepped inside. "Good morning." He greeted me sleepily, sliding his arms around my waist, his long hair loose.

I couldn't stop the flood of emotion at his words, and I bit my lip, trying to at least stem the tears stinging my eyes. "Good morning," I choked out, leaning back into him. "How long have you been awake?" he asked, nuzzling the side of my neck.

"Only for a few minutes. You were sleeping so peacefully I didn't want to wake you."

"Mmm. You feel so good first thing in the morning. Are you sore? I wasn't exactly gentle last night."

I blushed at his words, remembering a particularly rough moment. "I'm a little sore, but it's okay."

"I'm sorry, Fagan. I just couldn't get enough of you. I think I was making up for lost time," he teased gently.

I nodded in understanding and closed my eyes. "It's all right. I enjoyed every moment of it. What should we do today?" I changed the subject, not wanting to continue with the conversation while I was so close to crying.

"Hmm? Well I know I need to pack up what I'm taking and set aside what I'm not to donate to the Salvation Army. I also need to arrange for some movers to come in and get everything." Xavier hesitated, and then asked, "Are you sure you're okay about last night? You seem kind of upset."

Unable to take the uncertainty in his voice, I turned around, caressing his cheek lovingly. "Last night was beautiful. I was just overwhelmed by how much I love you, and I didn't want to wind up crying in front of you again."

His eyes widened and affection flooded his sterling-gray orbs. "Fagan." He gathered me in his arms and pressed his lips to mine in a soft kiss. "You don't ever have to be embarrassed about crying in front of me. Happy, sad, hurt, whatever you feel. I only hope it's not sadness or hurt because of my stupidity."

We finished the shower, had a quick breakfast, and then started packing. A few hours later, I looked up and saw the time. It was late afternoon. Trace's class would be just about starting right now. I went looking for Xavier, finding him in the kitchen, going through his dishes. "Hey, Xav, is it all right if I take off for a little while?" I asked, leaning against the doorjamb, watching him as he glanced between two sets of dishes, trying to decide which one to get rid of and which to keep.

"Sure, babe." He looked up at me and asked, "Is it all right if I ask where?"

"Of course!" I exclaimed, stepping farther into the room. "Why wouldn't it be?"

"I don't want to seem overly possessive," he stated, looking away.

I walked to him, sliding an arm around his shoulders and leaning my chin on his shoulder. "I don't mind if you want to be possessive, but just don't get obsessively so, babe. I intend to be a little possessive towards you when it comes to certain things. I'm going to go see Trace and talk with him for a short while, let him know what's going on." I felt him tense, and I pressed a kiss to his shoulder. "Don't worry. I don't have any interest in anyone but you. He is my friend, after all. I love you, Xav." Walking over to the kitchen door, I turned back to look at him only to see him watching me like his puppy dog was leaving him forever. I laughed and shook my head. "I promise, I will be coming back to you, Xav. Stop worrying." I grabbed my wallet and jacket, and headed out to the elevator.

I heard the front door open and he was beside me in an instant, sweeping me up into his arms and kissing me passionately, hotly. When he pulled away, I was in a daze, just staring at him. A heartbeat later I was alone in the hallway again. All this before the elevator even got to the floor! I stepped into the elevator and pressed the button for the lobby. I touched my fingers lightly to my lips. They were swollen from his kiss. I wanted him again. Sighing, I hailed a taxi once out on the street and gave the address of the college. Twenty minutes later I was opening the door to Trace's classroom, and stood there, watching him talking with a young man about eighteen or so. I saw the way Trace's eyes wandered down the man's body and I grinned.

I hoped he could find someone to love like I had found Xavier. He deserved to be happy.

He looked up and caught sight of me, surprise showing on his features. "Fagan! How are you?" He strode towards me with a big grin on his face.

"I'm doing great. I see you're checking out the new... talent," I teased, laughing at the slight red dusting his cheeks. "He's a little young, isn't he?"

"It's not like that!" Trace protested. "He reminds me a lot of you, though. Raw and untouched talent."

"Oh? Untouched talent, huh?" I laughed harder and he gave a chagrined smile.

"This class is almost over. Why don't you stick around for a little while and then we can talk?"

I nodded and took a seat in his desk chair, watching as he flitted from student to student, pointing out where they did a great job or needed improvement. The boy he'd been standing near kept glancing at him furtively and I smiled knowingly. So the kid had a crush on his teacher. Hmmm… I stood up and wandered over to look at the boy's painting. "Very nice," I commented, looking at the strong brush lines and the color scheme he'd chosen.

"Th-thanks," the boy stuttered.

"I'm Fagan. I was a student of Trace's as well."

"Austin." He smiled shyly.

"I couldn't help but notice you watching him," I stated easily, as though discussing the weather, glancing at the young man out the corner of my eye.

I smothered a grin as I saw the look of shock that crossed his features and then he blushed bright red. He spluttered, trying to come up with an obvious reason why he'd been watching him, but I guess he failed because he admitted it. "Is it that obvious?" he asked forlornly.

"No. He isn't aware of it, if that's what you're worried about." I looked at him seriously. "I just want to make sure you're going to be good to him. He's been through a lot in his life," I whispered to him, making sure Trace didn't hear me.

Austin looked at me and nodded also with a serious expression. "I know. I can tell from the way he distances himself from people."

I was pleasantly surprised this kid was so mature for his age, and I knew if Trace opened up, he would be good for him. "Well, just so you know, he's been watching you too," I hinted, sauntering away from Austin. His expression was comical.

Trace ended the class a few moments later, and I surreptitiously studied him as he watched Austin walk out of the classroom. "If you like him so much, why not make a move on him?" I asked casually.

"Because a kid like him doesn't need an old man like me who has a lot of baggage," he stated quietly, cleaning up some of the brushes the students had left behind.

"You're not old!" I protested, sitting up straighter. "You're only twenty-seven. That's only two years older than me!"

"That's almost ten years older than him. I also have a lot of shit I carry around every day, Fagan," Trace pointed out, setting the brushes into a canister to dry. "Let's go get a cup of coffee from the vending cart out front."

He led the way, buying both cups of coffee and handing one to me. "So how are things with Xavier?" he asked as we settled down onto one of the benches in front of the college.

"Great. He's moving to Boston."

Trace's eyes widened and he turned his head to look at me. "That's wonderful!"

We spent the next hour just talking with each other. He questioned me about everything to do with Xav. I actually got him to open up a little bit about his past and I felt so bad for him. He'd been through so much, and I leaned forward to hug him in sympathy. I felt him stiffen against me causing me to pull away in confusion. "What's wrong?"

"Your lover is here," he said calmly.

I grinned broadly and turned my head, but my grin faded as I saw the anger in Xavier's expression. Hurt flowed through me and I stood up. "I'm sorry, Trace. I'll talk to you later." I stalked over to where Xavier stood and before he could say a word, my own emotional dam broke and I started shouting at him. "God damn it, Xav! You have nothing to be angry over. When are you going to trust me?! I told you I don't want anyone other than you. He told me something about his past, something that hurt him very badly, and I hugged him to comfort him, nothing more!"

I glared at him in frustration. "If you can't learn to trust me, then I can't be with you." I started to stalk past him, but he grabbed my wrist and spun me around, straight into his arms.

He had a smile on his face and he settled his palm against my cheek. "You didn't even ask why I was angry. Talk about needing to learn to trust someone."

I was confused. "What?"

"I wasn't angry because you hugged Trace." He rubbed his thumb against my cheek, not caring that people might stare at two men caressing each other in public. "I was angry because someone almost ran into my car a moment ago. I was pulling up and they were on their cell phone, not paying attention. You know I love that car."

Understanding dawned and then shame flooded me. "Oh," I said quietly.

"Yeah. Oh." His voice was amused.

"I'm sorry." I looked down at the ground, not wanting to meet his eyes and see the disappointment.

He slipped his finger beneath my chin and lifted my gaze up to his. "I'm sorry I didn't smile when you looked my way. It's my fault for reacting that way in the past and I haven't given you a reason to think otherwise since we got to New York. I have to admit, it hurt with how easily you could walk away from me though."

I hugged him, hard. "Oh, my God. I'm sorry, Xav. I'm so sorry."

"Shh. It's fine. We'll get through this and any other rough

patches. It's just going to take time. Right?" He pulled back to look at me.

I nodded vigorously and replied, "I guess old habits die hard."

"I actually came to take you two to dinner. If you want to, that is," Xavier explained.

"Really?" My expression lit up and I glanced back to find Trace still sitting there. I beckoned him over and explained about dinner. He agreed, and a little while later, we were sitting in a Japanese restaurant, enjoying sushi.

Xavier surprised both of us when he thanked Trace openly for telling him where I was. I actually was surprised I hadn't thought of that myself. I seconded his thanks.

"Just be sure you both treat each other with love and respect," he said quietly. I knew he was remembering his past as he talked. "You never know how short life is until it's ripped away from you."

After we had dropped Trace off, we headed back to the apartment and as soon as the door was closed, I jumped all over him.

"I thought you'd be worn out!" Xavier exclaimed as I shoved him onto the couch and straddled him, kissing along his neck and running my hands down his chest.

"Xav?"

"Yeah?"

"Just shut up and make love to me," I commanded, with which he happily complied.

As he slowly stripped the clothes from my body, I knew it might not always be a gentle and easy ride with us, but I knew without a doubt that he truly loved me. And that was all I would ever need. To be loved by Xavier James, my own private Temptation.

EPILOGUE

"Xavier Anthony James!" I shouted with my hands on my hips.

He looked at me innocently. "What?" He stood in the doorway of our new apartment, dressed in nothing but a red bow around his hard cock, and holding a bottle of wine in his hand. His long black hair was out of its usual ponytail, trailing down his back.

"What are you doing? Trying to show your goods to the entire world?" I demanded, shoving him back inside and shutting the door behind us.

"I wanted to give you a housewarming gift." He grinned.

I shook my head, exasperated. Who would have known Xavier was such a clown? Since we moved in together a week ago, things have been great. Going to bed every night wrapped up in his arms, and waking up the same way, was the greatest gift in the entire world. He had already put in a bid on the storefront near the theater, and it looked like it was going to be a pretty good opportunity for him. He wanted me to help him choose how to arrange the office and everything. He also wanted me to paint him a couple of pictures to place around his office. I had been so excited when he'd asked me. There were already two drying in the extra bedroom at the apartment.

We have already set up half of the second bedroom as my studio and the other half as an office area for Xavier. At first, he'd insisted it only be my studio but I didn't need that much room right now. So I had finally persuaded him, after a night of amazingly hot sex, half the room should be his.

I stood there now, my cock stiffening at the sight of him with the cute red bow he had tied at the base of his penis. "What am I going to do with you?" I sighed.

"Come here and I'll show you." He smirked, crooking a finger at me.

I laughed huskily and slowly walked towards him, my fingers unbuttoning my shirt and letting it fall to the floor as I stopped in front of him. He helped me remove my white T-shirt I wore underneath, and I stood before him, naked from the waist up. He placed the palms of his hands against my chest and ran them over my flesh, eliciting a moan of pleasure from me. I could never get enough of his hands on me. He trailed them down to my pants, undoing the belt, slipping the button slowly out of its hole, and teasingly sliding the zipper down. The backs of his fingers brushed over my hard length, which was straining against the front of my pants, and I bit my lip, feeling my face flush with pleasure.

"I have a special gift for you tonight, Fagan." His voice was raspy with desire, and he pushed my pants and boxers down, revealing my aching shaft.

"Mmm. Very nice," he said, wrapping his hand around it and pressing closer to me. He slid his fingers back and forth on me, causing me to groan with pleasure. "So hot, so hard. If I didn't know any better, I'd think it's been more than a few hours since we last made love," he said teasingly.

I flushed at how hard he'd gotten me and then he pulled

away, causing me to frown in disappointment, but he carefully led me towards the couch by my prick. He pushed me down onto the cushions, kneeling in front of me. My cock jumped in anticipation as he locked his eyes on mine and I watched in fascination as he brought his lips to the head, pressing a light kiss against it. His pink tongue flicked out just lightly grazing me. I moaned and clenched my hands into fists as he continued to tease me, running the tip of his tongue along the underside of my shaft. A pearl of fluid seeped out and slid down my shaft, which he promptly lapped up. He nibbled along the shaft with his lips, using his tongue in between. Before long, I was so close to coming, but he felt it in the pulse of my cock and pulled back. I mewled in disappointment, frowning at him.

"Don't worry, love. I have something special for you tonight," Xavier stated, standing up. "Untie your gift," he demanded, straddling my legs, his hard flesh pointing at me.

I tugged the ribbon slowly, watching the red fabric fall away. I flung my head up to look up at him. "Such a beautiful gift. In fact, I think I'd like to kiss my gift." He smirked and put his hand on the back of my head, guiding me forward.

I reciprocated his earlier motions, pressing a light kiss to the head, and instead of licking along the shaft, I enveloped it completely between my lips, sliding down to the base and back up again. His head fell backwards as the hand at his side clenched into a fist. The other lightly gripped my hair.

"Ah... Fagan, that feels so good," he ground out, thrusting his hips forward and pushing his cock further down my throat.

I hummed, and he cried out, hunching over me slightly. "Oh, my God," he breathed. "Do that again."

I grinned as much as I could with his hard shaft in my mouth and hummed again.

"Holy shit."

He almost ripped himself from my throat, his breathing heavy and erratic.

"Give me a second. I don't want to come yet." He stepped away as I tried to reach for him again.

"But why? I wanted to have a cream smoothie." I pouted up at him.

I saw lust blaze even hotter in his eyes, and he growled, "I don't think I could ever get enough of you."

After a few moments of to breathe, he moved back to me, and pushed me back into the couch, straddling my legs with his knees again. "I told you I had something special for you."

He reached underneath the couch cushion and pulled out the tube of lube we'd stuffed there our first night here. I looked at him questioningly, but when I felt his fingers slathering the head of my prick with lube, my eyes widened as I realized his intentions. "Xavier, wait. Are you sure?" I asked, concerned. "Don't do this because you think you owe it to me or anything."

"I have never been more sure of anything in my life," he said, taking two of my fingers and slathering lube onto them. "Now get busy," he demanded, leaning forward to kiss me. His tongue fluttered along the seal of my lips as I pressed my fingers against his entrance. I felt his body jerk slightly, and I opened my lips, granting his tongue access and slipping my other hand around his throbbing prick to distract him as I slowly penetrated his ass with my fingers.

I heard and felt him groan against my lips as I slid them inside him, pushing in deep and pulling back out, only to plunge right back in.

"Now," he whispered against my lips, pushing my hand away and lowering his hips to where the tip of my dick brushed his tight hole.

My hands gripped his waist as he carefully lowered his body. He moved slowly until he sat upon my lap. "Are you okay?" I asked, concerned I was hurting him. I wasn't exactly small.

He gritted his teeth and nodded, his eyes closed, his head thrown back in pained pleasure. I watched in fascination as my cock appeared and disappeared inside him. I had never felt such tightness around me before and it was driving me insane with pleasure. "Is this how it feels when you're inside me?" I asked in wonder, my hands still guiding his hips up and down, back and forth.

"Does it feel tight, hot, and fucking incredible?" he rasped out, his eyes opening slightly to catch my gaze. I nodded. "Then, yeah. I hope you feel as good right now as I do when I'm inside you."

I started thrusting my hips upward to meet each of his downward plunges, groaning as I repeatedly bottomed out in his snug channel. "I don't think I can last much longer," I almost howled as I was getting close to orgasm. I could feel my balls tightening and a heat building at the base of my spine.

"Come," he groaned. "Come inside me." His eyes shut tightly as he pushed himself down one more time, and I cried out his name as I came, his hole tightening around me as his own spunk splashed over my chest and stomach. One spurt even hit my cheek. I shuddered, my body almost jack-knifing straight up from the couch cushions, as I filled him with my thick juices.

Seconds later, he collapsed on top of me and realized he'd come on my face.

"Oh damn, I'm so sorry, Fagan."

He used his fingers to wipe it off my cheek and was about to wipe it on the couch when I grabbed his wrist, bringing his hand to my lips and sucking on the two fingers, licking every drop of the salty-sweet fluid off. His eyes widened and I felt him shudder as my tongue bathed the come from his fingers. "I don't think I've ever seen anything sexier," his voice was strained with desire.

I smiled wickedly and scooped up every drop I could reach, cleaning my fingers hungrily. I felt him getting hard between us and my own cock responded, growing in size, still buried deep in his hot ass. "I think I could get used to this position," I said teasingly.

"We'll trade off."

His cocky grin turned into a grunt of pleasure as my prick slid free of his body. He grabbed my hand and yanked me off the couch towards the bedroom.

I couldn't help but watch his rear as he walked. My come was slowly dripping out and it was the most erotic image I'd ever seen. I let it burn into my brain, intent on painting the image later on. I couldn't believe how happy I was.

I love him with all my heart and I believe he loves me just as deeply. I am stunned he'd willingly let me fuck him, but it felt incredibly fantastic. It's something I hope to repeat later. Grinning, I wonder if he'd be interested in trying a little S&M. Well, I guess asking never hurt anyone.

Sorry, that's something you'll just have to imagine if it happens or not, because the story of how I found my temptation is over—and I want to enjoy his delicious body right now.

Craving more urban fantasy or paranormal? Spell of the Werewolf is available now on Kindle & Kindle Unlimited!

A werewolf seeks to sever the curse. A hybrid hunter wants him dead. Will the next moonrise be his last?

Looking for something contemporary? Try Touch Me Gently! Available on Kindle and Kindle Unlimited.

A scarred young man jumping at shadows. A big-hearted, sexy cowboy providing him a safe haven. But is he able to trust his cowboy with his heart?

A NOTE FROM J.R.

Thank you for reading Swift's Temptation. If you enjoyed it, I would truly appreciate if you could let your friends know so they can also enjoy the relationship between Fagan and Xavier. If you leave a review for Swift's Temptation on the site in which you purchased the book, Goodreads or your own blog, I would love to read it. Please email the link to jrloveless@gmail.com

ABOUT THE AUTHOR

J.R. Loveless began her adventure in writing at the young age of twelve. Her foray into creating her own worlds and telling her characters' life stories was triggered by her own love of reading. She currently resides in South Florida with her dog and two cats, and by day works as a manager for a financial lending institute.

Her journey into gay romance began in 2005 when she began posting her original fiction on a forum for feedback and readers' pleasure. In 2010, a good friend urged her to submit to a publishing company, and the day she received the acceptance and contract was the best day of her life. Since then, she has been noted to be one of the most purchased audio books after Fifty Shades of Grey on Audiobook.com and received best gay romantic fiction for Touch Me Gently in the 2011 TLA Gaybies.

J.R. adores her fans and loves hearing from them.

Never miss out on an update or sale by subscribing to J.R.'s Website. As a thank you, you'll receive a free short novelette called White Rain about two friends who become lovers!

J.R.'s Blog
J.R.'s Facebook Reader Group

- facebook.com/authorjrloveless
- twitter.com/J.R.%E2%80%99s%20Twitter
- instagram.com/jrloveless
- amazon.com/author/jrloveless
- bookbub.com/profile/j-r-loveless
- goodreads.com/jrloveless